Darren, Andrew and Mrs Hall

R J Gould writes contemporary fiction about relationships using a mix of wry humour and pathos to describe the life journeys of his protagonists. *Darren, Andrew and Mrs Hall* is his eighth novel. He has been published by Lume Books and Headline Accent and is also self-published. He is a member of Cambridge Writers and the Romantic Novelists' Association UK.

Before becoming a full-time author he worked in the education and charity sectors.

R J Gould lives in Cambridge, England.

www.rjgould.info

Darren, Andrew and Mrs Hall

R J Gould

Acknowledgements

There are several people who I would like to thank for their help with the publication of this novel. Joss Alexander, Thure Etzold and Angela Wray, fellow members of the Cambridge Writers Commercial Editing Group, provide expansive support ranging from consideration of plot and characterisation to micro proof reading. In addition to giving valuable feedback on my final draft, my readers launch team – Alex Elbro, Dr Karen Jost, Gwen Nunn and Mary Robinson – offer uplifting encouragement on my writing. Ken Dawson at Creative Covers has again done a great job in designing the cover. Finally, a thank you to Terry Chance for her patience and support together with perceptive tough judgement of my wilder ideas.

1

'No, no, no!'

'Yes, yes, yes … Yes!'

It was turning into a nightmare for Kelly Robertson to get her husband, Darren, to even consider moving to Muswell Hill. Wokeland he'd started calling the trendy, affluent London suburb.

'But what does Wokeland mean?' she'd asked him.

'Don't know exactly, but I've read about it in the *Daily Mail*. The wokes don't eat meat or drive a car, they're ashamed to be English – and they live in places like Muswell Hill.'

Kelly had identified two houses for sale on the same street, an attractive tree-lined avenue with tidy front gardens and Victorian elegance beyond. There was no way she was going to be deterred from viewing them despite Darren's reluctance. The appointment had been made to see both properties the following morning.

She googled the details of the first house, her fake nails clicking as she tapped her phone keypad. 'Look will you. This is perfect, wokey or not. And it's in our price range.'

Darren was sitting next to Kelly on the couch in the living room scanning his phone. He didn't look up.

'And here's the second property.'

Darren still wasn't engaging. He let out a long sigh.

Two of his less appealing traits – and of late there had been several to choose from – were moaning and sulking. These behaviours were often sequential. First the moan, a bitter whinge about something or other, and then the sulking with hours of silence interspersed by long drawn out sighs as was now the case.

'It's not fair,' he moaned, pointing his screen at Kelly. 'The bloody business. Look at this. I'll tell you what, I'm absolutely fed up with customers who have no idea what they're talking about giving me bad reviews.'

'Yes, it's not fair, is it?' Kelly offered in half-hearted, inattentive support. She was admiring the street view as the little icon walked along. 'It's a lovely spot. See.' She counter-pointed her phone at Darren.

'I'm not doing it. I'm not moving.'

'At least see the places.'

'No.' The sulking was kicking in, that little boy pout because he wasn't getting his way and was being ignored.

Darren turned towards the television; the early evening soap had begun. Kelly lifted up the remote and switched it off.

'What did you do that for?'

'Let me remind you, you were the one who said we had to move.'

'That's not true.'

'You know it is and you're right. We don't need such a big house or a huge garden, and top of the list, we need some cash in hand until the business picks up.'

Darren feared that his business would never pick up what with vindictive customers writing such spiteful reviews.

His security alarms company, *Stop Thief!*, had never shone on Trustpilot, but recently the star rating had plummeted to one and a bit out of five following the outrageous reviews that he was now scrutinising.

Extremely disappointed.

Useless customer service.

A terrible company to deal with.

Stay away from them.

Kelly looked across at her husband. Although frustrated by his despondency, she could understand the cause and was sympathetic. He'd worked hard to build up the company and initially everything had gone brilliantly well. There had been a wave of burglaries in the wealthy north London suburbs, meaning more and more households wanted alarm systems installed. But recently the business had been in freefall with Darren failing to match the new kids on the block, techie wizards prepared to be out and about 24/7 at their customers' beck and call.

Kelly recalled the times when Darren had come home full of funny stories about his customers. He'd been enthusiastic, loving the social side of the job. Not anymore. Now every client seemed to be a problem and it didn't take a Sherlock Holmes to work out that his responses to their complaints were rude. Bad reviews were his customers' revenge and quite possibly deserved.

'Remember this, Kelly. It's a disgrace.' Darren's phone was close to touching his wife's nose. 'After everything I did for that man.'

On a bitterly cold evening a month or so previously Darren was emptying the van ahead of the Christmas break when a customer called to request emergency help. He reloaded the vehicle in preparation for the visit. With the tank near empty he'd queued to fill up. He was stuck for ages in a traffic jam caused by last minute shoppers. The man had told him off for arriving later than arranged. Working outside in the dark and freezing cold he hadn't even been offered a mug of tea. And all this on Christmas Eve.

'I'm not happy with that box,' the man complained when Darren had finished. He was shining his phone spotlight upwards. 'It's askew.'

'It's right at the top of the wall, sir. No one's going to notice.'

'Well I am. It's out of line with the gutter.'

'I can't see that.'

'Then perhaps you need glasses.'

'It's the gutter that's the issue. It isn't level.'

'Clearly you *do* need glasses.'

Kelly interrupted Darren. 'You've already told me about this one – in fact twice.'

'But I haven't shown you the review.'

Kelly edged the phone away from her nose and read the text.

If I could give a no star I would it concluded.

'That is nasty.' Kelly was struggling to draw the fine line between pity and exasperation. 'However, deserved or not, you're getting bad reviews which means you're not getting much business which is why we're broke. So we have to move.'

Currently they inhabited Kelly's childhood home in Crouch End, a couple of miles down the road from Muswell Hill. It was a perfectly satisfactory neighbourhood though not as fashionable as where Kelly was hoping to live. Despite the business difficulties they could afford to leave the five-bedroom property with its vast garden that her parents had purchased almost forty years beforehand, the tiny mortgage paid off long ago. It was now theirs. If only Darren would appreciate how fortunate they were to have the inheritance, valued at over two and a half million pounds. They would be able to purchase a smaller place in a nicer neighbourhood and have plenty to live off while her husband got things sorted.

'Are you listening, Darren? Tomorrow we're viewing the two properties. Both of us.'

'I've had enough of you telling me what to do. I'm taking Tyson for a walk.' Their labradoodle, sprawled out on the living room floor, leapt up on hearing his master mention "walk". 'And I will not be looking at those Wokeland properties.'

'You can't just head off; we haven't finished. Just let Tykie out into the garden.'

'How many times have I asked you not to call him Tykie?'

'About the same number of times I told you I didn't like the name Tyson.'

'I'm not staying here to talk about houses – or dogs' names. I'm going.' Darren looked across at Kelly who had gone bright red. When she got angry she got really angry; it was time to flee. He stood up and Tyson followed him into the hall.

'It's not as if we'll ever need five bedrooms, is it, not with you refusing to consider IVF,' a furious Kelly called out after him.

'And it wouldn't hurt if you took Tyson out once in a while. It's bloody freezing out there.'

Kelly didn't answer. She was weighing up how she'd feel if her husband died of hypothermia. But then what about poor Tykie?

Her anger soon subsided. She knew Darren like the back of her hand. Of course he'd be joining her to view the two houses the next morning, she was always able to win him over. Despite his moods, the moans and the sulking, when it came down to it he'd do anything to please her. She was grateful for that and would apologise for what she'd said about IVF when he got back. It was a sensitive subject.

The last thing for Kelly to do that evening was text her boss to let him know that she'd be in late the following day. It wouldn't be a problem. Although she was the senior receptionist at the car showroom, the trainee was more than competent enough to hold the fort for an hour or so. Anyway, her boss fancied her and she could get away with blue murder.

~

As Kelly had predicted, Darren's opposition came to nothing and he joined her as they set off towards Muswell Hill the following morning. Pulling up in Brookland Gardens, Darren squeezed his *Stop Thief!* van between one hybrid and one electric car fifty yards away from the properties they were about to view.

'Unacceptable! If we lived on this street we wouldn't be able to park near our own house,' was his first moan of the day. Kelly decided against suggesting that the daily exercise from home to van and back again might be beneficial.

'Good morning, and what a cold one,' the estate agent greeted them, his attention directed at the attractive female in great shape rather than the man who clearly wasn't. Darren had an odd build: thin legs, large belly, and strong, muscular arms as a result of lifting weights at some sweaty, smelly gym in a converted snooker hall. Kelly's regular sessions to maintain her toned body were at an upmarket gym with pool, spa and coffee bar.

The agent was standing outside the house between the two for sale. 'I suggest we begin with this one,' he indicated, pointing to his left. 'It's a stunner. As soon as you step inside you'll see why.'

Darren glanced at the rectangular box high on the wall as they made their way up the path. It was one of his alarm systems though not one he was still servicing.

Once inside the house their guide sprang into admiration for décor and fittings that hadn't been modernised since the place was first built. 'Look at this,' he said, tenderly stroking the cast iron fireplace in the living room. 'These tiles are the originals and they're in perfect condition.'

Darren summoned up the pretence of a smile as he considered whether he would be able to salvage the lilac and green floral tiles when knocking out the fireplace. Someone on eBay might want to buy them. At any rate, this monstrosity would be the first thing to go; it was taking up a large chunk of wall when it wasn't even in use. The giant screen TV could fit there.

The tour continued. The place was a nightmare. Uneven creaking, polished floorboards. Floral wallpaper. Bedrooms without fitted wardrobes. And stupidest of all, a stand-alone bathtub in the middle of one bedroom, resting on ornate metal claws.

'Are you ready to move on to the next property?' the estate agent asked.

'Good idea,' Darren said. 'And as soon as possible.' Kelly poked him in the ribs in full view of the agent who smiled and gave her a knowing look.

They followed their guide outdoors, taking the few steps needed to reach the second house.

The estate agent paused outside the building. 'Some apologies needed for this place.' He pointed at the windows. 'Sadly, they were changed before planning laws were strengthened. Owners wouldn't get away with this now. But the good news is that there are companies in the area specialising in restoring windows to their original state.'

Darren had no idea what the man was on about because these sash windows were double glazed PVC. It was an improvement – low maintenance, better insulation, and from a security point of view, much harder to break into than the burglar's nirvana of wooden sash windows. It came to him all of a sudden, the estate agent must be a woke. Darren would have liked to have slammed each comment about original features with deep sarcasm: "While we're at it let's get rid of electricity and use candles". But Kelly would go ballistic.

When the agent opened the front door, Darren could see that this house was better than the first one, not brilliant but better. Downstairs walls had been knocked out to create a large open living space. The cornices were gone, the fireplaces taken out, the ceilings fitted with spots with the central mouldings absent.

'What do you reckon?' he whispered to Kelly as they made their way upstairs.

'Lovely, I think it's lovely.'

Entering a bedroom with a super king-sized bed, silky purple quilt cover and faux leather headboard, Darren's thoughts turned to sex. They often did.

'Some strange choices up here, I'm afraid,' the estate agent said as they moved on. 'They've turned a bedroom into a rather garish wet room.' Darren regarded the shower with its variety of sprinklers. There was a bottle of orange blossom foam on a shelf.

An orange blossom foam shower with Kelly. A nice thought.

When they returned downstairs the agent asked if they needed time to discuss the two properties in private.

'Not now, thank you,' Kelly said. 'We've not been looking for long, in fact these are the first we've seen. Mind you, we do need to find a place quickly, don't we, Darren?'

Darren didn't reply. It looked like he was in sulk mode.

'Well, a warning. That first house has only just come onto the market and it will be snapped up. If you're interested you need to act quickly. To be truthful, that's not the case with this one, it's been on sale for way longer than any property I've known in Muswell Hill. You can see why though, there's a considerable amount of remedial work needed to restore it to its original state. The good news is that the owners are getting desperate and are open to offers.'

Darren remained silent.

'Thank you for showing us round, we'll get back to you when we've had a think about it. You could have at least pretended to be interested,' Kelly added when the agent had left them.

'Why should I?'

'If you treat your customers like that it's not surprising they slate you. I'll carry on looking but the second place is definitely a possible.'

Over the next two weeks Kelly searched with nothing better coming on the market. The giant villas in the area were far too expensive except for the ones divided into flats that were too small.

Meanwhile, Darren's business was going from bad to worse with clients terminating their maintenance contracts. The seepage of lost business turned into a flood on the day the local paper ran an article featuring customers' dissatisfaction with *Stop Thief!*

Absolutely despicable – a nightmare. Trustpilot one-star review.

Worst company ever. Trustpilot one-star review.

A furious Darren came storming into the living room and dropped the newspaper onto Kelly's lap. Looking at the state of it, he must have scrunched it up and then attempted to straighten it out.

'Read this!'

'I already have. It's online.' She'd read the post through a hyperlink on the *Love Muswell Hill* Facebook group. 'It's not going to get any better in a hurry, is it? I think we should accept the offer we've had for this place.'

That offer, the first and close to their asking price, had come in a couple of days earlier.

'The man was a nutter,' Darren said.

'If we're moving why does it matter who's buying the house? Anyway, if he wants to turn the garden into one giant vegetable allotment that's up to him. It hardly makes him a nutter.'

'He reckons the country is doomed and everyone needs to grow their own food.'

'That's fine by me. It means we're getting a good price because of the size of the garden. So now we have to find somewhere and I think that house we saw on Brookland Gardens, the second one, is the best bet.'

'I'll tell you something Kelly, it's not fair. People are out to ruin my business.'

'Life isn't fair so stop moaning. I say accept the offer for here and make a low one for the Muswell Hill place. The agent said they're desperate to sell.'

'Or …'

'Or what?'

'We move well away from here, over the river where it's much cheaper.'

'No way, you know I love it here.'

'We'd have loads of money left over.'

'So you're happy for me to move somewhere to get mugged or raped?'

Darren was always going on about how parts of London were full of thugs, drug dealers, gangs and thieves. Kelly knew that trigger would work with Darren accepting her fear at face value while in reality she had no worries about safety. Her only fear was of having to give up the boutiques, cafés, gym and people living in and around Muswell Hill. It was a classy place, something Darren would never understand.

~

One gloomy afternoon in late February, on a day when it never quite got light, they signed the papers at the estate agency and the house was theirs.

'Let's be positive,' Kelly urged as they sat in the van outside their current home. Darren pressed the remote and they watched the garage door open. 'In fact, let's celebrate!'

'You do realise there's no garage at the new house,' Darren said. 'Not even a guaranteed parking place. Everything's going to get nicked from the van.'

'Apart from the ladder you never keep anything in ours overnight. And anyway, who's going to steal a vehicle off the street with *Stop Thief!* plastered all over it?'

'Maybe not.'

'Definitely not. Come on, inside. It's getting late so let's order a takeaway. Pizzas?'

'Yeah, good idea.' Still sitting in the van, Darren opened the app. 'The usuals?'

'Not for me. I've decided to cut down on meat.'

'No meat? What's up?'

'Nothing's up. It's meant to be healthier – and I want to be super slim by the time we move to our posh neighbourhood!'

'Posh? It's less than three miles away from here.'

'But an important three miles.'

Darren smiled and Kelly leaned across and kissed him, leaving a blob of red lipstick on his cheek. 'I'll try the pizza with vegan cheese.'

Darren put down his phone.

'What's up? You haven't put in the order yet.'

'Let's go to bed first.'

'No way, I'm starving. After we've eaten.'

When the Deliveroo boy arrived with their food, Kelly suggested they share half-half. Having declined the offer Darren attacked his pepperoni pizza while Kelly sliced and sampled a small triangle of her vegan offering.

'Darren, would you give me some of yours?' she said as she pushed her pizza to the side of the plate.

The single pizza was washed down with two bottles of Prosecco in celebration of the purchase of their new home. Upstairs, the naked Kelly watched her slow-moving, odd-shaped husband undress.

He has his ways, she was thinking as he slid into bed with her, but he's a good man.

of the front door. There was probably a reminder on his phone too.

She knew her husband loved her, he told her so whenever she asked. If only he paid her more attention though. Might that happen once they'd settled into their new home?

Andrew had laid out the requirements for their last meal on the kitchen table.

Two bowls.

Two mugs.

The cafetiere.

A Tupperware filled with just enough muesli.

A second one filled with sliced and chopped fruits.

A quarter-full packet of coffee.

He took the milk out the fridge which he then unplugged with a self-satisfied smile.

Incompatible emotions were spoiling Emma's excitement of the move to her dream house. On the one hand it was great that she had been able to rely on Andrew to plan and execute the perfect move. On the other hand, his faultlessness was unnerving. Where had spontaneity gone? The surprises? Even mistakes might be welcome, ones they could chuckle about together.

Brushing these thoughts aside, Emma lifted the kettle out of the cardboard box that had been marked with a thick red felt tip pen: *Removers – for immediate access please.*

'I fancied tea, but never mind,' she said, as much to be a nuisance as to declare a preference.

'I can get the teabags. They're over there. In *The kitchen – necessities.*'

'It's alright. Coffee will do.'

~

It was 12.07.

Darren and Kelly's removal van was entering Brookland Gardens, driving downhill towards number 34 from the east. Andrew and Emma's van was approaching number 38, travelling uphill from the west.

The vans edged closer. It didn't take a logistics expert to realise that they would neither be able to park nor pass on the narrow car-lined street. They came to rest bumper to bumper. After a brief impasse involving the drivers leaning out of their windows to gesticulate and shout, a crew member from each truck alighted from their passenger seats. Facing each other, it began amicably enough with smiles and laughs. The inaudible banter was observed by the women in numbers 34 and 38 who by coincidence had been in their front rooms, planning where furniture was to go.

The mood was deteriorating as the women stepped outside.

Emma called out to Andrew who was in the kitchen emptying the small *Absolute essentials* box that he'd carried to the new house in his pannier. 'Quick, see this. It's getting nasty, there's a bit of pushing going on.'

'They'll sort it out.' Being a practical person, Andrew was sure a solution could always be found. He didn't want to be disturbed while putting the

kitchen essentials away ahead of the arrival of the goods off the lorry.

'I'm not sure they will. Christ, their man has punched our man.'

'OK, I'm coming.'

Two doors down, Kelly had been yelling. 'You need to reverse!' she'd demanded from the driver of the rival van. 'Our removals got here first.'

Then the punch had come. Despite it being her man who had delivered it, Kelly wasn't convinced that this would help resolve the difficulty.

'Darren! Quick! You need to sort this out.'

Sitting on the floor against a wall in the hallway, her husband was on his mobile dealing with another difficult customer.

'I'm sorry you were burgled when the alarm failed, but I assure you the system was working perfectly well when I serviced it last week.'

'*The police said there wasn't a battery in the box.*'

'That's because one of them is always a dummy. The other one was working.'

'*But not the one connected to the back door which is where the burglars broke in.*'

'I dispute that.'

'*I'm only repeating what the police told me. The insurers have confirmed that's the case making our insurance invalid. Do you understand what that means?*'

Kelly was nagging him to see what was going on.

'Let me get back to you, I have an urgent issue to deal with here.'

'My theft is urgent! If you don't –'

Darren cut the call, switching off his phone as he joined Kelly by the front door in time to see four men pushing and shoving each other in the pouring rain.

'Our man's whacked him again. Good for you, mate!' Kelly cried out.

"Mate" looked across to Kelly, who he was later overheard describing as the doll by the door. He gave her a thumbs up. She waved back, the distraction giving the opposition removal man time to deliver a punch that was forceful enough to send Team Darren's member crashing to the ground.

With the drivers now out of their cabs, it was turning into a full on brawl.

In synchronised step, Andrew and Darren walked along their respective paths towards the melee, the one a bald, tubby yet muscular man, the other a wiry, bearded beanpole. They caught each other's eye, Darren laughing and Andrew offering a weak reciprocative smile in acknowledgement of the absurdity of the situation.

They called out "Stop that!" at exactly the same time. In a rare moment of rationality the crews must have recognised the need to comply with those paying their wages that day. The rival removal men brushed themselves down, where necessary wiping blood off their faces with the palms of their hands, leaving two of them to gingerly lift themselves up off the sodden pavement.

A crowd of neighbours had gathered to watch the spectacle which was yet to be resolved because the removal vans remained nose to nose on the street.

'We appear to have a bit of a problem,' Andrew said to his new almost-neighbour.

Darren considered a sarcastic response; the blindingly obvious comment merited it. Perhaps that wouldn't be the best of neighbourly starts, so instead he nodded in agreement. 'What were the chances of us moving in on the same day?'

'And at exactly the same time. What shall we do?'

'Tell them to fucking move their van,' Darren's driver called out.

'We got here first. You move out the fucking way,' one of the Team Andrew crew responded.

Some pushing and shoving started up again, broken when a knight in shining armour appeared. Well, hardly in shining armour; instead in a Paisley dressing gown with tartan slippers.

'Excuse me, I think we may be able to help.'

Andrew, Darren and six removal men looked across as the elderly gentleman meandered around puddles to reach the end of the path at Number 36.

'Apologies for my attire. We arrived at my son's late last night so we're having a lazy morning. But it appears you have a parking problem.'

A young man came racing out the house. 'Dad, I told you I'd sort it. Go inside, you're getting soaked.'

The older man stood his ground.

'Yes, come inside, Charles, or you'll catch pneumonia,' the elderly woman by the front door called out.

The son took hold of his father's shoulders, swivelled him round and gave him a gentle shove in the direction of the door. Like a wind-up toy the man took a few steps then collapsed into the outstretched arms of his wife.

'Sorry about that, he still likes to be in charge. I'm Luke Foster, your in-between neighbour.'

His outstretched arm obliged introductory handshakes.

'Andrew Crabtree.'

'Darren Robertson.'

'Here's the solution. That's my father's car,' the saviour said, pointing at a Renault Captur, 'and this monster next to it is mine. Remove both and you're sorted bearing in mind the huge gap Dad left between our cars and the spaces each side of them. Definitely enough room for both vans.'

'Sounds good to me,' Darren declared.

The removal men weren't listening. Now the best of mates they were sharing cigarettes and Mars bars, their whispered conversations generating chuckles.

Andrew, the ever-practical one, had spotted a flaw in the plan. 'How will you be able to move your cars when both sides of the street are blocked?'

'Easy, I've thought of that. That's the Gilberts' house over the road. They're away so we can park on their forecourt. If your vans reverse I'll shift both our cars onto it.'

Having been briefed, the drivers of the removal vans reversed the short distance needed to allow the inhabitants of Number 36 to swing their cars into the vacant space. It was then possible to park both vans and the unloading could begin.

'A strange start to life at Brooklands Gardens,' Luke said, having been thanked. 'See you around,' he added before heading indoors.

Turning, Andrew and Darren saw their wives on the Number 36 porch chatting away with a young woman, her pregnancy obvious.

'We've done our introductions and we're already the best of friends!' Kelly joked.

'We sure are,' Emma added with a smile.

'As soon as we're settled in we must organise a get together.'

'That would be lovely.'

Darren eyed Andrew and Andrew eyed Darren. Neither of them looked overwhelmed with enthusiasm.

4

Darren and Andrew stood on the pavement instructing their removal men where to offload their possessions. Indoors, the wives were modifying their husbands' directives. Finally, with the vans gone, boxes were being unpacked in what both couples regarded as their priority rooms – the kitchen and the main bedroom.

It was a little after six o'clock when Emma took the bottle out of the cooler bag that she'd carried in her panier.

'Let's call it a day. Time for Prosecco.'

'Now?' Andrew gave her a puzzled look.

'Yes, now. I'm shattered and it's time to celebrate the move to our new home.'

'I've got no idea where the glasses are.'

Emma rescued two mugs from the box labelled *Removers – for immediate access please*, half-filled them and handed one to her husband.

He set it down on the counter top. 'I will have a drink soon, but first I want to break up the damaged cardboard boxes and take them out to the bins.'

'You don't have to do that tonight.'

'There might be a recycling refuse collection early tomorrow morning.'

'Then do that later. Or should I have a one-person toast?'

'No, of course not. I'll take them out after our drink.'

'To us. To the house.' Emma stretched across and they clinked mugs.

There was a knock on the door. Barnaby started barking.

'I'll go,' Andrew said as Emma took hold of their dog. She heard indistinct chatter before Andrew returned to the kitchen.

'It's him,' he hissed, 'Darren, our neighbour. He wants me to go to the pub. This evening.'

'What did you say?'

'That I'd check if it was alright with you.'

'As in getting my permission? He'll think you're married to a tyrant.'

'Should I go then? I can't say I was enamoured by him this morning. He's hardly my type.'

'How can you tell? You've barely spoken to him. Anyway, you'd better go. It's probably a sensible move to get to know our new neighbour.'

'I suppose so. I'll tell him just for a quick one.'

~

The two men walked to The Broadway in silence, Andrew unhappy that he had been pressured into going out. He was knackered, there were the cardboard boxes to break up and put out, and he was with someone who he had already judged not to be

friend material. They would have nothing in common; this silent walk was proof of that.

Andrew already knew the area well. His favourite evening venue was A Street Café Named Desire, the trendy café during the day that seamlessly became a wine bar in the evenings. He had a particular loyalty to the place because it was here his publisher had discovered him while reciting poetry during one of the café's evening events.

Darren sailed past the side street where the café was located and was standing outside a pub no right-minded adult would frequent unless scoring drugs, wanting to watch sport on one of the massive TV screens, or was still behaving like a teenager, probably an underage one.

'Looks good here, don't it?'

Andrew decided not to challenge Darren's choice of venue. He would take Emma's advice and be neighbourly, and anyway, it was only for one quick drink. Andrew conducted a surreptitious scrutiny of the three young girls entering the pub to check that they weren't pupils from his school.

'What you having, mate?'

'A Grenache if they have it. If not, any rosé will do.'

'You mean wine?'

'Yes. Is that alright?'

Darren shrugged his shoulders before setting off to the bar, the gesture irritating Andrew beyond what it merited. His new neighbour returned with a pallid rosé and a pint of lager.

'They only have one type of *pink* wine,' Darren said, emphasising the word "pink" as if it were a condemnation.

'I'm sure this will be fine.' Lifting his glass, Andrew made a point of swilling the contents before drinking. 'Thank you.'

'Good to get out of the house, isn't it? I've left Kelly to do some more kitchen sorting. She's happy for me to be out of the way.'

Andrew intended to be involved in every aspect of their sorting out but refrained from admitting it. 'Quite some to-do today, wasn't it?'

'You bet. A fight in posh Muswell Hill.'

Andrew let that comment go, too. It wasn't all posh though; Friday and Saturday night fights spilled out from this very pub. He took another sip of wine as Darren gulped down half his beer.

Andrew took a further sip of his characterless drink.

Darren gulped down the remainder of his beer.

The silence was excruciating.

Andrew broke it. 'What do you do for a living, Darren?'

'I'm a stripper.'

'What do you mean?'

'I strip. I go round clubs, there's a gang of us. And we strip.'

'You mean take your clothes off?'

'Yep, that's what stripping means.'

'All your clothes?'

'These days it's no holds barred. I'm open-minded, you have to be in this job, but even I get shocked. You wouldn't believe what the audiences get us to do.'

'Like what?'

Stripping in front of a group of women was a long-standing erotic fantasy for Darren, not merely a spontaneous comment to shock his neighbour. 'Let's just say that I get home with lipstick on a rather private place.'

'Doesn't Kelly mind?'

'Actually I run my own business.'

'You mean you're a self-employed stripper?'

'No, I don't mean I'm a self-employed stripper. That was a joke, I was having you on. I run a security alarms company. Another drink?'

Darren was already up as Andrew struggled to deconstruct the joke. He couldn't see a funny side.

'I said do you want another one?' Darren asked.

The honest answer was no, he still had a half full glass of the acidic rosé to finish. 'One more then. But you sit down, it's my turn. What can I get you?'

'A pint of Kronenbourg would be good.'

Andrew returned with the pint and a small glass of Merlot.

'What about you, mate? Where do you work?'

'Down the road. I teach.'

'I couldn't imagine a worse job. All them kids.'

'I enjoy it, though admittedly there are good days and bad days.'

'Isn't it boring, saying the same things over and over again?'

'Not when it's with different kids each time. The fun is about how they react. Anyway, isn't fitting alarms doing the same thing over and over again?'

Darren had never thought of it like that before. The pink wine drinker might be right, not that he was going to admit it. There was a loud cheer from a nearby teenagers' table. They were playing some game involving clapping and slapping. 'Kids, eh. Do you have any?'

'No. We decided it would be irresponsible to bring a child into our overcrowded world. What about you?'

'Also no. It just never happened. Gives us lots of spare time though, doesn't it? You see all them dads chauffeuring their kids all over the place, playing with them, never enough time to do anything for themselves.'

'What do you do outside of work to keep yourself busy then?'

It was a simple question but Darren was unable to come up with a quickfire answer. He wasn't going to mention things that would make Andrew think he lacked class, like watching TV, going to football matches, playing snooker. He would have to say some bollocks like "Travelling the length and breadth of Britain to watch Shakespeare plays" to gain acceptance from this wokehead. He'd seen one Shakespeare play while at school. He remembered the teacher telling the class that it was a comedy, but there wasn't a single line to laugh at.

'Nothing much,' he settled on. 'What about you?'

'Well I do have a passion. Poetry.'

Two of the boys at the teenagers' table were yelling at each other. One of them lunged towards the other but was held back by a third boy. 'Calm down,' a girl shrieked and the dispute was over as quickly as it had begun.

'You mean like Humpty Dumpty sat on a wall, Humpty Dumpty had a great fall.'

'Not quite. That's more of a nursery rhyme,' Andrew replied, not a hundred percent sure that Darren was teasing him. 'Poetry doesn't have to rhyme – mine doesn't. It's more than a hobby though, I'm about to be published which is the reason why we could afford to buy the house.'

'Well I never; you get paid. Who wants to buy a poems book when they don't even rhyme?'

'Plenty of people. Poetry is becoming ever more popular so I'm hopeful for more success.'

'What is the world coming to?'

'Let's head back, I've got a busy day tomorrow. You too, I suppose.'

'Maybe, but as I said, Kelly likes to do all the sorting.'

~

'And?' Emma asked as Andrew came into the bedroom. She was propped up reading her Kindle.

'We ran out of things to say before we even started. I could never spend much time with him.'

'Well, you don't have to, but you do need to be on good terms with your neighbours.'

'I know, you've already told me that. Anyway, I've chucked the cardboard out but I'm going back down to sort a couple of things before bed.'

'Can't it wait until tomorrow?'

'I'd rather push on a bit.'

'You've got a nerve after I've stayed up waiting for you to come home. What was the point if you're going back downstairs?'

'I won't be long, I promise.'

The peck on the forehead was not appreciated.

Meanwhile, two doors along the road at number 34, Kelly's pretence of being asleep was interrupted by Darren prodding her.

'What are you doing that for? Get off me.'

'You'll never guess what. That Andrew.'

'What about him?'

'I knew there was something dodgy. He's a poet, a bloody poet.'

'What's wrong with that? We've never known a poet; it might be nice.'

'They don't even rhyme he told me, but he's still making money from it.'

'Then perhaps that's a career for you to consider.'

'What? Writing poe … very funny. We didn't have a thing to talk about. I don't even know which team he supports.'

'You could have asked him to recite one of his poems. I'm assuming you didn't.'

'Of course I bloody didn't. We were in a pub, not at someone's funeral.'

41

'I thought you'd learnt your lesson from living at our last house. We need to stay civil with our neighbours. His wife seems nice enough; I enjoyed our chat this morning.'

'I'm coming to bed now. We can … you know.'

'Darren, I'm asleep.'

'No you're not. We're talking.'

'Well I was asleep until you woke me up and I'm going back to sleep now. I'm shattered.'

'Goodnight then.'

'Sshh, I'm asleep.'

5

It was a week after the move and Emma was desperate for a break from rushing home after school to plough through the to-do list Andrew had allocated her.

'How long will you be?' he asked, his brush dripping Pavilion Blue paint onto the plastic sheet protecting the pine floor.

'Not sure but I do fancy a walk. You don't mind, do you?'

There was a pause as they watched a blob of paint run down his wrist. 'Of course not. Enjoy the sunshine.'

Maybe there wasn't a pause; maybe she'd been looking for one. Andrew was right to be taking advantage of the light summer evenings to race ahead with decorating after work. It was the perfect time to knuckle down, what with most of their pupils on leave for examinations, meaning little preparation or marking to do after school. She recognised the benefit of having a husband with such a strong work ethic. But all the same …

By the time she reached Alexandra Park she was feeling guilty about leaving Andrew to get on with it.

She should be enthusiastic to help, but the word "help" was the issue, a feeling that she was regarded as an assistant rather than a partner.

Barnaby was not enjoying the freedom of the park to roam. Maybe it was too hot. Maybe he was too old. 'Come on, Barnaby, it's time to get back. I've got decorating to do.' The dog was stopping by every tree for a sniff or a pee – and there were a lot of trees. As he came loping towards her, Emma was convinced she could see a look of relief that the day's exercise was over.

'Hello there.'

Emma turned to face Kelly whose own dog bounded up to Barnaby. There was some congenial tail wagging, circling and sniffing.

'Why don't you let him loose so they can have a run around together?'

'Barnaby run? I don't think so.' However, he seemed to have acquired a new lease of life in the company of Kelly's dog. Tyson, wasn't it? Emma unclipped the lead and Barnaby chased after his new friend.

'So, how's it going?' Kelly asked. 'Everything sorted in your house?'

'Getting there fast. It already looks like we've been settled in for years. Andrew's a steam train when it comes to fixing things. He's decorating the living room today. What about you?'

'I haven't got a steam train for a husband. More like a tortoise. A hibernating tortoise.'

Emma laughed. 'He's not that bad, is he?'

'Not really, not once you know how to handle him. Actually, he says he's got a bad back which might be true.' Kelly laughed, a contagious chuckle that made Emma smile. 'Maybe we should swap husbands.'

'No thank you very much!'

'I reckoned you'd say that.'

The dogs had finished their chasing and were by the women's sides.

'I suppose I'd better head back,' Emma said as she fastened Barnaby's lead. Kelly attached Tyson's lead and they walked along together.

'Do you know that place?' Emma asked, pointing down the side road off The Broadway. 'The café?'

'I've been past but I've never gone inside.' Kelly turned into the road and Emma followed. They stopped outside the café. 'A Street Café Named Desire. How on earth did they come up with that name?'

'It's a play on a play if you see what I mean.'

'Not really.' Kelly peered inside. 'It looks more like a chic wine bar than a café.'

'I suppose it's both really. Fancy going in?'

'What about your decorating?'

'It can wait. I'd only be getting in Andrew's way.'

'What about the dogs?'

'We can leave them outside and sit near the door to keep an eye on them.'

They fastened the dogs' leads onto purpose built hooks and entered.

'Wow, cool,' Kelly said. 'It's such an inviting space. I love the colour scheme and those paintings are amazing.'

'They're by Bridget, the owner. That's her behind the counter.'

'I used to do art. Textiles. A long time ago.'

'But not anymore?'

'Nah … life got in the way.'

No clarification was forthcoming as they made their way to the counter.

Emma and Andrew had been regulars at the café since the day it opened. Although not close friends of the owners, there was definitely a connection of sorts. Bridget acknowledged Emma with a broad smile.

'Bridget, this is Kelly, our neighbour.'

'Nice to meet you.'

'You too. I love your place – and those paintings.'

'Thank you.'

'What would you like?' Emma asked Kelly.

'A mint tea please.'

'That sounds good. I'll have the same, Bridget. So, how was your hugely deserved holiday?'

'The holiday was great. The aftermath less so, but that's another story. Shall I bring your teas over or do you want to take them with you?'

'Taking them is fine.'

The women headed back to the table with their drinks just as the café was filling with the post-work office brigade in their smart gear.

'It must be hard running a café,' Kelly said after she and Emma had sat down.

'For sure. This place has customers from early morning to late evening. Bridget looked exhausted before they went away. I'm so glad David persuaded her to take a break.'

'David?'

'He's the co-owner.'

'Darren told me you're a teacher. That must be hard work, too.'

'It keeps me busy but I love it.'

'More useful than what I do. Booking people in at a car showroom.'

'I'm sure it's not that bad.'

'Oh yes it is.'

The conversation flowed easily, moving on to their husbands' jobs, touching on Darren's business difficulties and Andrew's poetry, then to what they did in their spare time. Emma jogged and cycled; Kelly went to the gym.

'I hope it's OK to say, but you're in great shape. You look fabulous,' Kelly told her new neighbour and Emma blushed with the directness of the comment.

'You're not bad yourself!' she joked.

Kelly's response was to frown. 'I wish. The missing piece is my diet. Darren eats rubbish and for simplicity's sake I tend to go along with his choices. And look at the result.' Kelly was wearing a cotton sleeveless blouse with skinny jeans. Raising her top she tapped imaginary flab on her midriff with a tattoo briefly visible. 'But it's about to change. I'm thinking of going vegetarian, maybe even vegan. Darren doesn't know it yet though!'

'We don't eat meat but we do eat fish. I don't think I could go fully vegan though; I definitely couldn't survive without real yoghurt having tried the non-milk variety.' Emma glanced at her watch. 'I suppose I'd better go. Decorating awaits.'

The chatting continued as they walked home together, stopping to buy food at the M&S on The Broadway. Emma headed straight for the Plant Kitchen section and began filling her small basket. Kelly followed.

'I've been wanting to try things from this range for ages and now I think I will. I'll blame you if Darren starts moaning!'

Turning off the main road they travelled along side streets of Victorian villas, everything about them oozing affluence.

'Thanks for introducing me to that café,' Kelly said as they turned into Brookland Gardens.

'A pleasure. It really is a great place. I do wonder what Bridget was on about mentioning the aftermath of their holiday.'

'It was probably something infuriating like taking ages to get through customs.'

'Or losing their baggage. Still, whatever it was, I'm sure they sorted it. They strike me as an unflappable pair.'

They stopped outside number 34.

'This has been fun, let's do it again,' Kelly said.

'Definitely. Perhaps you and Darren can come over for a meal soon.'

'We'd love to,' Kelly agreed before launching into a farewell hug.

6

When David and Bridget took on the arts café they were full of optimism, but the level of success was exceeding their wildest dreams. They ran an upmarket café in a wealthy area that catered for different customer groups throughout the day and into the evening, a winning formula though skill and hard work were needed to bring that success. They were a perfect partnership, David with his accountancy background, enabling him to keep a keen eye on finance, and Bridget with her retail experience in the art gallery.

However, when Emma told Kelly that the pair were unflappable she was unaware of the full picture. There were tensions, in part because Bridget and David's relationship had just started when they immersed themselves into setting up the café. As a result there was insufficient downtime to spend together, made all the more complicated by having two sets of teenage children to look after.

'It's not possible,' were Bridget's first words when David suggested taking a holiday to celebrate her birthday.

'We could go on saying it's not possible for the rest of our working lives. We have to make it possible.'

'But how?'

'Engage experienced supply staff from that agency I told you about. Don't run any evening events while we're away. Consider reducing the opening hours during the holiday week.'

'We might lose customers for good if we do that.'

'Not if we give advance notice.' David handed over a sheet of paper.

Dear customers

This is a family run business. Having been going for a year we think we deserve a break! We will be reducing our opening hours for a week between ……… and during that period there won't be any evening events.

I'm sure you'll be understanding and will welcome back a rejuvenated Bridget and David after our holiday.

'If we put copies on tables and pin one up on the door everyone will get the message before we go. What do you reckon?'

'I might do some editing, but the gist is fine,' Bridget said, 'though I'm not comfortable leaving running the café to someone we don't know.'

'I've already contacted the agency; they have an ideal person in mind.'

'When would we go?'

'Like I said, during your birthday week. Actually, I've booked it.'

'What! Where?'

'I'm not saying; it's a surprise.'

We'll only be away for a week Bridget kept telling herself as she packed. Getting the holiday out of the way was her predominant thought as she stepped into the taxi taking them to the airport, and this notion lingered as they waited for their flight to be called at the terminal and even when they were boarding the plane.

As soon as they reached the hotel in Nice with its swimming pool and private beach Bridget's worries faded away – it was a wonderful birthday present and being with David without distractions was a tonic. They flopped by the pool or on the beach for hours on end and there was also the itinerary that David had planned.

'My lovely man,' she said, grabbing hold of his arm on their way out of the Matisse Museum. 'Where tomorrow?'

'A vineyard tour.'

Each evening they would stroll along the winding lanes in the city centre, select one from the huge choice of intimate bistros, and return to the hotel for passionate, unhurried sex that got better and better every night.

'I'm falling in love with you all over again, Mr Willoughby.'

The final day arrived far too quickly. Returning to their bedroom after breakfast, David was checking travel details while Bridget was having a final chill out on the balcony when *Message in a Bottle* played on the phone on the balcony table.

'Would you answer that?' he called out.

'It's Rachel.'

'Take it. See what she wants.'

Rachel was the girl who had nearly wrecked the opening night at the café. They'd been about to close, exhilarated but exhausted, when a policewoman turned up to inform David that his daughter had been arrested for drunk and disorderly behaviour. Bridget liked the confident, articulate girl but didn't approve of the way Rachel always got her own way with her father and she hadn't quite forgiven her for that evening a year ago.

'Do you think that's a good idea?' Bridget had asked David when he told her that Rachel had volunteered to house sit while they were on holiday. 'Wouldn't it be better if she stayed with your ex?'

'Hardly. They'd be at each other's throats before the week is out. It'll be fine. She won't have Sam to look after, he's staying with a friend.'

'I'd be inclined to trust Sam more than Rachel to look after your house.'

Sam was thirteen, Rachel eighteen.

'She's been more responsible lately. Joe's a good influence.'

'Will he be staying with her?'

'I haven't asked but I imagine so. She is old enough to have a boyfriend and like I said, Joe will make sure everything is OK.'

'If you say so.'

Her doom-laden "if you say so" was flashing through Bridget's mind as she took the call. 'Hi Rachel.'

'Hi Bridget. Is Dad there?'

'He will be in a sec. Is everything OK?'

'If I told you what has happened would you pass on a watered down version to Dad?'

'No, I'd tell him the whole truth. Assuming there's something to tell.'

'It's nothing major, no need to worry, but I had a party last night and ... and it got a bit out of hand.'

'Meaning?'

'Maybe I was silly but I couldn't be arsed to send out individual invites except to best friends, so I posted on Instagram. I didn't give the address, I'm not that stupid. I just said I'm having a party and message me if you'd like to come along.'

'And?'

'Some moron did put my address up.'

'Here's David, I'm passing you on.'

David put the call on speakerphone.

It was quite some party, about eighty turned up and Rachel had no idea who most of them were. It got unpleasant and Joe ended up calling the police, at which point the gate-crashers drifted off, but not without causing some damage. And taking stuff.

'Not much has gone, Dad.'

'What exactly is missing?'

'I don't want to spoil your holiday. You can see when you get home.'

'You have spoilt my holiday.'

'But I didn't want you getting back and it being a surprise.'

'You promised you'd look after the house.'

'I know. I'm sorry. There is one more thing though.'

'Go on.'

'Joe spoke to the police and they were really rude and unhelpful. It was that awful woman who arrested me last year when I wasn't doing anything wrong.'

'Let's not go into that.'

'Well, we handed over a list of the things that were missing or damaged and when Joe said we'd need a copy for the insurance company, Policewoman Know All said because we let strangers into the house we might not be covered.'

'I'm not happy, Rachel, not at all happy. I'll see you tomorrow. Make sure you're there when I get home.'

David cut the call and looked across at Bridget.

"Not happy" she was thinking, I should bloody well hope not. She wasn't going to be the first to speak.

'Oh dear,' David said. 'Still, at least no one got hurt.'

7

Despite some guilt, Emma was glad to have escaped the chores for a short while. Bumping into Kelly and chatting at the café had been a bonus. What a fun-loving woman her new neighbour seemed to be.

'I'm home,' Emma called out as she entered number 38.

There was silence.

'I'm back!'

She followed the sound of the hammering up to the spare bedroom. Andrew was crouched on the floor constructing an upmarket flatpack wardrobe. The whacks onto the wooden dowels seemed unnecessarily fierce.

'I suppose I can get by without one of them,' he said, holding up half a dowel in each hand. 'Good walk?'

What was it called when you disguised resentment with indifference? It came back to her – passive aggressive. Emma would have preferred Andrew to demand why the fuck she'd stayed out for so long while he was at home slaving away.

'Yes thanks. And guess who I met? Kelly from number 34. I like her; she's nice.'

'Is she?'

'Absolutely. I suggested she and Darren come over for a meal though we haven't set a date.'

There was no response from Andrew.

'I picked up a curry for dinner from M&S. I'll put it in the oven and then help with the painting.'

'I've finished it. That's why I'm up here doing something else.'

~

Two doors down at number 34, Kelly was telling Darren how much she'd enjoyed chatting with Emma.

'Better than me with her husband the other night then. The man's an idiot. And a snob.'

'You can't say that after one conversation; give the man a chance. They may not be like us but they're still nice. At least Emma is.'

'Did you know he's a poet?'

'Yes, I do know that, you've already told me. I don't see what you're getting at.'

'Nothing. Just that he is.'

'And you're an alarm fitter.'

'I run a business. I haven't got time to think of smart arse things to write.'

'Well, you might well have the time if your so-called business doesn't pick up. But anyway, why does Andrew writing poetry bother you so much?'

'His poems don't even rhyme.'

'And you've already told me that, too. So what? It's not as if you're ever going to read them. Some people must like them if he's selling books.'

'God knows how.'

'Look. They're our neighbours. I intend to be friendly even if you're not.'

'Neighbourly, yes. Friendly, no.'

'That's pathetic. Anyway, Emma's inviting us over for a meal.'

'When?'

'She hasn't said yet. And talking about meals, I've got us something from Plant Kitchen at M&S.'

Darren had started flicking through football headlines on his phone.

'They've got some interesting veggie stuff. Even you might like it.'

Darren had clicked into an article.

'We're having vegan beef wellington tonight.'

He had been listening, or at least half-listening, after all. 'Vegan beef? That's disgusting.'

'You can't say that until you've tried it.'

'You mean until you've tried it.'

'Are you going to starve tonight then? Sometimes I think you're the most unadventurous, boring person in the world.' There was a pause and a smile. 'I don't know why I still love you!'

~

Three weeks passed and the Crabtree's house was in perfect shape, furniture positioned; drawers and shelves filled; two rooms decorated, cardboard boxes flattened ready for the removal men to collect.

'Backgammon?' Emma suggested, this her Friday after school winding down ritual.

'Not yet, there's some paperwork I need to sort out.'

'Surely you don't have to do that now?'

'Backgammon might be relaxing for you, but not me because you always win,' Andrew teased.

'Not always.'

'Alright, one game. I'm feeling lucky tonight.'

'It's nothing to do with luck, Andrew. It's skill.'

Their conversations were often peppered with such light and amiable banter. Emma would have liked the occasional meaningful discussion embracing emotions but these had been off Andrew's radar for some time. Her concern had cropped up during a conversation with Kelly who told her that Darren was exactly the same and that it was probably a female-male thing. Emma hadn't said that her being the queen of sarcasm probably didn't help matters.

'I feel awful not having arranged a dinner for our neighbours yet,' Emma said as she slid the final black counter into her home area with Andrew still having one of his white pieces on the bar. The women had fallen into a regular Wednesday afternoon get together at the café and at each meeting Emma had promised to fix a date soon.

'I might as well give up,' Andrew said.

'You can still win if you get double sixes every throw.'

'Do I have to?'

'What? Get double sixes every throw?'

'Not that. Do I have to endure another evening with that man?'

'Yes, you do.'

'I struggled with Darren at the pub and since then, whenever we cross paths, neither of us can think of a thing to say other than "Hello. How's the sorting out going?" We have absolutely nothing in common.'

'We've talked about this, about how our friends share the same politics, like the same music, the same everything. It's not healthy, we need to mix with people who aren't identikit and here's an opportunity. Anyway, I like Kelly.'

'Deep thinking is she?'

'That's an awful thing to say. She might not be a university professor but she's no fool. I'm going to invite them over for next Saturday.'

'You'll regret it.'

Emma stood up. 'I'll get dinner ready.'

'What about the game?'

'I concede.'

When Andrew joined Emma in their bedroom that evening he apologised for being condescending. Yes, he was happy to have them over for dinner. Emma was already in bed reading. Her husband climbed into bed naked and shifted towards her. She wondered whether his apology was solely to facilitate the sex, but so what if it was.

She removed her nightwear.

~

The next morning Kelly got a text from Emma inviting them over for a meal.

Darren's first reaction precisely echoed that of Andrew. 'Do I have to?'

'Yes, you do.'

'I'm not going to talk about poetry all evening.'

'Fine. Tell them about security systems then, that's much more interesting.'

'No need for that.'

'Then be willing to make an effort.'

'I would if there was any point.'

'In that case spend the evening listening to Emma and me chatting because we've always got loads to say. Being so different makes our conversations fun. If you tried that might be the case for you and Andrew.'

'Tell me, Andrew, what was the first poem you –'

'Get lost, Darren.'

~

With hours to go before the dinner party Darren was still urging Kelly to cancel, in the end resorting to daft excuses that at least made Kelly laugh.

'Sorry, can't come, double booked with an award ceremony for security alarm fitters.'

'My mother's gone missing again, we're going to have to go over to search for her.'

Having declared that enough was enough, Kelly sent Darren off to buy wine and flowers.

'Wine AND flowers?' he complained.

'Yes, we want to make a good impression. Get going or else we'll be late.'

Darren wasn't a wine expert, usually sticking with Chardonnay, but Kelly had told him to get something interesting to impress. How was he going to do that though? He knew a particular wine went with a particular food but had no further understanding to influence his decision. And anyway, he didn't know what they would be eating that evening.

At the supermarket alcohol aisle he was thrown by a further complication – the wines were displayed according to country of origin. He had come to a stop by the small selection of Portuguese wines and chose a bottle of white based on its attractive label of an old sailing ship.

Next to the checkout he picked up a bunch of flowers for £6.99 and peeled off the reduced sticker as soon as he'd paid.

Kelly was on her way downstairs when he arrived home. 'You look gorgeous, love,' he declared in appreciation of her slim fitting navy dress. She'd piled her hair up, fastening it with clips. He liked it when she did that. Very pretty.

'Thank you. I do love it when you say nice things. You'd better get a move on though; we have to leave soon. Wear that nice jacket I got you.'

'Do I need to change? We're only going next door.'

'Yes you do, Mr Scruff. I'm not letting you out the house looking like that.'

'In that case I won't get changed.'

'Very funny. Move it, Darren. And I warn you, I'm on red alert this evening so don't let me down.'

Darren put on smart trousers and a shirt to go with the jacket that Kelly had suggested, these the type of clothes usually reserved for business meetings and pleas for help from the bank.

'How do I look?'

'Lovely. Come on, let's go. Sorry Tyson, you're staying here.'

Andrew greeted them in khaki chinos and a collarless navy shirt that wasn't tucked in, making Darren feel uncomfortably overdressed. Barnaby came bounding up to join them ahead of Emma who was wearing calf length black jeans and a T-shirt. *Frozen - for adults only* was the text on it with a picture of a gin and tonic glass crammed full of ice in front of a Disneyesque castle. Darren wondered if Kelly also felt overdressed. He'd check later.

He handed over the wine and Andrew examined the label. 'Portuguese, how interesting.'

Emma took hold of the flowers Kelly had proffered. 'Lovely. I'll put them in a vase.'

As Emma turned away Darren admired a scrawny yet attractive body, Kelly's prod on the small of his back indicating that she'd noticed him ogling.

'I love these colours, it's so moody in here,' Kelly exclaimed as Andrew led them into the dining room. Looking at the dark walls, the dark curtains and the waste-of-space fireplace, Darren couldn't think of anything further from the truth. Gloomy came to mind, the subdued lighting adding to the claustrophobic feel of the small room. How lucky they were that the previous owners of his place had knocked the downstairs walls out, saving him a job.

The table was laid with a maroon tablecloth and matching napkins. There were three lines of shiny cutlery and two slender-stemmed wine glasses by each chair.

Darren had been warned in advance that the food was going to be vegetarian, which he was prepared to accept, but he had zero interest when the others began talking about recipes. Kelly was acting like she cared. Surely this wasn't *his* Kelly.

'Oh, by the way, Bridget told me what the problem was about their holiday,' Emma was saying, her comment directed at Kelly. 'David's daughter organised a party at his house and it was a disaster.'

'His house? Don't David and Bridget live together?'

'Apparently not.'

'Who's Bridget?' Darren asked.

'One of the owners at A Street Café Named Desire.'

'Oh, that place.'

'Anyway …'

Darren had stopped listening. On his mind was the next day's big match. Who would he select to play if he was in charge? Dougie? Rubber Neck? Froggie?

He picked up snippets of conversation – how people could help tackle climate change through their food choices (apparently eating meat was one of the biggest crimes); the plight of asylum seekers; the over-reliance on Chinese imports; the best London art galleries. La-di da-di da.

'I'd love to go to the theatre,' he heard Kelly announce which was news to him, 'but Darren's not interested.'

'Then you must come with us,' Emma said. 'What do you like doing in your spare time, Darren?'

His silence generated a rephrasing. 'I mean what do you do when you're not working?'

Darren knew what had been asked the first time round. He was weighing up what to admit to. 'Football. In fact any sport.'

'I can see the attraction.'

'It's the unknown that I like. Before its played no match has a definite result.'

'And he bets on the uncertainty,' Kelly said.

'Gambling?' Andrew asked.

'Yes,' Darren's wife answered for him. Darren sensed the looks of sympathy being cast Kelly's way. 'It's OK though; he doesn't spend more than he can afford.'

'But does one ever win? Isn't it a fool's game?' Andrew asked.

So there it was, Andrew was calling him a fool.

Kelly was defending him. 'There's nothing wrong with a bit of a flutter. Provided you don't overspend it's fine if that's what makes you happy. After all, some people spend hundreds on a meal out. Or a fancy bowl,' she added, looking at the ornate serving dish on the table.

'Or going to the opera like we do occasionally,' Emma added, her smile directed at Kelly, the two of them out to avert confrontation.

The evening dragged on for Darren and judging by Andrew's resort to silence, for him too. The women nattered on, attempting and failing to engage their men.

When would this end? How would it end? Darren sensed it was up to him. 'It's getting late, shall we go?' he said on the dot of ten thirty. He stood up to prevent a rejection of his suggestion and was relieved when Kelly's offer of help with the clearing up was turned down by Emma.

'See, that wasn't too bad, was it?' Kelly said as they stepped inside number 34, her over optimistic assessment greeted by her husband's silence.

8

There followed another week of distress at work for Darren with customers out to ruin his attempt to turn the business round. He was thoroughly miserable.

The Zarkova woman with the barely comprehensible accent had been the worst of the bunch. All set to install an alarm system in a vast property, finally an opportunity to earn decent money, he knew she was bad news from the outset.

'If I know you were going to take so long to work I would have gone to the elsewhere,' were her clumsy unwelcoming words, her door having swung open a nano second after he'd rung the bell.

'A week and a bit is hardly long. I did need to order the parts.'

'My friend who is in the house opposite had someone fitting in hers the day after she call him.'

Darren looked across at the logo on the alarm box she was pointing to. It was the company set up by a lad he had trained.

'Have you been burgled?' he asked.

'Burgled?'

'Robbed. A thief. A break-in.'

'No. No thief, no break-in.'

'So what's your problem then?'

'My problem is you cancel me twice and I am left to, what is it you say – twisting my thumbs? I wait at home when I could be at work.'

'It's twiddling my thumbs,' Darren corrected her, noting the single ring on the woman's left thumb. No wedding ring then, hardly surprising considering what a misery she was. Mind you she was a good-looker, her red-with-anger face somehow alluring. He smiled, the much practiced cheeky chappy one.

'Do you think your incontinence is funny?' she snapped.

'Incompetence.'

'Yes, good for you to agree with me.'

'I'm not agreeing with you, I'm correcting you. Look, do you want me to do the job or not?' Darren asked, setting the ladder down against her wall.

If looks could kill. His smile may have charmed many in the past but of late it hadn't done the trick. 'My choice is zero so do it then,' the Zarkova woman said before closing the door.

Darren rang the bell.

'Yes?'

'I'll have to come in and out the house so you need to leave the door open ... please.'

The woman tutted, turned and walked off.

Sod's law, but a problem emerged. The control panel he'd ordered wasn't right for the system. He hadn't installed a new alarm for ages and was unaware that there had been an upgrade.

'I won't be able to get the job finished today; I need a replacement part. It's ordered and should be with me by Wednesday at the latest. Sorry about that, love.'

'You are not my love.'

He'd been calling women "love" since the year dot and no one had minded. How sad that the world was coming to this.

On the Friday morning, the day after the job was completed, Trustpilot pinged notification of a new *Stop Thief!* review, their message a chirpy congratulations, ignoring the fact that the review was another one-star assault.

Twice the company fail to arrive and when a not nice man finally came, he was without a part. I do not recommend this company because they are very useless and they should get rid of the rude one.

Darren showed Kelly the review. 'The woman can't even write properly,' he said.

'That's beside the point. The best thing you can do is apologise and see if she'll change her comment.'

'Apologise? For what?'

'For whatever she isn't happy about. Unless you want the negative review to stay as the most recent at the top.'

'And how do you think I'd be able to get her to change what she's written if she thinks I'm useless?'

'And rude, don't forget that. Let me see what I can do.'

Kelly emailed the customer explaining that the fitter had recently heard traumatic news concerning the health of his elderly invalid father. Consequently, he was suffering severe depression together with memory loss which explained his failure to attend appointments, order the correct parts, and his general rudeness. She offered a 20% reduction in price and a promise that any future work would be undertaken by another member of the team (unless there was a remarkable recovery of the man who, until recently, had been their star employee).

Kelly concluded: *I hope you don't mind this request, but would you be prepared to delete your current review and write something a little more neutral. I am assuming that the alarm system he installed is running properly which is, after all, the most important thing.*

The prompt reply offered sympathy, closing with: *I have changed my review to say that the alarm is working. I have made it three stars.*

'Job done,' Kelly announced. 'Listen to this.' She read Darren the new review.

'Thanks for helping out. Not that I did anything wrong.'

'Calling you useless and rude seems fair enough.'

Darren was unsure whether Kelly was joking or serious. She liked to tease him about things so was prepared to give her the benefit of the doubt despite her not smiling.

The next morning Kelly called down to Darren. 'Do me a favour, love. Pop over to that lovely French cake shop on The Broadway and get me some nice pastries. I'd do it but my hair's still wet and being a

Saturday I'm worried that they'll run out of the good stuff.'

'Yeah, I'll go. How many do you want?'

'A couple of the girls are coming over after their shift at work, so six for us should do. And anything you fancy.'

Darren set off, pleased to have an opportunity to help Kelly. He owed her one for her contact with the Zarkova woman, but that was beside the point because he was always happy to do things for her.

Reaching The Broadway, he came up to a ladder resting against the wall of a shop close to the cake place. He smiled as he watched pedestrians risk their lives stepping into the busy road to avoid walking underneath it. Cars beeped, cyclists swore. Superstition was for idiots; you made your own luck.

He strode under the ladder, hurrying to join the queue ahead of a couple approaching the shop from the opposite direction. No fancy pastries for him he'd already decided. He'd buy a pasty from the pie shop down the road once he'd got Kelly's pastries.

'Watch out!' came a cry from the top of the ladder.

Thick liquid hit the left side of Darren's face, immediately followed by something whacking him on the back of the head before dropping to the pavement. It was a plastic roller tray.

Plop.

Thud.

Splat.

There was a scurrying down the ladder. 'Sorry, mate. You OK? Good job it's only emulsion.'

'Good job?' he asked the man facing him, whose age and shape warranted a recommendation never to climb a ladder again.

'It's water-based so it should come away easily enough, though I'd scrape as much paint off as possible before putting anything in the wash. I wouldn't mix them in with other clothes either.'

'Thank you for that handy household tip. I'd hardly call it a good job though.'

'Just think. Gloss would be in a tin. That could have killed you. Well I'd better be getting on; I want to finish that window before lunch.' The decorator stooped to pick up his paint tray, seemingly unconcerned about the oozing mess left on the pavement, let alone about Darren's wellbeing.

Darren began picking off some of the already hardening paint from his scalp and cheek as he watched the man's precarious journey back up the ladder.

Joining the queue at the patisserie, he wondered whether he should get the decorator's contact details on his way home. Could he charge him for the cleaning? Sue him for injury?

'Did you know you're covered in grey paint?' the man behind him in the queue asked.

Darren blanked him out.

'What happened to you?' the girl behind the counter asked. She had a naughty smile.

'A bit of unsuccessful decorating,' Darren joked in that flirty way that was second nature to him.

'Perhaps it's better to get someone to do it for you. My grandad used to love DIY, but he's finally accepted that he's too old for it.'

Grandad! His flirting ended. 'Six pastries. A mix will do.'

Darren made a point of walking under the ladder again on his way home, though he did glance upwards before dashing through.

On reaching Brookland Gardens he saw Andrew at work in his front garden. Could he sneak past without being seen? Should he delay his return home until Andrew had gone away? Both options were non-starters; it might be hours before Andrew stopped and he wasn't going to wander round Muswell Hill covered in paint. No, he'd have to pass him and be silently ridiculed in the way that snobbish people do it.

To make matters worse, he'd be looking at the impressive display of flowers and bushes at number 38 before reaching the relative wilderness at number 34. Kelly had nagged him about it but gardening wasn't his thing; cutting back plants and weeding (as Andrew was now doing) had to be two of the most pointless activities imaginable because as soon as you'd finished you had to start all over again.

'Good morning, Darren.' Andrew always seemed so bloody cheerful when he was in his garden toiling away.

'Morning,' Darren called out, turning so that his non-paint spill side faced Andrew. He edged past, crablike.

'Did you know you have paint on your face?'

Did Andrew really think that he was such an idiot that he was wandering around without realising that he'd been splattered with paint?

'Yes, I do know thank you.' All he wanted was to go home, get out of his clothes and wash.

The inquisitor persisted. 'What happened?'

Darren told him, Andrew nodding gravely. 'My advice is to never walk under a ladder. The saying about it bringing bad luck isn't the issue, it's simply about taking precautions to minimise risk.'

'It's never happened to me before.'

'Until now that is. The incident today doesn't reduce the chances of it reoccurring the next time you walk under a ladder. Evaluating risk involves some understanding of probability theory.'

'Look, I'm not interested in theories.'

'It is emulsion though, isn't it?' Andrew said having moved closer to inspect. 'At least that's a positive.'

'I don't regard anything about today as a positive.'

'You should. Just imagine gloss in a metal tin landing on your head. That would have been an A&E job.'

'I'd like to go home now.'

With Emma appearing at the Crabtrees' front door, escape was now urgent. But it was too late; she was by his side with a cheery "Hello" before he could flee.

'What on earth's happened to you?'

'Andrew can tell you.'

'It's paint.'

'Correct, it's paint.'

'It's emulsion though, isn't it? That's lucky.'

'I'm going.'

They would be watching him with Andrew smirking as he told Emma the story. Fair enough though because if it had happened to Andrew he and Kelly would be pissing themselves laughing.

Darren called out as he opened his front door. 'Kelly, quick! I need your help.'

'What have you done; you're covered in paint?'

'I haven't done anything, it's what's been done to me.'

'It's a nice colour.'

'What?'

'I like the colour.'

'Is that a joke?'

'No. You promised to decorate the downstairs and this would be perfect. Do you know what the colour's called?'

'Someone dropped a paint tray over me. I was in a state of shock.'

'You could still have asked.'

'Well I didn't.'

'Maybe go back later when you've cleaned up to find out.'

'Or maybe you'd like me to go to the paint shop and ask for a colour match.'

'Would you? I could drive.'

'It was a joke, Kelly. A joke.'

'It'll probably change colour as it dries anyway, but I do have an idea. Stay there and I'll get my phone to take a pic.'

'I wasn't intending to move before taking these clothes off. Bring a bin bag will you and I'll drop everything into it.'

'Will do.' She was back in seconds. 'Smile. All done. Hand me the pastries, I'll take them into the kitchen.'

Darren passed over the box and Kelly peeked inside. 'Why are there two meringues?'

'What's wrong with meringues?'

'The three of us are on diets, that's what's wrong. You know they're full of sugar.'

'They didn't have much left.'

'Honestly, Darren!'

9

Had Andrew ever been happier in his whole life? A melodramatic consideration but quite possibly true.

On a purely mundane level, seeing Darren splattered with paint following his obstinacy in walking under a ladder had been hilarious. Emma told him not to laugh but he was sure that inwardly she was equally amused.

By coincidence he'd seen the very same ladder propped up against the wall of the charity shop three doors down from the patisserie earlier that day. Saturday was their treat morning as Emma liked to call it, her once a week release from a strict food regime ahead of running her first half-marathon. It was trivial things like having a treat morning that brought such joy. Usually it would be Emma leaping out of bed to dash round to the patisserie to get their baguette and croissants.

'Andrew, will you go this morning? I twisted my ankle and I think I'd better rest it.'

Happy to oblige he was up, dressed and out the house in minutes. Soon afterwards he was stepping into the road to avoid walking under the ladder. Yes, maybe ridiculous, based on an old wives' tale about bad luck, but it was a practice drummed in during childhood and there was some logic to the choice.

Back at home the Crabtrees enjoyed a relaxing breakfast before Andrew set to work in the garden and that's when he'd seen Darren. He'd spoken about risk, introducing him to probability theory, but Darren wasn't interested. Well, if Darren couldn't understand that another accident was waiting to happen, that it had no connection to a similar accident never happening before, that was his problem.

Moving on from the mundane, Andrew's happiness came from having finally reached the final project on his house move to-do list – gardening. He was right to have relegated the gardens to bottom place, prioritising all tasks in the house above it. Everything indoors was finished, all removal boxes unpacked, the decorating done, the attic lagged with insulation, the shelves fitted in the office, the paintings hung. Now, with six glorious weeks of summer holiday to come, he couldn't wait to take on front and back garden maintenance, starting at the front since this was the one visible to neighbours and passers-by. Actually the garden wasn't in too bad a shape already, but "not bad" didn't equate to good enough. He wanted it to be perfect, a place where people would stop to admire the bushes and flowers on display irrespective of the season.

With pruning and weeding complete he had begun to lay a bed for summer planting, reflecting as he worked on *the thing*, the one that was making him the happiest of all. He was about to be a published poet. Only a fellow poet could appreciate that this achievement was monumental, that getting an advance ahead of publication was almost unheard of.

The publishers had set an early winter date for release and all that was left for him to do was a final read of this first collection. All his favourites were included – *Knocking at death's door*, *How the wind howls*, *Never forget the children* – the poems he'd honed over the years were ready to go to print. A book tour and interviews were being lined up to promote the publication.

There was a nagging concern though. His publishers were pressing him to hand over a second collection as soon as possible. "To maintain the momentum" they had told him. How could he write about dystopian themes while he was in such high spirits? He loved the new house. He loved his job at school. He loved the additional education work he was doing across the city. He loved Emma, of course. It was impossible to write about death and destruction when everything was going so well.

It would have been reassuring to have completed at least one poem for the second set of works. Eight times over the past week, a mix of mornings, afternoons and evenings in the hope that a best time of the day to write would emerge, he'd sat at his desk with pencil and paper (he favoured handwriting over word processing) in an attempt to put down something of value. He tried to reflect on the depressing state of the world to rein in his happiness.

Climate change.

Persecution.

Inequality.

Poverty.

Economic catastrophe.

World conflicts.

It wasn't working, nothing could overshadow all the joy around him. Perhaps he should write a humorous poem or two if the publishers allowed it. He would need to find the right topics though and as yet nothing had come to mind.

When he sat down at that same desk with the still blank sheets of paper on the following Monday morning, keen to treat it as a full working day, he began by jotting down pairs of words that might induce humour.

Flower Power.

Bear Hug.

Beehive hairdo.

Barmy Army.

Darren Robertson! (He did include that exclamation mark).

Emma appeared at the office door. 'Fancy a walk? I'm going to the chemist to get some more of that spray for sprains.'

By then Andrew had come to the conclusion that sitting there was a waste of time. He was devoid of creativity and knew from past experience that inspiration would only come if he abandoned forcing it. A walk was a good idea.

'Absolutely. I'm getting nowhere fast with my writing. Hopefully a walk will clear my head. Are you OK though? I can get what you need.'

'I'm hoping to start running again tomorrow. This will be a good test.'

'Come on then, let's go.'

Six hours later Darren was getting out of his *Stop Thief!* van having successfully installed an alarm system for an elderly lady who was more than happy to let him get on with it without interrogation or criticism. She had supplied him with endless cups of tea and thick slices of a ginger cake that was rather good.

He lifted his ladder off the roof as a taxi pulled up outside number 38. He watched as Emma leapt out the back and raced to the other side holding a crutch. She eased her husband out of his seat. Andrew leaned on Emma's shoulder, struggling to straighten.

Darren went across to them as the taxi drove off. 'Can I help?'

'No need,' from Andrew, 'Yes please,' from Emma, their words mingling.

'Lean on me, mate,' Darren said as he took hold of Andrew. A bandage ran from his left foot upwards, disappearing inside his trouser leg. 'What happened?'

'Oh, it's nothing, only a sprain.'

It didn't look like nothing. There was the bandage and clearly Andrew was in pain. 'But how did you do it?'

'Can we go in, Emma? I'm rather tired.'

'You can go in, but it's Darren who's supporting you. You're too heavy for me.'

Kelly was coming down the road, her early shift at the showroom over. Andrew pushed to move on, Darren held him tightly and stood firm.

'Hi everyone. What's going on?'

Emma filled them in. They were on their way to the chemist when they came up to a ladder propped against the charity shop wall. She carried on walking under it but her husband pulled up and refused to follow her.

'I told him don't be silly but Mr Clever Clogs here insisted on stepping out onto the road to walk around it. He didn't just walk then get back on the pavement immediately, he stood in the road lecturing me about risk.'

'I was right on the edge of the road, not in the middle of it,' Andrew protested.

'Well, I was incredulous. The last thing I wanted was a debate about probability theory and I did tell you to get back on the pavement. Before I saw anything I heard yelling, the ringing of a bell and the screech of brakes. Then the cyclist hurtled into you, didn't it,' she added turning to face Andrew, 'sending you both crashing to the ground.'

'Help,' Kelly said.

'The funny thing is, when we're cycling we moan about thoughtless pedestrians who don't look where they're going. Mind you, we don't do the F-ing this and F-ing that like this cyclist. He wasn't even hurt. He got back on his bike and off he went.'

'But clearly poor Andrew here was injured,' Darren said, fighting off a smirk. 'How long did the ambulance take to arrive? They say they take ages these days.'

Emma glanced at Andrew before turning back to face Darren. 'Of course we should have called for one but this martyr said he was perfectly alright and insisted on hobbling home. By the time we got here his ankle looked like something out of *Elephant Man*. I was sure the walking had made it worse and the doctor agreed when we eventually got a taxi to A&E. We now have a badly sprained ankle, don't we Andrew.'

'Can we go in now?' her sheepish husband implored.

'Yeah, come on mate, I'll help you in.'

Kelly and Emma remained on the street chatting as the men walked on.

'I know it's not funny mate,' Darren said, the smirk having escaped. 'But as far as I can see your theories are all wrong. Walking round ladders brings bad luck.'

They'd reached the front door.

'I haven't got a key. Emma,' he called out. 'Come over please.'

10

Andrew's injury was responsible for improving the relationship between the two men.

Soon after the accident, as Darren was passing number 38, Andrew came hobbling out of his house using a crutch.

'How's Long John Silver today?'

'Fine, me hearties! Actually, my leg is on the mend. The doctor reckons the bandage can come off by the end of next week. How are things with you though? Were you able to get that paint off your clothes?'

Darren tolerated the tease; it was the sort of thing he might say. 'Yep, clothes are good thank you. I can't say the same about my mower though. I wanted to cut the grass today but the motor's packed up. I've been ringing around all morning to find spare parts but nothing's available for my ancient Flymo.'

'It's probably cheaper to buy a new mower than replace the motor though I'd want a better cut than a Flymo delivers.'

'I was wondering whether to get a new one.'

'I'll tell you what, until you do you can use mine. It's state of the art so you'll be able to see the difference between something ordinary and a machine even professionals use.'

Darren walked alongside his slow moving neighbour and lifted the impressive looking piece of machinery out the shed.

'Look mate,' Darren said having noticed that Andrew's back garden wasn't as manicured as usual, 'while you're out of action I'll mow your grass as well as mine.'

The deal was struck and Darren was presented with the shed key.

'No hurry to buy a new machine, you can use mine for as long as you want.'

'Cheers mate.'

The men looked up on hearing tapping on the kitchen window. Emma was signalling for Andrew to come in. He looked at his watch. 'That'll be coffee time, I'll leave you to it if you don't mind.'

Emma opened the back door. 'Come on in you two. Coffee.'

They sat round a small wooden table in the cramped kitchen. This was the first time Darren had been inside the number 38's kitchen since he'd viewed the house. He much preferred his open plan downstairs.

'I'll leave you to it,' he said having gulped down a strong, bitter coffee in a small cup. 'Mowing calls.'

'Thanks, Darren. Press that button and you'll be gliding along.'

Darren did as directed and the machine purred. After only a single push it was evident that mowing could be a quick, comfortable activity with the right equipment. He finished the two lawns in less than half the time it usually took to mow his own.

As soon as he got indoors he googled the make and model number and was shocked by the price. Taking up Andrew's offer for as long as possible was the sensible option.

He next saw Andrew while on his ladder at the front of his house.

'No bandage and no crutch I see,' he called out as Andrew was leaving number 38. 'That must be a relief.'

Darren noticed a slight limp as Andrew came over. 'I got the all clear a couple of days ago and I can't tell you how relieved I am to be back to normal. You be careful up there,' he added using a hand to shield his eyes from the sun as he looked up. 'Shouldn't you be wearing a helmet?'

'Nah, not for this. It's taken this long to get round to putting up an alarm in my own house.'

'Do you think we should install a new one? Ours doesn't work.'

'Definitely. It's the best deterrent against burglary.' It was an opportunity to return the favour for having the use of Andrew's lawnmower. 'I'd be happy to put one in for you – at cost price of course.'

'Are you sure?'

'I am.'

'Then yes please.'

'I've had a last minute cancellation. I could fit you in tomorrow afternoon.' There had been no cancellation, business remained dire. Darren hoped that the Crabtrees wouldn't do any research on Trustpilot.

'Brilliant. I'm at the publishers but Emma will be home. I'll let her know now.'

~

Darren hadn't realised how nice Emma was until he started working in the Crabtree house. Her friendly greeting, chatting away about this and that during his breaks for morning coffee and afternoon tea, trusting him to get on with the challenge of laying cables and fitting sensors in the old house without questioning what he was doing or why he was taking so long, as had been the case with other customers. He stuck to the task with an enthusiasm reminiscent of the past and made a good job of it.

Beep. Beep. Beep.

'That's letting you know it's active. So now put the fob against the control,' Darren advised Emma.

She did and the beeping stopped.

'It's as simple as that. You'd only need to use the pin number if something went wrong which is highly unlikely. And of course if it did you could let me know and I'd pop in to sort it.'

'Brilliant Darren, thanks ever so much. Andrew said you were only charging us for the parts but that isn't fair. It's taken you a full day to install.'

'I'm fine with that, it's what neighbours are for. I'm sure there'll be times when you'll be helping us out with something.'

'I'm not sure what. Nothing based on teaching, running or writing poetry comes to mind.'

'Well, there is one thing.'

'Sure. Just say.'

'There's been a bit of a conspiracy to diss my company lately. I'm sure it's a rival firm doing it. Would you go onto Trustpilot and write a positive review?'

'Of course, I'll do it straight away.'

Half an hour later there was the Trustpilot ping to notify Darren of the arrival of a new review. This five-star rating used words like competent, reliable and helpful to support the recommendation. Yes, Emma was really nice, it must be said easier to be around than with Andrew even though Darren's judgement of the man had softened. While they would never be close friends, neighbourly goodwill was possible.

That neighbourly goodwill flourished.

Andrew took the time to guide Darren through the basics of pruning and bought him a pair of secateurs on discovering that his weren't capable of cutting through the thinnest of stems.

'How much do I owe you, mate?'

'Don't worry, mate.' There was a mutual look of shock before both men burst out laughing at Andrew's use of "mate".

'But listen, this is a good pair so look after them. You need to wipe and oil them after every use otherwise they'll rust like this one.' With arm extended, Andrew was holding up Darren's tool like a dirty nappy. He dropped it into the dustbin.

Soon afterwards, Darren was in his front garden using those secateurs. He saw Andrew exit his house carrying two broken garden chairs which he dumped onto the pavement by his front gate. Indoors and out he went adding to the pile – a computer screen, a box of videos, pots of paint, odd pieces of crockery. A fascinated Darren ambled across to see what was going on as Andrew reappeared with a stack of saucepans.

'What's this about?' Darren asked.

'Take anything you want. It's stuff we're getting rid of after a final post-move clear out.'

'On the assumption that I won't be taking anything, what do you intend to do with all of this?'

'A few trips to the recycling centre. I can fit most in my paniers and for anything I can't carry I'll get someone to collect.'

When Darren's laughter had subsided he picked up the garden chairs and carried them across the road to his van without saying a word.

'Fancy helping with the carrying?' Darren asked having returned from the van.

'Are you sure?'

'Of course. If you bung everything in we can get the whole job done in half an hour.'

Together they loaded the *Stop thief!* vehicle and set off to the recycling centre.

The men discovered they had a shared sense of humour during the drives to and from the tip. They chatted about some absurdities surrounding recycling, mocking the goings on in Muswell Hill and agreeing that it was like living on a different planet when compared to places only a couple of miles away.

'I reckon an examination of recycling bags would reveal loads,' Darren said. 'Here there'll be Nespresso pods, Plant Kitchen containers, empty bottles of that wine you like, empty jars of artichokes.'

'And pizza boxes, beer cans and burger packaging down the road.'

'Exactly.'

More laughter.

Andrew reflected during a period of silence. A positive about Darren was his willingness to help – mowing the lawn, fitting an alarm system, this lift to the recycling centre. The man might be short on culture unless one regarded football, gambling and 1980s heavy metal bands as culture, but he wasn't as thick as Andrew had initially judged. Emma was right – he'd been a snob for thinking that.

One thing that did irritate though was Darren's attitude towards women. His "Cor, look at her" comments on their way to the recycling centre fuelled Andrew's speculation about how faithful a husband he was. He'd even spotted Darren leering at Emma when the four of them were together. Or was this a figment of his imagination? He could hardly accuse the man and to be honest, he enjoyed looking at the pretty

Kelly. Solely an aesthetic admiration of beauty, nothing more.

11

David had returned from their holiday in Nice fearing the worst following his telephone conversation with Rachel. The last thing he needed was having to cope with house damage, theft, the police and an insurance claim when running the café was such a full on task.

The holiday party aside, there was tension with Bridget who believed that he was too tolerant of his daughter's antics. She had a point since David had opted for leniency given the hard time Rachel had gone through when Jane walked out on the family. Rachel had remained resolutely loyal, laying into her mother so ferociously that David found himself placating his daughter despite his own anger. No doubt like the majority of teenagers she could be wild and thoughtless, but she had offered him more wisdom and support than could be expected from a seventeen year old.

Of course, David knew his daughter's personality better than Bridget did. Rachel was a good natured girl with a sensitive soul despite the outwardly tough veneer. He could never forget the floods of tears and the need for consoling in the early days after the separation.

At the airport, on the plane, in the taxi home, David was deep in thought about how to deal with Rachel following the party. That would depend, he concluded, on Rachel's attitude. His first task would be to assess the extent of the damage.

When he told Bridget his approach as the taxi turned into his street, her comment did little to put him at ease. 'It doesn't matter how much damage there is. The fact is she had a party when she was meant to be taking care of the house.'

It was alright for Bridget. Her nineteen year old son, Andy, was the epitome of common sense and had never caused any problems. But what was better, a computer-loving nerd or a free spirit like Rachel, despite the downsides? Hang on, it was unfair to think like that; Andy was fine. He and Bridget mustn't let the children create a rift between them.

Rachel and Joe came out the living room to greet them. It was early afternoon but Rachel was still in her T-shirt nightie. Joe was dressed, as usual in baggy jeans and shirt.

Set for a conversation about the party, David was distracted. Something about Rachel was different. 'Your nose.'

'Do you like it?'

'Not really. You're now stuck with a nose piercing for life.'

'It would close up if I decided not to use it.'

David looked across to Joe, perceived as the sensible one who might now say, "I told her not to have it done." That wasn't going to happen – he had a piercing too.

Joe took David's searching look as an invitation to launch the inquest about the party. 'Would it be a good idea to begin with a tour?'

David nodded and Joe led the four of them into the living room.

'Someone sat on this coffee table and busted a leg,' Rachel pointed out. 'I'll pay to replace it.'

'As far as we can tell,' Joe added as they stood in the dining room, 'the only things stolen were drinks – which we'll replenish of course. The gate-crashers weren't thieves; they were just idiots.'

They moved on. David was impressed to see cleaning materials scattered throughout the house, the hoover in the living room, a mop and bucket in the kitchen, bleach and a cloth in the downstairs bathroom, the extendable duster stick in the dining room.

'At least they've been clearing up,' he whispered to Bridget as they followed the youngsters upstairs.

'Or maybe the stuff's been left out to show us how hard they've worked to put things right.'

'Cynic!'

They entered the main bedroom, David's room. Bridget's too when she stayed the night.

'I think the duvet cover needs a good wash,' Rachel suggested.

'That's blood on it,' Bridget said. 'And God knows what else.'

'Perhaps chuck it,' was Joe's contribution. 'We'll buy you a new set of bedlinen.'

'Maybe a new mattress,' Bridget uttered.

Rachel led them back to the staircase.

'What about your bedroom. And Sam's?' David asked.

'We haven't finished clearing them up yet.'

'Sam's room? Why his?'

'Don't worry.'

'I'll be picking him up from his friend's soon. I want that room in perfect condition by the time he gets back.'

'Sure, Dad. Would you two like a tea or coffee while we finish cleaning. You must be tired after the journey.'

'No thanks, I can do that. You two carry on clearing up.'

'Aren't you going to ask her *why* Sam's room needs cleaning?' Bridget asked David when they were alone in the kitchen.

'I can't see the point.'

'Is that it then? Reprimand over?'

'What else? They've apologised, shown us what needs to be replaced and agreed to pay for the loss and damage – not that I'll be getting Rachel to pay for a new coffee table – and they're taking the cleaning seriously.'

Bridget's look was one of disbelief. 'Enough then.' Abruptly she changed the subject, turning to memories of their holiday, far safer territory as far as David was concerned.

Half an hour or so later Rachel and Joe came downstairs. 'We've finished Sam's room and I'll sort out mine later, but we need to head off now.'

'Before you go, one thing which is hopefully unnecessary to say but nevertheless I will. No more parties in this house unless I'm here and that includes when I'm over at Bridget's.'

'Of course, Mr Willoughby. And we apologise for all the inconvenience we've caused, don't we Rachel?'

'Yes, I'm really sorry,' Rachel said, edging Joe out the kitchen as she spoke.

'Don't look at me like that,' David said to Bridget as she was looking at him like that after the front door had been slammed shut. 'I'd better collect Sam. Do you want me to take you home first?'

'No I'll wait for you to get back. My mum isn't bringing my two home until late afternoon. I might walk round to the café to see how things are going. I'll be back by the time you get home.'

'We agreed to leave the checking until tomorrow morning. We've been touching base with them all week so there isn't going to be a problem.'

'Sure, but you know what I'm like.'

They remained seated, the silence drawn out and awkward.

David was the first to speak. 'Let's not let Rachel get in the way.'

'She doesn't. She won't. I reckon I'm a tougher parent than you but I get the father-daughter thing.'

'I'm not sure it's that. Anyway, I'd better get Sam.'

'OK, see you later.'

With David gone Bridget embarked on a proper house audit, carefully inspecting each room. She noted cigarette burns on the lovely rug in the living room, scratches on the wooden table in the hall, and a cracked pane of glass on the cabinet in the dining room. The bedlinen was disgusting; she pulled it off and remade the bed. And it appeared as if David had been satisfied with the state of the house!

Tidiness, or the lack of it, was one of the reasons why Bridget had declined David's offer to live together for the time being. She said she'd rather wait until Rachel was away at university even though she wanted to spend as much time as possible with him. Socialising with Rachel was enjoyable; inhabiting the same house might be hell.

David returned with Sam. As ever, the boy was bursting with enthusiasm in describing the time spent with his friend, a boy who seemed to have every electronic device available.

When Sam finally ran out of steam and went up to his bedroom to sort things out, David put his arms round Bridget. 'I know I'm too soft with Rachel.'

'It's nothing to argue about. I love her, she's a great kid.'

Despite the kiss that followed, for Bridget the holiday had been soured by the party and she was struggling to cope with the pressures of family life and work.

And here was David introducing a potential conflict concerning their children and the café.

'Actually Rachel texted me while I was waiting for Sam to sort out his things. She has an idea that I want to run past you. She's asked whether she can work in the café over the summer holidays. She's determined to pay for the party damage and that's how she's hoping to earn the money.'

'What are your thoughts?'

'We are short-staffed and to be truthful I think she'd be quite good.'

Bridget had doubts. Would Rachel always be polite to customers? She could turn on the charm when she needed to but switch it off just as quickly. Then there was another issue – would she keep her hands off the alcohol behind the counter?

'Then yes, but with conditions. A trial first week followed by a weekly assessment of performance.'

'Agreed.'

~

From Day One Rachel was an absolute star working at the café.

12

From unlikely beginnings some friendships grow from strength to strength. Others look like they are gaining in intensity only for all to come crashing down.

'He's quite a character,' Andrew said to Emma that evening after Darren had taken him to the recycling centre. 'It was an extremely generous act and we had a good laugh chatting. It was interesting though when he mentioned his gambling on the way home. I think he wanted my acceptance.'

'Or perhaps to understand why he has the interest?'

'Maybe. He was telling me about something called spot betting. You don't only bet on the result of a football match, you can put money on anything – which team scores first, which player scores, after how many minutes.'

'Sounds like you're hooked!'

'Absolutely not, you could end up losing a fortune.'

'Kelly wouldn't allow that.'

'She might not know.'

'From our conversations I'd say Kelly knows every single foible about her husband. I like being with her and you two getting on better helps us.'

'He's a complex man, full of contradictions and no fool. I might write a poem loosely based on him, covering the dark side of gambling.'

'Go for it.'

Two weeks later, Andrew was up on the podium at A Street Café Named Desire in front of a packed house. By then he was a regular contributor at the monthly poetry and literature night, a good place to test new material.

'Good evening. Those of you who have heard me before, and I do recognise many faces, will know that my themes tend to be dark. However, this new poem is rather frivolous though it does carry a serious message about the danger of gambling. It's called *Debt and Destruction*.'

Andrew began to recite utilising a rap-like rhythm.

White van man
Thinking it's fine
Spot betting every day
Frittering everything away
Leaving your wife in tears
Facing all those arrears.
White van man
Stopping thieves if you can –

There was a burst of shrill feedback and Andrew paused. David, the café owner, was dashing into the office to sort things out. The sound system was often playing up.

Scanning the audience he caught Emma's look of horror and immediately he could see why: Kelly and Darren were by her side. They'd never come to a poetry reading before. Why that evening? They were not smiling.

The high-pitched whistling abated and there was silence, all eyes upon the performer. The audience weren't to know that the last thing Andrew wanted was to be on stage. He had no idea what to do. He looked at Emma in the hope that she would somehow be able to sort things. Maybe grab hold of their neighbours and drag them out.

Andrew was conscious of David's you-should-be-performing cough.

Continuing with *Debt and Destruction* was out of the question, not with the lines to follow:

His wife has had a bellyful
When what she want is a belly full
But no money means no baby
And it's driving her crazy.

'I'm afraid I've forgotten the words, ladies and gentlemen. I wrote it last night, it's all been a bit of a rush. It was only an experiment anyway and it's unlikely I'll ever use it. Apologies. Let me move on to a favourite from my first publication, *Our shattered lives.*

He saw Kelly and Darren get up and leave as he began to recite. They still weren't smiling. The damage was done.

'That wasn't clever,' Emma said as they were walking home after Andrew's nervy performance.

'How was I to know they'd be there? It's not as if they've shown interest in the past.'

'Kelly has and she finally got Darren to give it a go.'

'The poem though, it was only tongue in cheek. I thought it would be fun writing something lighter than my usual stuff. And it rhymes.'

'They weren't to know that you were experimenting with content and form. Accusing Darren of frittering away all his money gambling and suggesting that Kelly wanted a baby, that's what they'll have taken away from this. And you told me it would be loosely based on Darren, not obvious that it was him.'

They had reached the outside of number 34. Andrew paused. The living room lights were on. 'Should I knock? Apologise?'

'Best not to. Let me try and sort it out when I next see Kelly. We have a catch up coffee on Wednesday, assuming she's still prepared to meet me. I might say that the poem is about a friend who gambles and by coincidence has a partner called Kelly which I assume you were about to rhyme with belly in that poem of yours.'

'Very funny.'

'Maybe you should give up on humour and stick with dystopia.'

'Hopefully they'll see the funny side.'

13

It was the start of the new academic year and Emma's first day back at school. There was loads to do but she wasn't going to miss turning up for the Wednesday afternoon catch up at A Street Café Named Desire. She fully expected to be sitting there alone following what had happened at Monday's poetry evening. Emma and Andrew had dithered about how to go about apologising. A note through the door? A text to Darren? A text to Kelly? An email? Dare they knock on the door? They decided to see what transpired on the Wednesday first.

Emma sat in their regular table by the window peering out as Kelly came into view, on time with a wave and a smile.

'Before you say anything I want to apologise for the other night,' Emma got in before Kelly had had a chance to sit down. 'Andrew didn't mean to offend. He was trying to be humorous which is not his strong point. Mind you, if you'd heard him read the full poem you would know that there was praise for the man for stopping gambling and supporting his wife.'

Sometimes it was reasonable to tell a tiny white lie. A dark grey lie.

Kelly kept quiet, forcing Emma to continue making things up. 'It was a coincidence that Darren had told us about his little bit of gambling because Andrew had already written the poem based on the mess a close friend got into with his gambling addiction. Which of course is not the case for Darren; as you said, he might enjoy a bit of a flutter but nothing more. You can tell that Darren is completely responsible because –'

'Stop Emma! Slow down. Take a deep breath. It's fair to say that Darren was pissed off but I told him it was no big deal. He'll get over it.'

'But what about you?'

'Me? I haven't got anything to get over. Actually I'm perfectly happy to be a character in one of Andrew's poems even if I am hard done by. Do you think he'll give me a signed copy of the book?'

Not unless he rewrites that poem. 'I'm sure he will.'

'Everything's fine then. A famous author writing a poem about me – us. That's one for Instagram! But you do need to be aware that Darren doesn't spend a fortune gambling; I'd know if he did. He realises lives can be ruined; that's happened to some of his mates. He only bets a bit to make watching football more exciting.'

'I get it – and I'm grateful that you're OK about the poem. I didn't want to wreck our friendship.'

'No way is that going to happen. I'll get the drinks; what do you want?'

'Sparkling water would be good. I was desperate to catch you but I won't stay for too long. I missed my run yesterday because of the awful weather so I have to make up for it today.'

'Would it matter if you didn't go running for a few days?'

'Usually not, but I'm doing a half-marathon next month and I've got a schedule to follow.'

'Blimey, that's huge, isn't it?'

'About thirteen miles.'

'That's like running from here to the West End and back. And there's me struggling to walk from home to The Broadway to get to the shops!'

'I'm not a fast runner, but I am building up stamina.'

Smiling at her friend's modesty, Kelly went across to the counter.

There was a new girl serving. Her hair was dyed streaky purple, there was a piercing on a nostril and several piercings with studs and rings on her ears. An elaborate *J* was visible on one arm, the rest of the tattoo concealed under her black T-shirt.

'What does it say? Kelly asked, pointing at the arm.

The girl lifted up her sleeve to reveal *oe*.

'Who's Joe?'

'My boyfriend.'

'I hope he stays your boyfriend now that you've done that.'

'He will. He's the love of my life.'

Kelly considered how many times she'd said that when she was this girl's age. She had one tattoo herself from that era – a long story!

'I've got this one too,' the girl said, half turning to show some italic scrawl on the back of her neck. 'It's the first line of a Nirvana song.'

'Nirvana! They were from my day.'

'I love them. Joe's in a band and they play some of their songs. Anyway, what can I get you?'

'A sparkling water and a mint tea, please.'

'Coming up.'

Kelly liked the polite and cheerful girl but sensed that she was going through hard times. She added a pound coin into the tips tin.

'I've not seen her before,' Kelly said as she sat down, nodding in the direction of the counter. 'Hardly the expected employee in this place.'

'That's Rachel, the owner's daughter.'

'You mean the party girl?'

'That's the one.'

Kelly handed over the sparkling water. 'I bet there won't be another house party in a hurry.'

'Not if Bridget has any say. She told me that David always caves in when Rachel wants something so she might have a battle on her hands.'

'But it's his house, right? Not hers.'

'That's true. They don't live together permanently.'

'Changing the subject, I think you're amazing doing a marathon.'

'Half-marathon. I'd never be able to do a full one though running is addictive. You manage to go five miles so then you set a new target for six. You reach a certain time and then you want to beat it.'

'Well I'm impressed. I used to watch you setting off when we first moved in. We had those gale force winds in March and I thought you were mad.'

'I must admit, it was a challenge then. Funny too, because I'd fly along in one direction and barely be able to advance against the wind on the way back.'

'I'd like to try it, running outdoors. It's boring being on a treadmill in the gym, especially while the weather's OK. Yeah, I want to give it a go.'

'Start today then.'

Kelly laughed.

'I mean it. I'm running this afternoon so you can come with.'

'Yeah right. Race against you?'

'You don't need to run for long but we can at least set off together and then I'll keep going after you've stopped. There's a simple training programme for you to try out. It starts with a one minute run then a minute walk repeated for … I think it's twenty minutes on the first day.'

'I'm not sure about today but another time …'

'Come on, let's go.'

Half an hour later Emma was standing outside her house waiting for Kelly to appear. A fashion icon stepped out, Emma recognising the *Sweaty Betty* gear – a headache inducing pair of yellow, navy and orange leggings – with Veja running shoes that Emma knew cost a fortune.

'Ready?'

'Ready.'

Emma ran close to her usual pace and Kelly was keeping up. Five minutes. Ten minutes. Fifteen minutes.

Kelly stopped and called out. 'I'm puffed out. I'll see you back home.'

There was a text waiting on Emma's return.

I loved it but stupid me forgot I had to go all the way back. You're brilliant though.

Hardly, but I do enjoy it. Actually I was mightily impressed by you.

Must be all the gym running. Come with me one day to see what it's like there. I can use one of my guest passes. There's a pool – and a coffee bar.

The following Saturday Emma took up the offer and the experience made her wonder why she was out in all weathers when instead she could be using a zillion clever exercise machines, go for a swim, relax in the sauna and steam room, and end up in a comfortable coffee lounge.

While they were in the lounge together Kelly picked up a flyer laying on the table. 'I've been thinking about doing this,' she said, handing the sheet over to Emma. It was advertising a spa break with a discount offered to gym members. 'We're allowed to bring a friend for the same price. What do you reckon?'

'Go for it, it looks great.'

'Fancy it then?'

'You mean me?'

'Yeah.'

'I don't think so.'

'Why not? We could go midweek after your half-marathon – as a reward.'

'I'm not sure.'

'Didn't you say your run was at the start of the half-term break? It would be a great chance to relax before going back to school.'

Emma wasn't convinced. Simply flopping out at home after the run was tempting. Then there was the cost, despite the special price offered. There was Andrew's reaction to consider and going away with someone she barely knew was risky.

Why put up barriers though?

'Yes, it's a great idea. I'll come with you.'

14

Ahead of the spa break with Kelly there was Emma's half-marathon. Would all that training be good enough to enable her to run the full distance? The answer was yes because she'd run the distance several times, but this first timed, competitive run was different.

Andrew travelled with Emma to the Leicester venue. He'd booked them in close to the starting point at one of those anonymous hotels that belonged to a chain.

'Look at everyone,' Emma said as they joined the queue at reception. 'They're so fit they could run a full marathon and not even get out of breath.'

'Don't be silly.'

'I'm nervous. What if I can't do it?'

'Remember what you've told me. It's not against the rules to walk part of it and it's not a race so even if you come in last it doesn't matter. And if you have to stop, well, so what?'

This was hardly the "Of course you'll be able to do it" encouragement she had wanted. Expected.

'So you do think I'll end up walking, coming last or stopping?'

'You've twisted what I said. I was merely repeating what you've told me.'

An uncomfortable silence followed, leaving Andrew to consider whether what he'd said had indeed been out of order. He concluded that it had not.

There followed a restless night, Andrew kept awake first by Emma's gentle fidgeting then what seemed like her running. One foot collided against his shin before the other whacked against his knee. He cried out in surprised pain and Emma turned to face the other way. Judging by the continued intense movement, she was still running but at least it wasn't against him.

'You probably did the half-marathon in bed last night,' Andrew joked at breakfast. Preoccupied with her Fitbit, Emma didn't respond. She'd purchased the glorified watch to help her prepare for the run and as far as Andrew was concerned it was a waste of money. Assessing state of readiness might be of value to a medical research scientist working in a laboratory but surely not for an amateur jogger using evidence generated by an upmarket wrist contraption.

He was irritated to the point of anger by Emma's fixation on it, resulting in her inability to hold a normal conversation during breakfast.

'One positive,' she was saying as he was spreading a generous helping of strawberry jam onto a slice of toast, 'is that my SpO2 has reached the perfect Daily Readiness Score.'

He took a bite. 'SpO2?'

'I've told you, Andrew. Oxygen Saturation Level.'

'Oh yes. That.' A waitress set a cup and saucer down. 'Thank you.'

Ridiculously he was feeling guilty having ordered a second cappuccino to go with the oversized croissant in front of him, while Emma was nibbling an energy bar and drinking gallons of water.

Four hours later Andrew was at the finishing line to cheer Emma on as she ran down the home straight. Her fear about needing to walk was obviously unfounded; looking up the road he could see a horde of runners way behind her.

'I'm proud of you,' he said as he reached his wife. Emma had been bent low catching her breath but on seeing him she stood straight and fell into his arms. They hugged. 'A massive well done.'

'Thanks. Let's look at this.' She was holding up her wrist.

'What are you doing? Surely it's time to relax and enjoy the moment.'

'I will in a sec but I need to check that I'm in a good state.'

'Meaning?'

'How long it's taking for my heart rate to return to normal. And that my HRV score is OK.'

'HRV?'

'Heart Rate Variability. I think I've told you about that.'

Andrew considered reminding his wife that he was a poet and a special needs teacher, not a health statistician.

'Emma, you've just run lots of miles in a good time without collapsing from exhaustion or dehydration at the finishing line. You are still alive. Surely you don't need a Fitbit to tell you that.'

'No, you're right.'

'So now what are you doing?'

'Last thing. A calorie burn check then I'm done.'

'You can put your calories back on if we get some lunch.'

'Sure.' Emma continued to fiddle with her Fitbit.

'Now what? I'm beginning to feel unwanted, Emma.'

'Sorry. I'm trying to return to the clock display. I can never remember how to reset this thing.'

'I can help out with the time,' Andrew said, glancing at his analogue watch face. 'It's a little gone twelve. Time to get changed and then we can find a place to eat.'

Sitting in a cosy Greek restaurant round the corner from their hotel, Andrew was pleased that the smiling and relaxed Emma had disengaged from her Fitbit. He was smiling too as he reflected on how well things were going with his poetry. There had been a flurry of correspondence with the publisher as the launch date neared. They had organised an LBC interview on the day of the release of his book and there was talk of a BBC2 television appearance.

'I should know one way or the other next week,' he told Emma.

'The way things are going you might be a TV celebrity as well as a poet soon.'

'Hardly. If it happens it'll be a one-off.'

Emma's look made him realise that her comment about stardom had been a tease. Her leg-pulling was always benevolent and he was never upset about being the recipient.

'And I've got my spa break which I can finally look forward to now that the run is over. I think I deserve a break; working flat out at school and training like mad for the half-marathon has taken it out of me.'

Andrew had been surprised when Emma informed him that she was going away with Kelly. He didn't mind because there was plenty to get on with at home, but going with Kelly? His wife had loads of friends so why choose a neighbour she'd only just met and who seemed to be from another planet? 'I hope it goes well.'

'It will, I've looked the place up online. It's amazing. So posh.'

Andrew decided against explaining that he was referring to the company not the place. 'If it's that posh perhaps you'll meet one of those millionaire influencers we read about the other day.'

'Now you're a TV star you might become one yourself.'

'I wouldn't know what I was meant to do.'

'You'd just need to act cool. Serious for a sec. There is one thing I'd appreciate while the two of us are away. Could you and Darren do something together? You've hardly spoken since you know when.'

'There won't be time,' Andrew said abruptly. 'What with having to plan for my book signing tour.'

'That isn't until late December.'

'I still need to prepare.'

'Prepare what? How to sign your name?'

'It's more than signing. There are speeches to make and I need to be ready to respond to awkward questions.'

'You're a teacher, an extremely articulate one. You can make things up as you go along and answer anything they throw at you. Let's face it, you simply don't want anything to do with Darren.'

That was the truth. Andrew remained silent.

'I'd like us to do things as a foursome sometimes rather than only me and Kelly socialising. For a start it wouldn't hurt if you apologised to Darren; he'd appreciate that.'

'Is that what Kelly told you?'

'No, it's what I think. Never mind, let's drop it.'

Andrew was happy to. If Emma wanted to be friendly with Kelly that was fine, but he and Darren? Never.

~

Emma had wanted to use public transport to travel to Brownley Lodge Spa, but when Kelly pointed out that it was in the middle of nowhere and would take at least six hours by trains and taxi but only two by car, Emma conceded.

Joining Kelly by the Ford Fiesta that had seen better days, Emma realised that using public transport could never have been an option. She was carrying a single backpack, admittedly the large one used for hill-walking. The boot and back seat were crammed full of Kelly's cases, holdalls and bags. How could anyone need so much for a two-night trip?

Kelly explained the logic – a different outfit to suit every conceivable occasion and a portfolio of make-up choices to get the right tone for each event and mood. Then there were the magazines, more than could ever be read during their short break, plus several paperbacks "just in case". And favourite snacks, another "just in case".

The women were so different and that's what Emma liked.

Brownley Lodge Spa was located in a converted stately home reached through a dramatic ramrod-straight driveway of cedars. Finally there was a lurch to the left, a sharp turn before catching sight of the magnificent Virginia Creeper clad house – the brilliant crimson red leaves at their autumn best. The symmetry of the house was broken by a large glass structure on the left-hand side, this presumably the spa. Maybe not quite the scale of the Louvre pyramid, it was nevertheless impressive.

They were greeted and shown to their room by one of the Hello Team (the spa's term, not theirs). This woman's starched white uniform with her jet black hair tied back in a severe ponytail reminded Emma of a film she'd seen set in a sanitorium. At the outset calmness prevailed before all hell broke loose, the red of the residents' blood gushing against the white uniform a striking image. Silly though it was, Emma was pleased to see the back of their guide following a farewell fake smile which was a further memory from the film.

They'd agreed to share a bedroom to keep the cost down from outrageously exorbitant to exorbitant. Their room was vast with the potential to house many more than the two double beds pushed close together, only separated by a low cabinet. They'd been provided with a demonstration of the hi-tech features in the room by the psycho Hello Team woman. As soon as she'd left Kelly began testing and Emma had a moment of trepidation as she watched her excitable neighbour. She barely knew the woman and was about to spend a couple of days and nights with her.

Kelly was trying out the voice commands.

'Wall lights on.' On they went.

'Wall lights off.' Nothing. 'I said wall lights off.' Off they went.

'Room temperature twenty degrees.' The fan started whirring.

'TV on.' Located on the wall opposite the beds, it was as big as the smallest screen at the Muswell Hill cinema, the one in a room large enough for eighty seats.

'TV off.' Off it went.

'Play David Bowie's *Changes*.'

Still don't know what I was waiting for, and my time was running wild...

'Volume up. Bloody hell! Volume down.'

'Maybe that's enough for now,' Emma suggested with a broad smile, Kelly's fun-loving nature having put her mind at rest concerning spending time together. 'But you can leave the music on – quietly – while we unpack.'

'Right, I'm sorted,' Kelly announced ten or so minutes after Emma had finished putting her own things away and was now sitting in an armchair reading her Kindle. 'Since we're here we'd better suss out the spa.'

Kelly picked up a two-piece swimsuit off the bed while Emma gathered a dressing gown, slippers, towel and hair products in addition to her own swimsuit.

'What are you doing?' Kelly asked as she watched her friend cram everything into a canvas bag.

'For the spa. I assume we're going to use it rather than just look.'

'Yes, but they supply everything. You'll only need that,' she said, pointing to the black Speedo swimsuit resting at the top of Emma's bag. 'Actually, would you like to borrow one of mine?'

'Nope, this is fine.'

'Are you sure?'

'Come on, let's go. I'm dying to see everything.'

And everything was amazing, madly over the top amazing, the saunas, steam rooms and relax zones replicating the sights and smells of countries across the world. There were seven pools! Who needed seven pools? But you did because there were hot ones for floating, jet ones for massage, ice cold ones, and even one for swimming.

Relaxing on a tropical island hammock, the surrounding walls painted with strips of azure blue sea and golden sands, they browsed the menu of massage options for the following day.

'I'm not sure about the afternoon session yet but I'm going to start with a mud treatment.'

'I'm as tense as hell after my run so it's a back and neck massage for me.'

After a light meal, both opting for steamed fish, rice and a heap of stir-fried vegetables, they retired to their bedroom early. Doing nothing had been exhausting and sharing a cocktail and bottle of wine over dinner had further knocked them out.

'I'm surprised they serve alcohol; I could have done without it really,' Emma declared.

'They tried not selling it but that lost them customers so they reversed the decision. TV on.'

On it came with a fanfare and they were presented with a spoilt-for-choice menu offering what could well have been every subscription channel going, though when it came to television viewing Emma was no authority.

Deciding what to watch was a challenge, in part because of the vast choice, but also since the women's tastes were different. The resolution between Kelly's pick of a romcom on Disney+ and Emma's preference for a French New Wave classic on BBC iPlayer was to view a bland whodunnit on Netflix, at the end of which both admitted to it being rubbish.

Emma wasn't shy but was surprised to see Kelly undress in the bedroom and stroll around naked, she having planned to get changed in the bathroom. She couldn't avoid looking and Kelly noticed.

'Are you looking at this?' Kelly asked, pinching her midriff in an attempt to expose excess fat that wasn't there. 'I know I've got to get rid of it.'

Emma wasn't focusing on Kelly's slim waistline. She was intrigued by the presently distorted (Kelly was still pinching) lizard tattoo that was making its way from Kelly's stomach down towards her bald labia. From what she'd read and seen, going pubic-hairless seemed to be the norm for Millennials and Generation Zs, but a woman close to her forties?

'Oh, this. I got it done years ago. I had a thing about lizards back then.'

'And you shave?'

'Yeah, once you start you might as well carry on or else it looks like a man's stubble.'

'But what made you do it in the first place? Actually, never mind, I don't need to know.'

Emma went into the bathroom to wash and get into her nightwear – a baggy T-shirt.

'I never bother with nightwear,' the naked, prancing Kelly told her when Emma reappeared.

'Don't you get cold?'

'Cold? No, there's always Darren to keep me warm.'

Kelly climbed into bed and took hold of a pile of magazines from the stack on the floor. Emma commenced reading her Kindle. After a minute or so of page rustling she heard Kelly drop a magazine and pick up another one.

Emma continued reading.

Another minute, another magazine discarded and a new one picked up.

Emma read on.

A third magazine came and went.

'Nothing worth reading?' Emma asked, looking across.

'Emma. Have you ever, you know, with a woman?'

'No.' This wasn't a hundred percent true if you counted some messing around with friends at university, but it was accurate enough. 'Have you?'

'Only a bit. Fancy giving it a go?'

Emma was unsure whether Kelly was asking in the wider sense or whether she meant with her that night. 'I don't think so. Goodnight, Kelly.'

~

Andrew had been thinking about Emma's request for him to engage with Darren during the women's spa break. His excuse of being too busy to socialise was rubbish. There was nothing to prepare in advance of the book signing tour and he was finally making headway with the writing of the second collection of poems. Emma's logic made perfect sense – it's always sensible to stay friendly with your neighbours. He recognised that it would be up to him to take the initiative. At the very least Darren deserved an explanation about the poem he'd written, if not an apology.

That evening there was an open mike session at A Street Café Named Desire, music this time, not poetry. That would be the perfect option for socialising with

Darren; they could do something together without needing to talk much.

Early afternoon Andrew walked down to number 34 and rang the bell.

'Hello, mate. What do you want?'

'I was wondering whether you're doing anything this evening. It's open mike night at the café down the road and the musicians are usually pretty good.'

'Tonight?'

'Yes. Listen though. Before saying yes or no I want to apologise for that poem I read out. It was meant to be funny but I appreciate that it could be taken as offensive.'

'No worries, mate. Write whatever you like, it doesn't bother me.'

'How long are you going to be?' He hadn't noticed the woman sitting at the dining table on the far side of the open plan space.

'Only a sec, love.' Darren turned back to face Andrew. 'That's Kelly. Not mine of course, another Kelly. She does my accounts. There are some issues we're trying to sort out today.'

'Oh,' was all Andrew could come up with as he considered which of two very different scenarios was the more likely.

'Yeah, I'll come along this evening. It'll be good to have a break from all this working with figures.'

Andrew glanced at the woman. "Figures" Darren had said. Did he grasp the irony? The part of the woman's figure that he could see inside the skimpy blouse was quite something. 'Great. I'll pick you up a little before eight.'

'Fine. And look, it's probably best you don't tell Kelly – my Kelly – about this Kelly being here. You know what women are like.'

'I won't say a thing.'

'Thanks, mate. Perhaps don't mention it to Emma either what with them being friends.'

Andrew wasn't sure about this supplementary request and left it open. 'I'll see you around eight then.'

The other Kelly was still there when Andrew returned that evening and Darren seemed perfectly relaxed when he introduced them. 'We've been working our socks off all day so we've earned a break, haven't we?'

Kelly2 nodded.

'So I hope you don't mind Kelly joining us.'

'Of course not.'

Andrew couldn't work out what was going on as the three of them made the short walk to the café. If Darren was being unfaithful surely he wouldn't be introducing the woman to Andrew and taking her to a crowded public venue. Maybe he was telling the truth then – she was an accounts person, a young female accounts person with a pleasing figure, nothing more.

It was an acoustic night so there was more scope to chat than he'd anticipated but being with the pair of them turned out to be OK. Kelly2 was laughing away at Darren's jokes and anecdotes, leaving the smiling Andrew conscious of tolerating language and themes far removed from his usual political correctness. The heavy intake of alcohol was possibly a factor narrowing the cultural divide.

The three of them walked back to Brookland Gardens together, the unsteady Kelly2 holding on to Darren's arm for support.

'Coming in for a coffee?' Darren asked his part-time young female accounts manager with the pleasing figure and she accepted. There was no invite for Andrew, leaving him to wonder whether there was more to it than bookkeeping. Might she be staying the night? Back at home he peered out his bedroom window for a while to see if a taxi rolled up. None appeared. Exhausted, somewhat intoxicated, he abandoned his spying.

Having spent some of the night fantasising about Kelly2's body, he decided it was best to do as Darren had asked, not mention anything to Emma.

~

Andrew was in the garden piling up leaves and Darren was getting out of the *Stop Thief!* van when the Ford Fiesta turned into Brookland Gardens and Kelly beeped the horn. She parked and the women jumped out of the car and opened the back doors. Emma lifted up her backpack and hooked it onto her shoulder before taking hold of one of Kelly's cases. Kelly was taking out possessions from the boot as Darren ran across the road to greet them. Andrew abandoned his gardening to join in.

'We had a great time,' Kelly announced to no one in particular as the four of them stood by the car.

'Yes, absolutely great,' Emma echoed, this directed at Kelly.

'Well give us a hug then, darling,' Darren said, his arms outstretched, and Kelly rushed into an embrace. Kelly2 was on Andrew's mind as he watched them kiss.

'Err, I'm here too,' Emma said.

'Yes, of course.' Andrew wrapped an arm round his wife's shoulder and planted a kiss on her cheek. 'Welcome home.'

Darren, Andrew and Emma followed Kelly to number 34 in convoy carrying her bags and cases.

On reaching her front door, Kelly dropped the bag she had been holding and hugged Emma. The men stood by.

'Perhaps we should go home,' Andrew said as Emma broke free.

'Good idea. See you soon. Both of you.'

15

The Robertsons at number 34 and the Crabtrees at number 38 regarded Luke and Alex Foster, their in-between neighbours at number 36, as a lovely young couple even though there had been little contact beyond greetings whenever paths crossed.

The same polite conversations were had again and again.

Are you settling in OK? (Asked by one of the Fosters when the residents at number 34 and 38 first moved in).

Yes, we're getting there. (During the first month or so).

Have you settled in OK? (Still being asked four months later).

All sorted. Finally. (How much longer could this be the topic of conversation?)

How's the pregnancy going? (The counter question from the residents at number 34 and 38).

Tiring, but touch wood everything is fine.

One Saturday morning in November, Emma and Kelly were on the street about to start their run. Despite the inclement weather Emma was only wearing black leggings and a short-sleeved T-shirt. Kelly, in a multi-coloured combi set topped with a bulky orange gilet and an orange beanie, looked set for an Antarctic expedition. They paused on seeing Alex leave her house, her hand resting on her belly.

'How's the pregnancy going?' Kelly asked.

'Kicking like mad. He's taking the wind out of me and that's only by walking from the front door to here.'

'Not long to wait though,' Emma said.

'No. A couple of weeks then the real work begins. Not the best of weather for running, is it? Anyway, enjoy it.'

Kelly had become Emma's regular running partner. Emma had initially thought that it might be a fad with Kelly soon dropping out. She was wrong; her friend's determination and rate of improvement were phenomenal.

They set off at a pedestrian pace, having decided to only run flat out when they reached the safety of the gravel paths in the park, the recent rain and fallen leaves having made the pavements lethally slippery.

'I can't say I'm enjoying this,' Kelly said as an icy drizzle bore down before they had even reached Alexandra Park.

It was rare for Kelly to suggest giving up and even more unusual for Emma to think the same, but that day was exceptionally unpleasant, the wind now driving the stinging sleet into their faces.

Emma stopped. 'Agreed. Let's head back.'

They walked, heads down, chatting about whether to try again later that day if the weather improved.

'I don't think it will get better,' Kelly said, looking at her weather app. 'Home for a quick shower then I'd better start getting our meal ready. It's Asian fusion, are you both OK with that? I should have asked before I bought the ingredients.'

'Sounds great, it's one of my favourites. Andrew's too.'

When they turned into Brookland Gardens they saw Luke driving away at speed. As the car shot by there was a half-hearted wave from Alex, slumped in the passenger seat.

'That's the baby on its way,' Kelly said.

'I think you're right.'

'So we won't be able to ask her how the pregnancy's going anymore.'

'And they've stopped asking us about the move.'

'Then what's left to talk about?'

'Easy. How's the baby?'

'Yeah, there'll be that. Maybe the conversation will go beyond one or two sentences because actually I'd be happy to help them. Perhaps with babysitting.'

'I'd like to do that too,' Emma agreed.

There was an exchange of glances as if there were something unsaid, but the moment passed.

'OK. See you tonight then,' Kelly said. 'Around seven thirty would be fine.'

It was the Robertsons' turn to host the dinner party, unofficially a monthly event. Emma and Kelly were still attempting to bring their husbands together, an uphill struggle despite having looked like things were improving at one stage. They were persisting – they got on, so why couldn't the men?

'Because men lack the emotional intelligence that we have,' Emma had once explained.

'You mean they're all tossers,' was Kelly's flippant response.

'That's one way of putting it.'

Kelly was particularly anxious about that evening's get together because Darren had spent the whole day in the house moping and was in a foul mood. There hadn't been a single *Stop Thief!* customer or enquiry all week. 'Maybe I should write poetry,' he wisecracked as they were getting ready to greet their visitors. 'There's obviously money in it. Did you know they're planning to have a kitchen refit? That won't come cheap.'

'I don't think his poetry brings in tons of money. Emma told me he got paid when he signed the contract which meant they could afford the house, but she doesn't think he'll be earning much in royalties.'

'Royalties? What have the royals got to do with it?'

'It's what you get paid for selling books. And like I said, Andrew won't be making a packet.'

'So how come they can afford a new kitchen?'

'They teach so there's that regular income coming in. Why don't you ask them what their schools are like this evening?'

'That's no better than talking about poetry.'

'So what's left? Football? At least be polite. You make it obvious you aren't interested.'

'That's because I'm not. What do you want me to do, invite him to read them to us?'

'You have to admit that it's exciting. He's going to be on telly soon and during the school holidays he's off to bookshops to sign copies.'

Kelly pecked her husband on the cheek, as amorous as a peck on a cheek could be. There had been lots of kissing and more since her spa visit. Darren wasn't to know that being away with Emma had made her feel sexy and that he was the beneficiary of her lust.

'If you're well behaved this evening who knows what might follow,' she joked.

Good behaviour was not immediately apparent. The meal got off to the usual disappointing start with easy chatter from the women, vain attempts to involve their husbands, and subsequent periods of silence.

Andrew broke one such silence by asking where Darren and Kelly's favourite places to visit were. At least he was trying even if Darren wasn't.

It was left to Kelly to respond. 'We used to go to Wales a lot, to the coast, didn't we Darren? We haven't been for ages though.'

'Why not?'

'I don't know, money I suppose,' Kelly said and it looked like her eyes were welling up as she left the others at the table.

'We like the coast, too,' Andrew was saying as Kelly returned with a tray. 'We usually end up in Norfolk.'

Kelly set four smallish sharing bowls onto the table.

'This looks delicious.'

'Thanks. Two more to get.'

'Need any help?'

'No thanks, Emma. I'm fine.'

'So you're off to sign books next month,' Darren blurted out, his first contribution that evening beyond taking drinks orders when the Crabtrees arrived.

'Yep, as soon as the school holidays start. Local first, London that is, then if all goes well, to other cities.'

'That's your Christmas sorted then,' Kelly said, having rejoined them. 'Just help yourselves to the food please.'

'Yes, our Christmas adventure and we're happy about that. The alternative would have been spending the holiday with either Emma's sister or my brother or both of them, surrounded by over-excited kids.'

'Don't you like being around kids then?' Darren asked.

'I wouldn't be teaching if that were the case.'

'But no children yourselves?'

'No. We decided not to. We think the world's crowded enough without adding to it, don't we Emma? You don't have kids either. Any particular reason?'

A silence erupted, the wives looking across at each other wondering how to deal with Andrew's insensitive question. Kelly had told Emma that Darren might be infertile but that he wasn't prepared to investigate or consider options. And Emma had told Kelly that Andrew's decision about children based on overpopulation wasn't fully shared. She was unsure. Anyway, approaching forty it was probably too late.

'Can you imagine it,' Darren was saying. 'Having to deal with babies. The crying, the feeding, the pissing and pooing. I don't think Kelly would be up for all that, would you love.'

There was another look between the women. Emma had introduced Kelly to the concept of subliminal sexism and Kelly had taken the concept onboard.

Emma stepped in. 'I think Kelly is a hundred percent capable of doing anything.'

'Thank you, Emma.'

'I wasn't saying she couldn't,' Darren replied.

'You implied it,' his wife countered.

'Well, I didn't mean to. Of course you can do everything.'

'Then perhaps it would have been nice to say so first time round.'

'I … I …'

'Just eat, Darren.'

The evening came to a speedy end, Emma instigating the departure by declaring exhaustion and the onset of a cold.

~

'God, did you hear how Darren put Kelly down,' Andrew slurred when they got home. Alcohol had been his salvation that evening.

'Not unexpected from a bloke. It's only the level of subtlety in undermining women that differs.'

'You're not suggesting that I …'

The pause was deliberate; Andrew was waiting for a response. He didn't get one.

'Surely you're not likening me to Darren.' Andrew took hold of his wife's hand. 'Come on, let's head upstairs. I'm in the mood.'

Emma was hardly "in the mood", daft as the expression was, but once upstairs she softened. They kissed, undressed and made love and she enjoyed it as much as ever.

Meanwhile, at number 34, a row was brewing with Kelly accusing Darren of insulting her in front of their neighbours. 'Of course I'd be capable of taking proper care of a child. I had a good mind to tell them that not having children was because of you.'

'That's not definite; it could be you.'

Kelly knew that was unlikely. She had fallen pregnant while still at school. Refusing to say who the father was and he unwilling to admit it, her parents got her to have an abortion. Not forced her. Not quite forced. Darren knew the story, perhaps it was on his mind too as he drew close to her. 'Let's not argue, love.'

She could feel his hardness as he pressed against her. If Darren ever found out that she had discussed the topic with Emma he'd go bananas. She was feeling guilty. 'Upstairs Mr Robertson. We can leave the rest of the clearing up until tomorrow.'

~

Four days after the dinner party the Robertsons and Crabtrees were invited to meet the Foster's baby. Alex

133

looked remarkably in control and relaxed as she cradled the sleeping Arthur in the crook of her arm.

'You're witnessing a lull before a storm,' she said when Emma complimented her. 'He's not a brilliant sleeper.'

Kelly handed over their joint present, a Jellycat soft book and a lion comforter. Luke poured out glasses of champagne. 'Well, we did it,' he said as glasses clinked together.

'More a case of I did it after your initial contribution.'

'Can I hold him?' Clasping the tiny being, Emma embraced the warmth, the smell, the sense of need to be protective. The realisation that she wanted a baby came from nowhere.

'Come on, pass him over. Quick, before he wakes up,' Kelly ordered.

As she was about to, Arthur's eyes opened, pale blue inquisitive eyes. Emma had to deflect her reluctance to give him up.

'You are a sweety pie, aren't you,' Kelly said as she gently rocked Arthur.

Emma regarded the three men, showing interest in the baby but perhaps not that much. And then there was Kelly cuddling the baby and Alex, alert and on guard, ready to spring into action if need be to protect him. She wondered whether there was a difference between women and men after all.

Luke was outlining their plans to Andrew and Darren. With Alex intending to return to work after maternity leave, his parents had agreed to be the principal baby minders. 'They're both retired and more than happy to help us out.'

The logistics were complicated because the grandparents lived a couple of hours' drive away, making a daily journey unrealistic.

'We've gone round and round in circles considering options. Our initial plan was to move near to them in Suffolk. It has advantages, cheaper house prices for a start. You wouldn't believe what we could buy out there for what we'd get for this place. But the commute to work would be a nightmare. Impossible. We don't want to change jobs, so when it came down to it we realised that leaving London wasn't on, not for the time being anyway.'

The resolution was for the Fosters to move to a place with an adjoining annex and for Luke's parents to stay there for four nights a week, returning to their Suffolk home for weekends. 'And we've already found the perfect place.'

'Where is it?'

'Further away from Central London but well served by the Underground.'

'When do you think you'll be moving?' Andrew asked.

'Sooner than we thought. You know what Muswell Hill is like. The house went on the market last Wednesday and we sold it by Friday. The estate agent hadn't even put up the For Sale sign. He contacted clients on their books desperate to move to the area and there was a bidding war.'

'Who won?'

'A Mrs Hall, that's all I know about her. I saw her the once, for about ten minutes but didn't take any notice when the estate agent was showing her round. Why would I when I had no idea she was going to be the purchaser at the time? Apparently she's in a hurry which suits us. We'll be gone by the end of the year, I'm sure of that.'

With Alex having gone upstairs for Arthur's feed, Emma and Kelly turned their attention to the discussion about houses.

'We'll miss having you as neighbours,' Emma chipped in, more out of politeness than anything else since she'd barely spoken to the Fosters over the past five months.

As soon as Alex came back downstairs the four departed, taking the hint that the parents were desperate for some quiet time while Arthur was asleep.

'Who did they say was moving in?' Emma asked Andrew as the four of them stood on the pavement outside number 36.

'A Mrs Hall.'

'I suppose there'll be a Mr Hall and children too,' Kelly said. 'It's too big a property for one person. We'll find out what's what soon enough.'

16

The pressure on Darren was relentless as one disastrous week was followed by another. There was no new business and past regular customers were turning on him. Mrs Harwood, a long-time client, was questioning why the alarm maintenance charge had soared since the previous year.

'Materials,' he told her, but that single word wasn't considered comprehensive enough. Mrs Harwood demanded elaboration.

'Like I said, prices have soared,' he explained. 'It's all to do with the supply chain.'

'But how can it be a supply chain issue when nothing's been added or replaced? All you've done is gone up a ladder to check the boxes and then pressed a few buttons on the control panel.'

Living in a double-fronted Victorian villa in one of the most expensive streets in north London, this woman was loaded; you only had to look at the antiques crammed into each room where sensors were installed to know that. Yes, he'd upped the service charge by twenty-five percent in a desperate attempt to bring in more income, but she could afford to pay.

'I've done some research, Mr Robertson, and I have to say that your prices are way higher than anybody else's. This will be the last year of our agreement. I'll be cancelling the direct debit.'

On his return home the Trustpilot app had pinged to signify a new review.

More expensive service charge than any other company in the area and unwilling to take customer concerns on board. One star.

'Look at this, Kelly,' he said as he passed across his phone that evening.

'What happened?'

'Nothing. I did the service, tested everything, was polite – and then she writes this rubbish.'

'Maybe it's time to consider what you can do to improve how you communicate with your customers. I could even help; I've been trained to death about that at work.'

Darren was so despondent that Kelly's offer of help wasn't acknowledged, let alone taken up. His sullen sulk persisted during dinner and lingered as he hopped between channels in search of something he considered worth watching.

'Here, give me that,' Kelly said, taking hold of the remote and switching off the TV. She snuggled up against him. 'Things will get better; I know you'll work something out. I trust you.'

That night she undressed him – he always liked that. He removed her clothes – he liked that too. But having tumbled onto the bed Darren seemed distracted and was unable to perform.

'What's up?'

'You're not interested in me anymore.'

'Don't be daft.'

'I can tell.'

'I love this – and this –'

'Hands off please.'

'Darren!'

He moved apart.

'Stop being silly. Get back here at once, Mr Robertson!' Darren had swung round and was sitting on the edge of the bed. 'OK, don't then. I'm going into the spare room.'

Kelly got out of bed and marched towards the door.

'Sorry, Kelly. Come back.'

'Get lost.'

'Jesus, I've got heart palpitations.'

'I'm sure you'll be fine.'

Darren was left to contemplate what was going on. The thing is, he was thinking as he lay back down in bed, Kelly's right to be angry with me. And if she wasn't interested in him anymore – and he was convinced that was possible – he deserved it. He used to be a joker and she would be laughing uncontrollably by the end of one of his stories. He'd always wanted to please her, lavishing her with praise, with gifts. Why had that changed, or had it? He loved her and was in danger of losing her.

It was work that was dragging him down. When he first set up the company customers relished his cheery can-do attitude. He played up to it, the cheeky cockney (which he wasn't) who related comic adventures, usually made up, about fitting alarms.

So the next thing I knew there were two police cars shooting round the corner, sirens blaring and screeching to a halt, all because a nosey neighbour had reported a thief up a ladder because he knew the occupants were away on holiday.

Testing the alarm set off the barking and when I turned there was this vicious dog going for me. I've never moved so fast and I made it to the downstairs loo just in time. I had to stay there until the customer came home after work.

God, how sour it had got. It would be easy to blame it on financial difficulties, but no, boredom and dissatisfaction had set in well before then. The money problems were the result of his attitude, not the cause of it.

Not surprising Kelly was fed up with him because all he did was moan: he had to change.

~

Andrew was on Cloud 9. On reaching home after school he'd ripped open the cardboard packet that had been squeezed through the letterbox, to unearth the proof copy of his book.

He loved it.

That cover! Dense woodland with moonlit shadows making the winding path through a bottle green and purple landscape appear both frightening and tempting.

Andrew Crabtree! There was his name in bold off-white font.

He was so excited. When he heard the key in the lock he rushed to the front door. 'Take a look at this.'

Emma took hold of the book, examining the front and back covers before opening to a random page. 'Wow, I love it! I'm so proud of you. Just a sec.'

She returned with the bottle of absurdly expensive wine that they had purchased for publication day. What the hell; they'd buy another bottle for then.

Sitting together on the sofa they flicked through the book, appreciating the achievement rather than doing any checking – that could wait. Having pigged themselves on crisps, nuts and chocolate, Emma stood, took hold of Andrew's hands and tried to yank him up.

He resisted.

'I'd like to continue the celebration in bed with my famous poet husband.'

'Soon. After *QI XL*.'

The affronted Emma's lustful thoughts dived, fully disappearing as trivial scientific facts were rolled out during the TV programme. Usually amused by the comic antics of the panel, she was utterly disconnected. Clearly this wasn't the case for Andrew who was engrossed on discovering the dietary habits of toads and frogs.

'Finished. Come on then,' Andrew said as he yanked Emma up.

The failure of her own yanking attempt was on her mind but nevertheless she stood up. Her husband was pulling off his clothes as they made their way upstairs (it was always upstairs, always in the bedroom), stumbling as he pulled off his trousers, grabbing the bannister to remove socks. It was more comic than erotic.

Finally reaching the landing he made a beeline for Emma.

'That's my job,' Andrew said as Emma was unbuttoning her blouse. Under normal circumstances she would have been happy with that but these weren't normal circumstances – putting watching a TV show ahead of her needs had festered.

He was fiddling with the clasp at the back of her bra. He'd always been cack-handed at taking her bra off. 'Ow, you're pinching. Let me do it.'

Neither sensuality nor sensitivity appeared to be on Andrew's radar that evening. Both naked, standing in the centre of the bedroom, he took hold of his wife and kissed ferociously.

'Jeez Andrew, go easy. Your beard is so rough when you snog hard.'

The aroused Andrew was working his way down Emma's body.

'I get chafed there too. Be gentle.'

By the time they were on the bed, Andrew pressing down on her, Emma was not optimistic about the scope for a high-quality experience.

'Maybe it's time to get rid of the beard,' she suggested after her husband had sped to orgasm and rolled to her side.

'Rid of it? No, I like it.'

'But if I don't?'

'It's fitting for a poet to have one.'

'What! That's mad. Is fame going to your head?'

Andrew tutted as he got out of bed.

'Where are you going?' Emma asked.

'Downstairs. I forgot to hang out the washing.'

'Now?'

'Yes, now.'

'I'll be in the spare room when you come back up.'

Andrew ran his hands up and down his face on his way downstairs. It was rough against his palms and so might well be uncomfortable against Emma's soft skin, but he liked the aura a beard created. And anyway, loads of men had them these days.

As he pulled the damp clothes out of the machine he reflected on Emma's mood. Maybe she had a point: they'd been comfortable in each other's arms and he'd abruptly pulled away. He'd been selfish because he'd had his orgasm and she hadn't. He could have delayed hanging out the washing until the morning. Yes, Emma's anger was merited because he should be worrying less about getting things done and more about making his wife happy. This was by no means the first time he'd resolved to change, always in the past slipping back to his old ways.

The dishwasher was beeping, the cycle complete. He might as well unload it before going back up.

~

Having been on a run, the dogs with them, Kelly and Emma were back in the café.

Hot chocolate and apple cake might not be the healthiest of choices for runners, but it was a chill late November day and both the drink and the snack were wolfed down.

'Anything of interest to report since last week?'

'Nothing much. We've sold cars which is good because I get commission. And don't we need it what with Darren's business in freefall.'

'You thought there might be some improvement.'

'I was wrong and it's getting him down big time. We had a bit of a bust up last Friday but I had to smile the next morning. He left me a note by the side of the bed. Here, have a look, it's top secret!'

Kelly took out the sheet of paper and handed it to Emma.

'Are you sure it's OK?'

'Yeah, as long as you don't tell Darren.'

'This is so sweet, apologising and saying he's going to change.'

'Problem is it might be too late.'

'You're not saying between you and him, are you?'

'No, I was more talking about work.'

Bridget was on duty and came across to clear their table. 'Hi, ladies. Sorry I can't stop, we've got a comedian in this evening and I'm up to my eyeballs trying to get everything ready.'

'She looks knackered,' Emma said after Bridget had moved on. 'The place is getting more and more busy.'

'Maybe they should get another person in to help. Anyway, that's for them to sort. How's your week been?'

'Hit and miss really,' Emma said as she rubbed her itchy chin. 'Andrew's happy. He's read the proof of his book. It's fine so ready to go to print. The TV interview is a definite and the bookshops have been sorted for the signing sessions. So everything's great.'

'I'm so happy for you both.'

Emma burst into tears.

'What's up?'

'Nothing really. It's me.'

'It doesn't seem like nothing. You're usually as tough as nails.'

'Thanks for that! It's just that Andrew is so obsessed with getting things done that our relationship takes second place. I wish there was more emotion in him, a bit of romance again. Oh, I don't know. I suppose it's inevitable after we've been together for so long. It's not as if we aren't still in love.'

'You had romance? Lucky you!'

Emma laughed, Kelly once again diffusing tension with a light-hearted quip.

'I'm not sure what's worse, your husband with his non-stop jobs or mine who never does anything. The end result is the same though. No surprises. No romance.'

Emma nodded in agreement. 'I think we deserve a glass of wine.'

'Definitely. Hang on, what's going on in there?'

Raised voices were emanating from the back office.

~

Bridget had made an S.O.S. call to David requesting his help because there was so much to do in advance of that evening's show. It was good fortune that the woman they'd booked had featured on the ever popular *Would I lie to you?* a fortnight before she was due to appear at the café. With demand likely to be high they took the sensible decision to make it an all-ticket event, but this brought extra work in creating an audience list and engaging a temp to check admissions at the door. It would be mobbed. Was there enough food and drink available? Had they allowed enough time to induct the temporary staff? Having Rachel around would have been a huge help but she had a college commitment and was unavailable.

Bridget was furious because she'd warned David that the lack of managerial back up was going to be their downfall. In his usual way he'd stayed calm and non-committal, his "You could be right" deserving a throttle. Now he had turned up to help and she should be grateful but was too far gone so wasn't. And she was uncomfortable about leaving two children, her Kay and David's Sam, home alone until late at night. She had started shouting in the café in front of customers, her rage intensified when David wasn't shouting back. God knows what people must have thought.

David had led Bridget into the office and closed the door but Kelly and Emma were able to catch snippets of the heated conversation in the otherwise silent café.

'... we've no choice ...'

'... we need help! ...'

'... not convinced that's viable ...'

'... but we're making loads! ...'

'... turning over loads, that's not the same thing ...'

'... pedant! ...'

'... I'm just saying what it is ...'

'... perhaps spare a thought for me; I'm drained! ...'

'... ok, I'll take another look, but a manager isn't going to come cheap. What do you want me to do tonight? ...'

'*... nothing, forget it! ...*'

'*... don't be silly, Bridget. I'm here to help.*'

'Yikes, that doesn't sound good,' Kelly said after they saw Bridget leave the premises.

'No. it doesn't. I don't think I've ever heard a cross word spoken before now.'

'Ha-ha, just like us! Shall we skip the wine and head back to our amazing husbands?'

17

Football was Darren's escape from the struggles with his business. The fact that he supported a team with loads of money but an inability to spend it wisely could at times be deflating, but he could always hedge against the disappointment of defeat by betting on his team to lose.

Grant, a friend from his schooldays, was a fellow United supporter. Nowadays they had little else in common, their post-school trajectories being poles apart. Grant was a serial entrepreneur and each time they caught up at a match it seemed as if there was another venture added to the list – food, furniture, clothing, medical supplies, hospitality. It wouldn't be a surprise if Grant was put on the *Dragons Den* panel.

The man was rolling in it and was generous. He never bragged, never showed off, just quietly did all the paying – for taxis to the ground, for meals, for tickets. 'Yo Darren, listen up.' Now in his mid-forties, Grant spoke more like a teenager than he had done when he was a teenager. 'Fancy a Paris trip, Monsieur Robertson?'

'You mean for the match?'

United's performances in the league had been dire but somehow they were doing better in the European competition.

'Right on.'

There was no way Darren could afford it. Kelly would kill him if he wasted money going and he had too much pride to expect a full handout for the trip.

'I'm not sure.'

'Mate, if it's the money don't worry. It'd be on me but it doesn't cost me a penny. It's all corporate stuff – the tickets, even the flights and hotel. All you need do is turn up – and maybe get me a burger at the ground as a thank you.'

It was too good to miss and when he told Kelly she was delighted that there was this chance to take his mind off work.

When Grant called him three days before their departure, Darren was expecting the final details about flight times and the like. Instead he was told that something urgent had cropped up at work. Grant couldn't go.

'Look mate, I don't wanna waste the tickets and don't wanna dump one of my boring old business farts as your travelling companion, so listen up, you choose who to go with and I'll make the necessary arrangements.'

'But Grant –'

'Must go. Sort it out and text me.'

'You know what I think about football,' Kelly said when she was offered the trip.

'But it's Paris.'

'Paris for two nights with the city full of beer drinking English fans? No thank you.'

'Who can I ask then?'

Kelly's suggestion was instant, as was his response.

'Andrew, you're joking! He isn't interested in football. Maybe if it was lacrosse he might be, but not football.'

'You won't know until you ask. Anyway, who else would you go with?'

'One of the lads.'

'I'd rather there was someone responsible to keep an eye on you.'

Since accusing Kelly of not being interested in him there had been an apology and a promise not to let frustrations at work threaten their relationship. Things had improved and Darren didn't want an outright rejection of her idea to hinder progress. He could go along with her suggestion because Andrew was bound to decline the offer.

'OK. I'll text him.'

'No. Pop round and ask him.'

'Tomorrow though, it's too late now.'

'What's the time, Darren?'

'Nearly nine o'clock.'

'I think they'll still be awake, don't you? He'll need as much notice as possible to organise things.' She stood up. 'Don't move.'

Kelly returned with the pair of shoes Darren kept by the front door. Kneeling, she pulled off his slippers. 'You can do the rest.'

When Darren knocked at number 38 it was Andrew who greeted him.

'Good evening, Darren. Is anything wrong?'

Wrong, yes there was because I'm about to ask you to come to a football match. 'No, everything's fine. I've got a spare ticket for a United match in Paris and thought you might like to join me. I realise it's probably impossible what with you teaching and all the poetry events coming up.'

'Paris? With you?'

Darren nodded, wondering whether his ask would find its way into another insulting poem. What rhymed with Paris? Embarrass?

'When is it?'

'On Wednesday.'

'This Wednesday?'

'Yes.'

'I'll have to do some diary checking. When do you need to know?'

When it's over Darren wanted to say. 'As soon as possible.'

'OK, I'll get back to you by tomorrow. Err, thanks for the offer.'

Darren headed back to number 34 with a broad smile. He was confident Andrew would say no. His neighbour had a range of excuses to choose from and Darren wasn't intending to mention that the trip would be free.

'I've asked him,' he told Kelly. 'It's going to be difficult though; it's such short notice.'

Meanwhile, at number 38, Andrew had sat down next to Emma.

'You'll never guess what,' he began.

'So, of course I won't be going,' he ended.

'Why not? I had doubts about going away with Kelly, but when I did it was great.'

'But Darren isn't Kelly.'

'He might surprise you; it could be enjoyable.'

'I'm sorry, but I don't think so.'

'Paris for two nights? You'd be mad not to do it. What could be a better start to the school holidays and it's not as if you've got much else to do?'

'That's not the case.'

'It is. You said yourself that everything's sorted for the book signings and now that they've rescheduled the TV interview you can put planning for that to the side for a while.'

Andrew was thinking about the argument they'd had recently with Emma claiming that getting jobs done always took precedence over socialising. Early days, but having promised to take her criticism on board, their relationship was improving. Emma would appreciate his willingness to accept the offer but he had a plan that would make joining Darren impossible. The match was imminent. If he delayed his response Darren surely would be finding someone else.

'OK, I will go. I'll let him know tomorrow. There's a full day meeting at school so it'll have to be when I get back.'

'Haven't you heard of texts and phone calls? Actually it would be nicer to tell him face to face. Go round now.'

'Now? It's late.'

'What time is it?'

'Gone nine-thirty.'

'That's not late. Go.'

The women had pushed the men together and the stage was set for a trip to Paris to see United play.

~

Andrew was prepared for a nightmare flight, shoved in with alcohol-fuelled, foul-mouthed supporters. How wrong he was because their tickets were business class. From the calm check-in desk to the exclusive lounge, to the comfortable seating at the front of the plane, to the high quality refreshments, the trip was a delight.

It was only at the Paris airport that they were first confronted by the alcohol-fuelled, foul-mouthed supporters. By no means everyone, but enough to make him embarrassed to be associated with them.

Honestly, what was the purpose of taunting the police and chanting anti-French songs?

'Great, innit?' Darren observed.

'What's great?'

'This atmosphere. I love it.'

The next evening Andrew did love the atmosphere – not the walk to the stadium escorted by police, but the match itself. The skill and intensity of the players, the chanting of the rival supporters, the sheer scale of it all.

However, the excitement of the match couldn't make up for the dreadful twenty-four hours beforehand. Arriving at the hotel, an attractive building in a quiet neighbourhood, Andrew's worst fear was realised – he'd be sharing a bedroom with Darren. It was a nice enough room, large with double beds close together.

'Kelly reckons I spend all night snoring and farting so you might want to move away a bit.'

Andrew was on the case in seconds.

When Darren outlined his proposed itinerary for the evening Andrew faced a no-win choice. Either accept Darren's appalling suggestions or go their separate ways which would be discourteous given that he was Darren's guest. It was obvious which of the two options Emma would expect him to choose – stick with Darren. But would she be so sure if she were aware that the plan was to visit the seediest bars around Place de Pigalle and remain until the early hours of the morning?

The area was teeming with men, United supporters included. As they passed the Moulin Rouge Andrew recommended a stop there: the place was legendary and presumably moderately respectable.

'Too pricey, mate.'

Darren had done his research and Lulu and Dirty Dick were on his list.

Four excruciating hours followed.

'Think of Kelly,' Andrew yelled against the thud of the music before pulling his intoxicated companion away from the naked woman he'd been dancing with at Lulu.

At Dirty Dick Andrew intervened when Darren invited a woman back to their hotel.

'Think of Kelly!'

Finally, the wasted Darren was persuaded that it was time to get a taxi back to base.

Andrew dragged Darren to the lift then pulled him along the third floor corridor to their bedroom, leaving him on the bed to snore and fart the night away.

At nine the next morning Andrew went down to breakfast alone and at ten he set off for the Musée d'Orsay, leaving a text for Darren to contact him when he woke up.

He ended his message with: *I'm going to the Louvre later. Text me if you want to meet there or else I'll be back around four.* The mention of the Louvre was his tactic to guarantee that he wouldn't be seeing Darren until it was time to get ready for the match.

Darren wasn't an idiot though and the atmosphere was frosty when Andrew returned to the hotel. There was no thaw during the match, the rest of the evening or the next morning on their journey home.

Andrew bought Darren a bottle of whisky at the duty free, an expensive one, as a thank you for the trip. Hardly a word was spoken on the drive home from the airport in the *Stop Thief!* van.

When Emma asked Andrew how it had gone he found himself close to tears. 'I can't talk about it. Maybe later.' He would not be telling her about Darren's behaviour the night before the match. What would be the point?

Darren was more vocal when Kelly asked the same question. 'That's it, never again.'

18

At last! The book was out, the critics had praised it, and Andrew was on his tour to bookstores across London to sign copies.

Between Christmas and the start of the new school term there were twelve events scheduled. Emma had agreed to join her husband and at the outset was full of enthusiasm. Before long, standing by his side with a fixed smile was proving to be tiresome as was observing Andrew's cosy chats with fans.

'Who are *you*?' several of them asked her.

'His wife,' she told them; it grated that she was defining herself as a wife.

The twelfth event was identical to the previous eleven. Although there was no queue snaking outside the shop in Bloomsbury in anticipation of meeting the great poet, there were sufficient customers to regard the occasion as a success. That was certainly the opinion of the member of the publisher's team acting as chaperone, her smile as fixed as Emma's. Despite being together on a daily basis the women didn't converse much. Emma never could remember the youngster's name, but the words "Isn't everything going well" were embedded in her brain having heard it repeated two or three times at each event.

The organisation was slick and Andrew played his part well. Following a brief introduction it was his turn to speak and he turned on the charm, expressing delight that more and more people were appreciating poetry. A light-hearted quip came next, surprise that enjoyment was still possible despite his dark subject matter. A round of thank yous followed – for his editors, the cover designer, the tour organisers, the bookstore staff.

'And finally, huge gratitude to my dear wife, Emma, who is here with me this evening. She has provided immeasurable support on my journey to publication.' At which point Andrew drew attention to her, an arm extended, his body deferentially slightly bowed, this generating a round of applause. Emma's fixed smile remained on a reddening face. It was a thoughtful gesture, but "dear wife"! Twelve times. She'd had enough.

Back at home on the evening after the final event, Andrew told Emma about the plans for another round of signings during the February half-term. He was on a high, seemingly wanting to continue with author appearances forever more.

'How did the bookshops go?' Kelly asked Emma when they were together at the café. It was the first

Wednesday of the new school term, only a few days after the final signing event.

'A big success. Andrew's struggling to get back to the mundanity of work. He loved every minute of it. He wants to be a full time poet.'

'Is that on the cards?'

'No.' There'd never be enough income to make up for the loss of his teacher's salary, but Emma left that unsaid.

'What about you? Did you love every minute of it?'

Kelly was always asking the right questions.

'I should be over the moon happy for Andrew – and I am really.'

'But?'

'I think he's behaving differently since his poetry's been published. I'm not sure what to make of it.'

'In what way different?'

'There are positives. He's chattier, more sociable, but he's forgotten how to listen. To me at least. I'm asking myself whether the fame, not that there's much of it, has gone to his head. Like I said, I am glad he's doing well, but there's no need to be so pompous. He's hardly a Ted Hughes, is he?'

'Ted who?'

'Exactly. A famous poet, but how many people know anything about any poet?'

'I think it's fair enough for him to be excited for a while when something like this happens. Give it a few weeks then I'm sure he'll be back to his old self.'

'Yeah, and maybe that's the problem.'

'Meaning?'

'When he was obsessing about the launch of his book I was relegated to a distant second place. His old self will still have me in second place even if the distant rating goes.'

'Oh, that's not good.'

'No. I shouldn't complain though. Nothing's bad between us.' Emma sprang up. 'Mint tea? Or alcohol?'

'Tea please.'

Bridget was on duty. She beamed on seeing Emma. 'We've recruited a deputy manager and I think we've found a gem. He starts at the end of the month.'

Having heard Bridget's heated debate with David, Emma was pleased it had been resolved. 'Great. You'll be able to relax a bit, though knowing you I doubt whether you will.'

'Let me tell you, I intend to and I'm looking forward to it.' She waved her arm across the room. 'Look how crowded the place is and this is supposedly the quiet period. The after work group will be here soon and this evening it's folk night.'

Emma returned with the teas and handed one to Kelly.

'I'm thinking about what you said, about always being second in Andrew's thoughts. I must say, I don't see that when you're together. He strikes me as being attentive and considerate, the things I could do with.'

'Maybe I'm being over sensitive. Never mind us, how are things at number 34? Darren's business for starters.'

'Actually better lately. I've been working on him and finally he's realising that being nice to customers is a good idea. He got a Trustpilot four star rating the other day.'

'Brilliant. Five stars here we come!'

'There's another thing which I think is good news. A bloke he trained left to set up his own company and it's growing so fast he's struggling to find staff. He asked Darren if he could freelance a bit and Darren said yes. He's not over the moon working for someone who used to work for him so I'm proud of him for not letting pride get in the way.'

'Agreed.'

'And although he won't admit it, I think he's enjoying being part of a team again. Good job we got a short run in,' Kelly continued as sleet whacked against the café window. 'Unless the weather improves quickly I'll never be able to do that 5k run you've forced me into.'

'Hardly forced. You wanted to give it a try.'

'But I'm not ready for it. There's less than eight weeks to go.'

'You're already more than good enough.'

'It doesn't matter if you miss a couple of weeks of training, Little Ms Half Marathon, but I'm a beginner.'

'We can still run if the weather's bad, but maybe it's better to drive to the park and run on gravel.'

'That might be safer but it would still be cold, wet and miserable.'

'Just wait until you cross the finishing line. You'll know it's all been worth it.'

'You're not coaching me like you promised.'

'That's because we can hardly stand and chat when the weather's like this. All we can do is run then dash indoors.'

Thwack! A blast of sleet slammed against the window.

'Fancy another drink? I'm seriously considering a glass of red wine to warm me up.'

'Not really. Oh, go on then.'

Emma looked across as Kelly chatted with Bridget.

'She's won, she's got her deputy manager,' Kelly announced when she returned.

'I know, she told me earlier. Sorry, I forgot to pass on the news.'

Kelly lifted her glass then put it down without drinking. 'I've had a thought. Why don't we get out of London, go somewhere in the countryside for a few days of full-on training? If we had whole days available we could do our runs in between blizzards or whatever else was thrown at us.'

'Err, I'm a teacher remember. I'd like to get away, I think I deserve a proper break after that book tour, but I can't.'

'And I'm selling cars, but so what? I'm sure our workplaces can survive without us for a few days. Our men can too.'

'I can't miss school.'

19

'That sounds nice,' Andrew uttered when Emma told him that she would be away for a short while. He was barely listening as he scanned tweets on his newly set up poetry account.

Having booked the countryside retreat, Kelly had suggested that they tell their husbands that evening to prevent one finding out from the other. Not that that was likely as the men had hardly spoken since the football fiasco.

'It's only for a couple of days.'

'Great.' Andrew had switched to his Facebook poetry group. He began typing.

'Next week.'

Andrew looked up. 'During term time?'

'Like I said, it's an emergency conference because they've changed the French syllabus with hardly any notice before this summer's examinations.'

'But what about your teaching?'

'I've been encouraged to go. They can get supply cover.'

'I suppose so.' He wasn't listening again.

'So you'll be alright?'

'Alright? Of course I'll be alright.'

Down the road, Kelly was informing Darren about her phantom event. 'I've got no choice really. There's a software update for the car dealership nationwide and the training is vital.'

'When is it?'

'Next week.'

'That's a disgrace, giving such short notice. Say we had something on?'

'But we haven't.'

'That's not the point.'

'It is the point. Anyway, it's only for a couple of days.'

'Would you buy some microwave meals?'

'Of course, love.'

~

Following the Paris trip the men were on undeclared non-speaking terms except if passing each other on Brookland Gardens when there was little option other than to say hello.

It was late on Friday afternoon, the final day of the wives' work trips. There had been texts but no phone calls, both women claiming they were so inundated with information and evening homework that it would be best to await hearing about their respective courses until they returned.

'Hello Andrew.'

'Hello Darren.'

Barnaby and Tyson were hindering a rapid moving on. It wasn't clear just how friendly those dogs were. When out with Emma and Kelly they seemed playful. When with the husbands there was suspicious circling and growling as if sensing the hostility between the men.

After what seemed like an endless observation of the dogs interspersed with 'No, Barnaby' and 'Stop that, Tyson', there was no choice but to converse.

'Everything alright with you?'

'Yes, good thanks. Everything alright with you?'

'Yes, fine. How's the poetry going?'

'Good. I've see you out and about in your van a lot. Business going well then?'

'Yeah, it is.'

'Glad to hear that.'

'Isn't it Emma who usually walks Barnaby weekday afternoons?'

'True enough, but she's away for a couple of days. At some conference.'

'Kelly's off too. At a training course.'

There was a silence. The women had become close friends and now both were away. Should they share their suspicion?

Andrew decided against. 'It looks like rain. I'd better get going before I'm hit by the worst of it.'

Darren likewise. 'I'm lucky, our walking's done, isn't it Tyson.'

It had begun to drizzle. 'Lucky indeed. Bye Darren.'

'Yeah, see you Andrew.'

There was only one thing on Andrew's mind as he walked on. Was it a coincidence that Emma and Kelly were away at the same time? Their friendship was such that they were meeting several times a week since Kelly had taken up running, but Kelly wasn't a French teacher so would hardly be joining Emma at an examination board conference.

Darren had no time to think things through. As he stepped indoors the landline phone was ringing, a rare occurrence. He dashed across to take the call but was too late. Kelly's boss was leaving an answerphone message.

Hi Kelly. I'll call back after I've collected my daughter from choir practice.

An hour or so later the phone rang again. Kelly's boss wanted to know how she was feeling. He'd tried her mobile a couple of times but it had gone straight to voicemail.

'Her health comes first, but if I could get an idea of how long she might be away I can decide whether to make do with the staff I've got here or get a temp in.'

'She's definitely on the mend. I'm sure she'll be back in on Monday.'

'That's good to know. Thanks. Send her my best wishes will you?'

'Of course I will.'

Training! She'd lied. Was she with another man? Or was it something involving Emma?

The last thing Darren wanted was a conversation with Andrew but this was an emergency. He hovered by his own front door for a while before making his way to his neighbour's house.

'It's a lie,' he blurted out as Andrew opened the door. 'A lie.'

Andrew had reached the same conclusion and was weighing up whether it was worth involving Darren despite the friction.

'Come in.'

They stood in the hall as Andrew called Emma. She didn't pick up so he left a voicemail.

It would be lovely to hear from you. Just for a quick chat to check everything's OK.

There was an immediate reply text.

Can't speak but everything fine thanks.

Good conference?

Hectic but brilliant. Picking up loads of new ideas.

Where are you staying?'

Somewhere up north. I'd better go – see you tomorrow.

Darren read the exchange before taking his phone out of his back pocket. He pressed the Kelly button. Andrew noted the image of Kelly in skimpy underwear. He wouldn't dream of having something like that against Emma's name. Kelly did have a lovely body though.

Kelly didn't answer: Darren left a voicemail.

Just a hello. I'm coping ok. Hope your training up north is going well. Bye love.

Andrew nodded and smiled. "Up north." Clever; give credit where credit is due.

'I've got a giant pack of microwave macaroni cheese back at home if you're interested,' Darren offered.

Together they walked back to number 34 and shared the culinary failure, washed down with sufficient beer to raise Darren's interest in poetry and Andrew's understanding of the burglar alarm business. Their conversation went on until the early hours of the morning.

~

The women knew the game was up, the calls one after the other and the reference to up north being obvious giveaways.

'I would have got a bollocking from Andrew if I'd said I was about to skive school,' Emma said in an attempt to justify her lie. 'But it was still a stupid thing to do.'

'And I should have just told Darren the truth. It's not as if I've got anything to hide. Not really anyway.'

Maybe not, Emma was thinking, but as far as she was concerned, close to it.

On the first day they'd arrived at the hotel, dumped their bags and gone for a run across gently undulating Chiltern hillsides.

'That was a killer,' Kelly said as they returned to their bedroom. 'I'm totally knackered but I absolutely loved it. A quick shower then I must eat or else I'll die of starvation.'

'Go on then. You first.'

Kelly's clothes were off in a flash and she was parading round the bedroom naked as she had done during their stay at the spa.

Emma could have turned away but didn't. 'Good to see the lizard looking so well,' she joked.

'Yep, he enjoyed the run.'

'So it's a he is it?'

'Has to be. Look where he's heading!'

As soon as Kelly came out the shower, dropping her towel, Emma peeled off her running gear and the two women faced each other. Kelly stepped forward and hugged Emma who thought it was nice, extremely nice.

'Are you sure you don't want to join me there?' Kelly asked, looking across at the bed.

Pressed together, Emma was tempted, but pulled away. 'No, it's not for me.'

'Go on, have your shower then,' Kelly said without a hint of disappointment, leaving Emma to reflect on the offer as they walked into the centre of the village. They discovered an ancient pub with thatched roof, oak beams and a roaring fire a short distance from the hotel and their meal was amazing quality though at an astonishing cost. When they told the receptionist back at the hotel where they'd had dinner she let them know that it had a Michelin Star rating.

'Maybe MacDonalds tomorrow,' Kelly quipped.

They watched a TV film and the rest of the evening passed amiably.

The next morning they were full-on tourists in the nearby town, wandering in and out of shops and visiting the museum with its permanent exhibition of Anglo Saxon artefacts. After a light lunch they returned to the hotel, changed, and set off on an afternoon run that demonstrated that Kelly would have no problem coping with the 5k race.

Sitting on a bed together, the two of them caked in sweat, Emma was monumentally aroused. This seemed to be the case every time she was alone with Kelly. There was something about her, an aura, that sparked it. It couldn't be to do with wanting sex with the woman because she was straight and she loved Andrew.

Nevertheless, it was Emma who instigated the hug, sliding her hands down her friend's back. She might well have gone further, a kiss on Kelly's luscious lips, perhaps still further.

Then came the husbands' phone calls.

So Kelly claiming she had nothing to hide from Darren was just about true, though Emma was riddled with guilt.

A discussion about how to confront their husbands ensued, continuing until the early hours of the morning.

'Simply tell the truth then,' Emma reasoned. 'That we needed time to train for the run.'

'A huge apology for not being open about it. We'll need to add that.'

'Agreed. And a promise that we'll never lie again.'

'We sound like a pair of schoolgirls caught doing something ever so slightly wrong.'

Emma paused to reflect on Kelly's comment. 'But we're grown-ups so do you know what, I'm not sure a humble apology is needed.'

'Exactly. It's hardly a crime to go away for a couple of days.'

'Or bunking off work when we're usually 100% committed.'

'So we say we had a great time training for the run. End of.'

'Yes, end of.'

Night was turning to day, a dull grey day, as they prepared for their return home. Kelly was the first to get out of bed and dress. 'Come on, let's have breakfast then get going.'

Emma had yet to dismiss thoughts of how things might have ended up the previous evening. 'You do know that I love Andrew,' she began as she dropped a blob of jam onto her toast.

'That's fine, you don't have to say. I love Darren. He has a heart of gold; he'd do anything for me.'

'One thing though. I do wonder whether I'm too quick to criticise Andrew – which could explain why he never seems to listen.'

'I know what you mean. I've made a career out of telling off Darren.' Kelly stirred the frothed milk into her cappuccino. 'I'm going to stop doing that, starting tomorrow. God, I sound like a teenager again – from now on I'm going to be nicer to my mum and dad!'

'When you've lived with someone for a long time it's not a bad idea every so often to reflect on how you behave rather than be on automatic pilot.'

'As long as they're willing to do the same. We'll find that out when we get home and we've done our explaining.'

They loaded up the car ready to set off.

'Do you think I should get Darren an apology gift?'

'You mean something from up north like Bakewell Tarts or Wensleydale Cheese!'

'Maybe not. Come on, home for the inquisition.'

The journey home was slower than expected with traffic reduced to low speeds on the saturated road surfaces. Kelly switched from station to station on the audio system, Emma was mesmerised close to sleep by the windscreen wipers.

'I've just realised it's our monthly meal together tomorrow,' Emma said as Kelly was parking outside number 34.

'We could postpone. I doubt whether the men will have remembered and if they have they'd be delighted to cancel since they both hate the evenings.'

'Andrew will have remembered; he never forgets anything.'

'Then let's go ahead. Assuming they're still talking to us.'

20

Kelly intended to launch into gushiness the second she arrived home.

'I'm back, love,' she called out as she opened the front door.

Silence.

She checked each room upstairs. He wasn't there. She went back out in search of the *Stop Thief!* van. It was missing.

Darren didn't pick up when she called, her voicemail a schmaltzy one telling her husband that she couldn't wait to see him because she'd missed him so much.

He texted. *I'm working.*

Well, at least he'd responded despite the brevity.

On a Saturday? Great you're getting customers again. See, being nice to people is helping like I told you it would. When are you home? Her message was littered with emojis.

Later.

You do remember that Emma and Andrew are over tonight for dinner.

Yes. I know.

Can we speak?

Not now. Busy.

Kelly was unperturbed by the abruptness, confident that would change as soon as he was back. A flirtatious welcome, maybe sex before the guests arrived.

No problem. I'm popping out to get food then I'll be here cooking. See you when I see you.

She waited a while with her phone in her hand thinking that there might be a reply.

There wasn't. She set off to The Broadway.

Emma had arrived at number 38 with an equally upbeat greeting to Kelly's. 'I'm ba-ack,' she called out, her tone jolly. 'Andrew? Where are you?'

She went from room to room in a fruitless attempt to locate him: if he was there surely he would have emerged to greet her. But if he was out where was the note in the kitchen? Andrew always left a note to explain where he'd gone and what time he'd be home.

No note.

Taking her phone out of her back pocket, (the new storage place picked up from Kelly despite the fear of sitting on the device and cracking the screen), she clicked onto the Andrew photo, one of him beaming, his beard much shorter than now, more like a trendy few-day stubble. It struck her that he hadn't done much smiling of late, not with her anyway, though there had been plenty of smiles for the fans queueing to buy his book. Why so few smiles for her anymore? Was he bored? Dissatisfied?

Kelly had told Emma that she was confident Darren would immediately forgive her for lying, leaving Emma to wonder what tactics her friend used to prevent the boredom and dissatisfaction that she feared. By flirting probably. If flirting worked for Kelly then maybe that's what was needed with Andrew. It was a pity they had the dinner date with the Robertsons that evening – a serene, candlelit romantic meal, just the two of them, and then early to bed would be better.

Why serenity though? If she was Kelly it might mean talking dirty, a raucous alcohol-fuelled evening, ripping clothes off, licking food off each other, sex in the dining room. Yikes! These thoughts were turning her on, but somehow she couldn't imagine Andrew embracing the scenario.

What did she imagine instead?

"Watch out, Emma, you'll rip my new shirt."

"Careful, don't get the chocolate sauce on the carpet."

"Shouldn't we adjourn to the bedroom?"

She pressed that lovely smiling face photo on her phone to call him.

'Yes?'

'It's me.'

'I can see that. Your number came up.'

Andrew was in punishment mode. She considered ending the conversation.

'Anyway, I'm home.'

'OK.'

'Where are you?'

'In the West End. I've been visiting bookstores to see how well they're displaying the book.'

'I was hoping you'd be here when I got home. Are you heading back soon?'

'Not yet, I'm on my way to Tate Modern. There's a Walter Sickert exhibition on.'

'I know there is, we both read the newspaper review. I thought we'd decided to go together.'

'Well, too late now. You could always go with Kelly.'

Yes, it was punishment. With immaturity thrown in.

'Maybe I will. I'll see you when I see you but remember we're at Kelly and Darren's for dinner tonight.'

'I haven't forgotten. See you later.'

Didn't calls always end with "Love you. Bye."? This one hadn't.

If I'm prepared to make an effort to reconnect he also needs to Emma was thinking as she headed down to The Broadway to buy flowers for the hosts.

~

Darren got home at six-thirty, pecked his wife on the cheek, passed no comment about the body-hugging dress she had on, and mumbled about the need to take a shower before heading upstairs without further conversation. He reeked of beer.

Andrew got home a little after seven, accepting a welcoming hug from his wife with minimal contact: it was more like a pat on the back. Stepping away, he informed her that the exhibition was breathtaking.

He was already on his way upstairs, preventing any clarification about why it was breathtaking.

He called down from the landing. 'What time do we need to leave?'

'In a few minutes.'

'OK, I'll skip a shower or a change of clothes. Who cares if we're only going to Darren's house.'

Emma had got dressed up, squeezing into the tightest, shortest dress she possessed, one she hadn't worn for ages. She had on her only pair of true heels, far more make-up than usual, and an outrageously expensive perfume reserved for special occasions. Had Andrew even noticed? Was he thinking that his woman was drop dead gorgeous, that he couldn't wait to get home after the meal to make love? Or sex right there and then, even if it meant getting to Kelly's late? Simply a "You look lovely" would have been nice.

Emma hid in the utility room, pretending that she was sorting laundry, until she heard Andrew by the front door.

'Ready then?'

They walked to number 34 in silence.

'You look amazing,' were Kelly's first words as she took hold of Emma and hugged.

'Never quite right compared to you,' Emma said, stepping back to admire her friend.

'Don't be silly. Look boys, before anything else we both want to apologise for not telling the truth about our trip.'

'Yes. It was silly but we thought the easiest option was to go without over-complicating things.'

'Anyway, let's start eating and we can tell you all about our trip.'

Not all, Emma was thinking.

Kelly did most of the describing of how well the running had gone, her tone light and jolly as she endeavoured to engage the men. 'Your Emma is a right old taskmaster,' Kelly told Andrew.

'Did you know your wife is a bloody brilliant athlete?' Emma told Darren.

It wasn't working. The husbands, now seemingly the best of friends, had stopped listening and were holding their own conversation. Andrew was showing considerable interest in a tricky installation Darren had dealt with that afternoon. Darren was fascinated by how dystopian themes played such an important role in western world literature.

'In fact not solely in the west. Literature and drama across the world.'

'Is that a fact.'

'I'll help,' Emma volunteered when Kelly began stacking the dinner plates.

In the kitchen area the furious women spoke quietly about their discontent.

'Wankers. What do they expect us to do? Beg for forgiveness?'

'Well, they'll have a long wait for that.'

'I'd happily abandon this evening but then you'd be gone and I'd be left with my idiot of a husband.'

'And I'd be at home with a real life dystopian nightmare.'

They laughed; for now they could see a funny side.

The men looked across before returning to their own conversation.

'That looks delicious,' Emma said, examining the dish Kelly had taken from the fridge. 'What is it?'

'Blackberry and lemon fool. Named in honour of my husband!'

'Mine's more like a vinegar and sourdough fool.'

Kelly stuck a finger into the dish and sucked the gooey mess.

Emma copied her.

They were still laughing as Kelly carried the dessert across to the table. The men were stern-faced.

'It's time you two grew up,' Kelly said as she sploshed the creamy substance into the bowls. 'We've said sorry for what is hardly the biggest crime ever committed.'

'Agreed. Just move on.'

'We can't understand why you lied to us,' Andrew said.

'Is there something going on that we don't know about?' Darren added.

'Something else? What? That we hired a couple of male escorts?'

'We were on a secret spying mission?'

'We sniffed coke all day long?'

'We popped over to watch Sting perform in Berlin?'

'For fuck's sake. Get over it.'

'Enough!' Andrew stood up and stormed out the room. Darren chased after him. Seconds later the front door was slammed shut.

'Not a great success,' Emma said.

'Do you think that dramatic exit was planned?' Kelly asked as she tucked into her blackberry and lemon fool. 'Don't worry, Emma, it'll soon boil over. This could even be a good thing; they're now the best of mates it seems.'

'Yep, finally we've found a way to bring them together. By hating us.'

'You'll be OK with Andrew, won't you?'

'I'm sure I will because Andrew's a conflict avoider – we never argue. Sometimes I think it would be better for resolving disagreements. And you and Darren?'

'We do argue – loads – but it always blows over. Perhaps not tonight though, I'll be using the spare bedroom.'

'And I'll be in our spare bedroom. I'm shattered, do you mind if we call it a day?'

'Sure. Look,' Kelly added, taking hold of Emma's shoulders, 'we were right to challenge their stupidity even if it's set back our resolution to be nice.'

'We are nice; they're the idiots.'

They hugged, Emma quickly pulling away.

~

'I don't understand it,' Darren said as the pair strode away from the house, as much to himself as to Andrew.

'Don't think of it as Kelly and Emma acting strangely. Think of it as womankind's way of dealing with discord.'

'What are you on about? Are you talking like in a poem?'

'No, of course not,' Andrew said as they reached the end of Brookland Gardens. Without discussing it they set off for the main road. 'Women are different to men.'

'Of course they are.' Darren was eyeing the two teenage girls approaching them in ridiculously skimpy clothes for the time of the year. 'Evening, darlings,' he said as they passed.

'Fuck off, pervert!'

'Cor, they were something and a half. Different to us men alright.'

'I don't mean different physically. I mean emotionally.'

'Well there was definitely something up emotionally with Kelly tonight.'

'I think it's to do with perceptions of right and wrong. The thing is …' They were passing youngsters queueing to get into a nightclub. Darren had stopped. 'Are you listening?' Andrew asked.

'I'll tell you something, tonight I'm wishing I was twenty-five years younger. Look at that one.'

'They're teenagers for God's sake.'

'Be truthful, Andrew. Wouldn't you like to be younger and have the pick of that lot?'

'I'm not playing that game. Stop it.'

'Here's one more question though. Are you getting enough with Emma?'

'And I'm not answering that either.'

'Let me tell you then. Of late I'm not with Kelly and that's new.'

'What, not at all?'

'I didn't say that. Just not as much.'

They were still by the nightclub entrance. 'What are you doing? You can't join the queue.'

'Why not?'

'You're too old.'

'There isn't a senior age limit.'

'Stop it, Darren.' Andrew grabbed his neighbour's hand and steered him away to the sound of catcalls from the youngsters.

'When you're in love …' a boy sang and there was laughter as they walked on, Andrew quick to release Darren's hand. The fragrance of cheap perfume and the glimpse of bare midriffs remained with him as he reflected on his own marriage. No, lately he wasn't getting enough with Emma but no way was he going to tell Darren.

They ended up in a quiet pub among a scattering of oldies.

Andrew was attempting to return the conversation to cerebral matters. 'Like I was saying, it's all too easy to forget that women are wired differently to men. They're more sensitive, more sociable, more thoughtful about others than us.'

'So what are you getting at?'

Andrew didn't quite know. 'I think we need to respect those differences,' he uttered. 'I know what I need to do. Listen more carefully. Spend more time with Emma doing the things she likes doing.'

'Yeah, me too with Kelly.'

'Hashtag metoo.'

'What?'

'Never mind. Let's go home.'

'Soon. One more for the road.'

21

As they walked unsteadily home after several more for the road there were pledges and vows to put things right.

'From now on I'm going to listen to Emma.'

'And I'm going to take Kelly shopping.'

'I need to take more of an interest in Emma's running.'

'And Kelly's running. Who would have thought it?'

'I have no idea how Emma's getting on at school. I've stopped asking her. That's wrong.'

'I'm sure Kelly would like more sex. I would too so I'm not sure why it isn't happening.'

Similarly absurd alcohol-induced statements were formulated before they reached home.

'Good luck, Andrew,' Darren offered as they leaned on each other outside number 34.

'Thank you, Darren. And the best of luck to you.' Andrew moved to one side and extended his arm. The men shook hands, the sudden sobriety and politeness causing both of them to step further back in shock.

They parted, soon to take up occupancy of two double beds currently unoccupied.

~

With the men pledging to be more attentive to their wives' needs and the women determined to put more effort into their marriages, improvement was surely imminent. However, changing patterns of behaviour they'd drifted into over many years was no easy task.

Confrontations prevailed, nothing dire, no flaming rows, simply frustrating bickering which could be draining.

At number 34 Kelly complained when their Fiesta was left near empty after Darren had used it.

'What's the problem? You know where the garages are, Kelly.'

'You knew I was already late for work.'

Conversations at number 38 were equally mundane.

'Where are onions? They were on my list.'

'It's hardly the end of the world, Emma.'

'No, but it's another example of –'

'Of what?'

'Oh, never mind.'

Work issues were causing additional tension for all four of them.

Andrew's publisher had shortened the already tight deadline for producing his second collection of poems. A third publication hinged on him delivering on schedule.

Darren wanted time to re-establish his own business but had to agree to longer hours when his ex-employee turned boss threatened to replace him unless he accepted the new terms.

Another bright young trainee at the car showroom had quit, leaving Kelly with longer shifts as a stop gap until a replacement could be found.

Emma's problems at school were threefold – having to cover staff absences, an abysmally behaved Year 9 class, and her nerdy head of department making a pass at her.

Despite time pressures, Emma and Kelly stuck to their Wednesday afternoon get togethers at A Street Café Named Desire in addition to two or three runs together each week. The January freeze had turned into a February low-hanging mist.

'You know what?' Kelly said on one of the Wednesdays as they looked out at distorted headlights flashing by, 'I'm going to abandon doing that run. I'm not ready for it.'

'I don't think I'll bother either. I'm not sure why I booked us in for one this time of the year. They're much more fun in summer.'

'Don't worry about me dropping out. You should still do it.'

'Perhaps, but I don't much fancy going to Sheffield to get freezing cold and soaking wet. Mind you, I'd love to have something planned to get away for a few days. Andrew has another book signing tour over Easter. He's assuming I'll be joining him but I don't think I can face it.'

'I'd love to get away, too. God, I'm desperate to escape for a while.'

'Escape? Are things that bad?'

'No, I suppose not.'

~

Things were that bad. Darren had lied to Kelly and she was furious.

Having told anyone and everyone, Emma and Andrew included, that her husband's gambling was confined to the occasional flutter when his football team were playing, she now knew that this was not the case. She'd discovered he had a separate bank account in overdraft when she opened a letter that looked official. There was part of a line of red text visible under the address window on the envelope. Red meant bad news; she knew that. Since there were no secrets between them when it came to finances, she wasn't being underhand in checking the correspondence to see what was what. If necessary she would deal with anything requiring urgent attention. Perhaps Darren hadn't provided details of his new credit card to their energy company or internet provider or some other organisation.

This particular letter was from a bank which until then she didn't know they used. The account was two thousand pounds overdrawn with the statement indicating only one payee – a betting company. The accompanying letter was a request to either settle immediately or contact the bank to discuss a repayment schedule.

Kelly kept the letter in the back pocket of her jeans while she prepared a meagre meal of baked beans and jacket potato for him, but tuna steak on a medley of stir fried Asian vegetables for her.

'I'm busy thinking,' she told Darren when he returned home from a job. 'Do something and I'll call you when the food's ready.'

The meal was ready and she was still furious. She dropped a plastic picnic plate with a potato topped with baked beans in front of him before setting her own meal down. A knife and fork from the best cutlery set rested on a crisp linen napkin. She poured wine into a cut glass tumbler and took a sip before making eye contact with Darren.

He was holding his plastic fork and a paper towel.

'Why are we eating different meals?'

'Because.'

She took another sip of her drink.

'Can't I have some wine, love?'

Kelly fetched a paper picnic cup, filled it and set it down without saying a word.

'What's up?' Darren asked.

'This.' She pulled out the letter, unfolded it, and laid it out in front of him.

'It's addressed to me; how come you've opened it? No, forget that. This is embarrassing.'

'So it should be. Number One is that you've done this behind my back.' She held up the statement. 'And Number Two is that you've done it at all. Here am I scrimping and saving because of your business failure and you're wasting money betting.'

'It has got a bit out of hand.'

'I can see that! How did you think you were going to pay this without me finding out? By raiding our holiday fund – which I've built up without any help from you? Or were you going to bet some more in the hope of winning, like all the idiotic addicts do?'

There were a lot of apologies that evening, some illogical reasoning too.

'The thing is, as you know, United aren't doing well this year. Well, I thought if I bet on them losing I was going to end up happy whatever the result of a match. If they won I'd be pleased and if they lost at least I'd be getting money to compensate.'

'You really are stupid, aren't you? More than I ever realised.'

'Come on, Kelly, I've said I'm sorry. I'll make an appointment with the bank to arrange repayment and that's it as far as betting goes. I promise.'

'So once you've repaid what you owe you'll close the account?'

'I've said yes. I promise.'

'And never open another one without telling me?'

'I promise that too.'

'And if you lie again I might kill you.'

Darren took this humour to be a sign of a thaw. He walked round to Kelly's side of the table and attempted to caress her.

'Get off, will ya! I'm serious. I'd kill you even if it meant spending the rest of my life in prison!'

'You won't have to do that.' Darren knew Kelly wasn't serious but at the same time it wasn't quite the friendly tease he liked to hear.

'I'm going to use some of *my* money in the holiday pot to go away. Alone,' she said.

'Why? Where to?'

'I might tell you. I might not.'

~

'To be honest, Emma, things aren't great with Darren,' Kelly began. 'He hasn't been truthful.'

'An affair?'

'No, not that. It's to do with gambling.'

Kelly stirred her empty teacup vigorously, the spoon clattering against its side. It was her habit whenever she was deep in thought. She had intended to leave the explanation at that, but now that they were together it seemed right to give more details – she valued Emma's opinion and might get a suggestion about what to do next. She took a sip of the fresh tea.

'That's awful,' Emma said having heard the story, 'but it does sound like he's learnt his lesson. Having said that, a break using *your* money would cement your warning in his brain.'

'If he's got a brain.'

The smiling Kelly was back to jesting; she was a star at bouncing back to her fun-loving self.

'Any idea where to go?'

'Actually yes. There's something I haven't told you about me.'

'God, Kelly. What's going on this afternoon!'

'I absolutely hated school; I was pretty useless at everything really –'

'You're one of the brightest people I know.'

'Hardly. I left school as soon as I could and got a job. I was OK at art though; I'd enjoyed those lessons and soon after starting work I joined an evening class. The teacher was brilliant and he suggested I was good enough to do a foundation course at art college.'

'You've got a degree in art!'

'No. I began a textiles course but soon after meeting Darren I packed it in. I wish I'd carried on.'

'It's never too late to start again.'

'Exactly. And I was thinking of dipping my toes in the water. There's stuff like this around.'

Kelly opened her phone and passed it across to Emma. It was on a page showing details of a two-week weaving course held during the Easter holidays. Emma flicked through and was struck by the photos of the stunning location in the Scottish Highlands. She flicked again to see the accommodation, wooden chalets with views to die for across a shimmering lake edged with golden heather.

'This looks amazing! You must go.'

'I am seriously considering it. Come on, we'd better go home. It's beans on toast for Darren tonight!''

~

On the short walk home Emma decided not to tell Andrew about Darren's gambling problem. The men had more than tolerated each other of late and she didn't want to ruin it. All she'd get back from Andrew would be a contemptuous "I'm not surprised" which she really didn't want to hear.

There was a note on the kitchen table.*I've run out of printer paper so out to get some. Love you. Bye.*

Possibly Andrew was the only person who still wrote notes rather than send texts. She liked it though, his neat handwriting, the formal language, the "Love you" at the end.

There was a ping on his laptop which he'd left in the kitchen. With no particular purpose, not even curiosity, she bent down to look at the screen. His gmail account was open, the one he used for his poetry correspondence. The email that had shown was from a dirtydaisy.

Emma clicked into the correspondence, cursoring down to the first message.

Hi A. Was at your book signing – what a cool smile you have. Loved what you read, those poor women marooned on that island. Got me thinking. Click the pic! Love, Dirty Daisy.

Emma did as requested. It was a photo of a woman in a plain beige dress, more like a sackcloth really, ripped to shreds to reveal considerable cleavage. Her face was blanked out in a fuzzy cloud.

Andrew had replied the following day.

Dear Dirty Daisy. I'm glad you enjoyed the poem. It's one I'm much attached to given the current state of the world. Many thanks for the photograph. While not quite how I envisaged the main protagonist, it certainly is imaginative. Best wishes, Andrew.

There was a week's pause.

Hi again A. Glad you liked the pic. I'm thinking they're on a tropical island where the women would be getting overheated. See the pic! Love, DD

Emma clicked on the attachment. The same woman, again the face covered up. The dress was off, the underwear was skimpy.

There was a two-day pause before Andrew had replied.

Dear DD, your imagination has certainly run wild. Although the poem refers to global warming in passing, I hadn't envisaged the woman escaping to a tropical island. I was thinking more like the Faroe Islands, but the beauty of poetry is that it is open to interpretation. Thank you for your interest in my writing. Best wishes, A.

Ten days passed.

Hi A. Tropical works best for me, I'd hate to live anywhere cold. I love taking everything off and walking around naked. Here's a pic! DD xxxx

There were no surprises when Emma clicked into the photograph of a naked Dirty Daisy, lying on a bed in a rude pose which to Emma looked more sad than seductive although she wondered whether Andrew would agree.

'Emma?' Andrew was by her side. 'What do you think you're doing?'

'Checking out your fan mail.'

'There's nothing to hide but it is private.'

'I'm sure it is. Your turn to write I see.'

'And I was going to tell her not to correspond with me anymore.'

'Do you remember her from the book launch?' Emma asked, peering down at the image and trying to assess the woman's age, difficult without seeing the face.

'No, of course not.'

'Have you met her since the book signing?'

'Don't be silly.'

Emma believed him. Unless there were text exchanges as well as these emails, his replies were hardly chat up lines. In fact his responses were so dull it was surprising that Dirty Daisy had persevered. But one thing didn't sit comfortably.

'You're savvy with IT. You didn't have to reply, you know how to block an email address, to report it as spam. Why didn't you do either of those things?'

Andrew reddened, leaving Emma to feel that while he might be innocent, he was getting a buzz from the correspondence.

'Never mind,' she continued. 'I do trust you even if I don't like it.'

She left him with his laptop, wondering what he was going to do. Write back to DD? Block her? It struck Emma that the publication of his poetry had given Andrew a whole new outlet to enjoy while she was stuck doing the same old things.

~

'Yes, I do trust him.'

Emma had left it until the following week at their coffee catch up to tell Kelly. 'It's just that ... oh, I don't know.'

'You are never lost for words. What do you want?'

'I suppose I'm bored. Teaching. Running. Teaching. Running. I'm not unhappy but I wish I had something else.'

'Like weaving?'

'What?'

'That course I told you about. I keep wavering but I think I am going to go for it.'

'Good for you.'

Kelly began to stir her tea vigorously.

'Yes,' Emma announced.

'Yes what?'

'Yes, I will come with you. Not that I can weave.'

'Please come. I've looked it up; there's a beginners option. I doubt whether I'm much more advanced than that.'

'I've already said I will,' Emma replied before it hit her that Kelly might have been hoping for that all along. It would explain why she had investigated classes for beginners. 'Doing something completely different is exactly what I need. I bet it's a great place for running, too.'

'It is, I've done some investigating. The weaving classes aren't for the whole of each day so there's plenty of time for running. There's even someone to advise participants about the best routes for walks and runs.'

'Brilliant. I'm already excited.' Emma took out her phone and googled.

'What are you doing?'

'Booking.'

'But I haven't definitely decided.'

'Well, I'll decide for both of us now. We should get a move on, we don't want the course to fill. And if I book before speaking to Andrew it'll make it easier to deflect any opposition.'

~

In case the newfound buddies were in regular communication, Kelly and Emma agreed to tell their husbands about the trip at the same time. No hanging around – that evening.

Whilst Emma knew that she didn't need permission, after the deceit of the last trip she was going to be open and honest. The conversation with Andrew turned out to be far easier than expected. He was happy to do the Easter book signing tour to Manchester alone.

'To be truthful, as well as the tour you being away suits me fine. I'll be up to my eyeballs finalising the new collection. Some peace and quiet will be welcome.'

Despite being pleased with Andrew's quick acceptance, Emma felt slighted. She was the one who he bounced ideas off, she was the one at his beck and call to make tea and coffee, she was the one given the responsibility to proof read the final draft. And now it seemed as if she was redundant.

'Are you going to meet up with Dirty Daisy while I'm away?' was her pathetic attempt at a joke. It didn't merit a reply and didn't get one.

Two doors down Darren had been served a meat-laden feast.

'You know I used to do art?' Kelly began.

'Yeah. A waste of time that was. Packing it in was the best thing you ever did.'

Avoid conflict. Avoid conflict at all costs. 'Maybe you're right, but now that we're settled and I've got a reasonable job I'm thinking of doing some art again. Just for fun.'

'Dabble away, darling.'

She explained that her dabbling away was at a two-week weaving course in the Scottish Highlands.

'Why up there? What about me?'

'You could come with,' Kelly replied, taking a chance on his likely response.

'I'm not going to do weaving, am I?'

'I suppose not; I can't see you taking to it. So stay here and enjoy yourself. Maybe hang out with Andrew.'

'For the millionth time, we are neighbours, not mates.'

'Whatever. It's only for a couple of weeks, I'm sure you'll find something to keep you busy.'

'Sorting the accounts is one thing I'm going to have to do; they're in a right mess. Maybe I could submit my tax return early this year.'

'There you are then. You've got that woman to help, haven't you?'

'Yes.'

'And this could be your golden opportunity to extend your culinary repertoire.'

'What?'

'Move on from fried eggs, baked beans and sausages. Become a *Masterchef* contestant. Don't look so worried, I'll get stuff for the freezer that you can microwave.'

'That'll be helpful.'
'And Darren. No gambling.'
'I know. I promise.'

22

'Andrew didn't seem that bothered that I was going away,' Emma said when they were sitting in the café the following week. They'd texted each other about their husbands' reactions but left further details until they were together.

'Do you suspect anything?'

'Absolutely not. I think me finding out about Dirty Daisy has scared the living daylight out of him. I expect exemplary behaviour.'

'My Darren was more concerned about food than anything else. He's intending to do accounts which he hates, though there is a woman who does most of the work. In fact I do have my suspicions about that, but more about her motives than his.'

'Andrew's biggest confusion is why I'd want to go away with you. "Kelly? Weaving? Scotland?" That's what he said and in that order.'

'I also got a bit of a funny look when I told Darren I was going with you.'

'We've nothing to feel guilty about for wanting a break together, after all, they're the ones who let us down with their secrets. We've never done anything behind their backs, well, apart from those couple of days training for the run.'

'Hang on, Kelly! We nearly did. I nearly did.'

'But we didn't. And anyway, that's beside the point. I think us going away will do all four of us the world of good. We'll get home with renewed … passion.'

'Yeah, I fancy a bit more passion.'

'Me too.'

They laughed.

'Good afternoon, ladies. I'm pleased to see you so happy.'

'Hello, David.'

Emma liked David, a friendly and helpful man even though not as gregarious as Bridget. Kelly had rarely spoken to him; he was usually in the back office when she was at the café.

'We're happy because we're discussing plans for a holiday. We're going weaving in Scotland.'

'Nice one, it sounds like fun.' He started clearing their table.

The women were in their running gear, the weather having improved sufficiently to enable a twenty-minute jog through the sodden path in the park.

'Did you enjoy your run?'

'I didn't,' Kelly said. 'It was my first for ages and I discovered I'm dreadfully unfit. I'm putting on weight by the minute. Look.'

She raised her top a little. Kelly seemed keen to show the world her flat stomach.

David did look but didn't comment despite seeing a brightly coloured lizard winding its way down into Sweaty Betty joggers. He lingered by the table, but it wasn't Kelly's lizard that he was focused on. 'Actually, while you're here I'd appreciate your opinion about something.'

'Fire away.'

'Thank you. We've – well, more Bridget really – we've been considering the café name. What do you think of it?'

'It's certainly different!' Kelly responded immediately with a broad smile.

'I think it's really clever alluding an arts café to the Tennessee Williams play,' Emma added.

'Tennis-ee what? I don't know what you're on about, Emma.'

David's smile was rueful. 'Exactly. Not everyone recognises it as such. To add to that, it's rather long, a pain for everything – our email address, business cards, posters, the lot. However, it is the name my uncle suggested and I wouldn't want to upset him.'

'But he hasn't got any stake in running the café, or has he?'

'No, not at all.'

'Then it has to be your decision, not his. My Darren thinks the name's ridiculous, in fact he can never remember what it's called. He's always saying, "That café with the daft name."'

'Whereas my Andrew would be mortified if you changed it. He thinks it's brilliant.'

'Yeah, but he's a poet,' Kelly countered. 'Most people coming here aren't poets.'

'They aren't literature buffs either,' David added.

'There you go then. You should change it.'

'Kelly! It's not as simple as that.'

'Why not?' Kelly turned back to face David. 'What would you call the place instead?'

'Bridget was thinking of Dream Café.'

'Brilliant. The place where dreams are made and can come true!' Kelly exclaimed. 'Like us going on holiday.'

'Mmmm, I never thought of it like that,' David said. 'Thanks for your thoughts, I'll pass them on to Bridget.'

'I bet Bridget gets her way on this,' Kelly said when David was out of earshot.

'He's no pushover but I think you're right, a name change does make sense.'

'And it really is a place where dreams are made and come true. Your Andrew found a publisher, I found a lovely friend – and we're off to Scotland together!'

~

It was a busy week for both women, Kelly still doing extra shifts ahead of recruiting a new person at the car showroom and Emma covering for more and more colleagues because of a wave of colds and flu.

You still on for a run and café after work? Kelly texted Emma on the following Wednesday morning.

OK though might be bit late back from school.

No probs, text when you're ready.

By the time they'd finished their run it was dark; it had hardly got light on this late February day.

'Let's skip anything soft and go straight for wine,' Kelly suggested.

'That won't help us rehydrate, in fact alcohol has quite the opposite effect, it … I'll have a glass of red.'

'Coming up, coach.'

Bridget was on duty and a smartly dressed young man stood behind the counter by her side. 'We're in celebration mode,' Kelly announced. 'We're off on holiday together over Easter.'

Bridget nodded but didn't further engage beyond taking the order.

Kelly came back with a bottle and two glasses. 'I'm thirsty,' she said when Emma gave her one of her teacher looks. Kelly began listing the clothing she intended to take to Scotland. Emma relaxed and as was often the case, a round of giggling ensued.

They were in fits of laughter, Kelly having told Emma the one-liner she'd heard at work, as Bridget and her young shadow came up to them.

'What's so funny?' Bridget asked.

'A not at all funny joke.'

'Come on then, fire away.'

'What do you call an Italian who's a bit of a nuisance?'

'No idea.'

'Pesto.'

Kelly and Emma started laughing again; Bridget and the young man's smiles were merely polite.

'I'll pass that on to the children, I'm sure they'll like it. Let me introduce Doug, our new Deputy Manager.'

There were nods of acknowledgement.

'These are two of our nicest customers,' Bridget continued. 'And I need to thank you both for winning David over to a name change. We've decided to go with Dream Café.'

'Andrew will be devastated!'

'And Darren will be delighted!'

23

Dinner parties in the past had been tense affairs but this mid-March one, the last before Kelly and Emma's departure for their Scottish Highlands weaving course, was an unprecedently good-humoured event. Instead of the chatty women desperately trying to engage their sullen and argumentative husbands, on this occasion the four of them were in fits of laughter as they shared anecdotes.

Kelly told of an enraged customer when the car that he had purchased was unveiled in the showroom.

'Ready for the countdown, Mr Sharples?' Kelly's boss had announced, having handed the man a plastic beaker of cheap fizz.

All the staff were there, ready to roll back the tarpaulin.

'Five. Four. Three. Two. One. Zero.'

Kelly recognised the problem before the man spoke because she was the one who had processed the order – for a Flame Red car.

'It's black,' was the simple phrase uttered by the crestfallen customer. This before he got rather angry.

Andrew's story concerned a member of the audience during the half-term book signing tour. He was reading a poem about how a decent, ordinary family were facing starvation during a global warming induced famine.

The slow, slow end, the children's howls, their sunken eyes, their wasting away ...

The woman had burst out crying and urged him to stop.

'But I can't. It's my poem.'

'You must!' she screamed.

'No.'

The woman ran out of the shop.

'I can't say I blame her,' Kelly quipped.

'All his poems are bleak,' Emma added.

'Then what did you do?' Darren asked.

'Carried on reading.'

'We shouldn't laugh. That poor woman.'

Darren described how he had come to the rescue of a disgruntled householder after a rival alarm company had severed the electricity supply.

'Thank the Lord for you,' the woman declared. 'It's such a relief to have an experienced workman rather than one of those youngsters who think they know it all.'

'I'm told that again and again, madam. I'm wondering, perhaps you'd be so kind as to write a review on Trustpilot.'

He got a five-star rating with some weird text about being a miracle sent by God.

Finally, Emma described the antics of her dreadful Year 9 pupils who had managed to hack into the French tutorial displayed on the whiteboard. Some IT genius had set up a graphically violent battle between French emojis with berets and navy hooped jumpers and their English counterparts wearing the national football kit. It wasn't funny at the time, but on retelling in the staff room it generated hoots of laughter and a sense of pride for the Computer Studies head of department.

There were hugs and kisses all round at the end of the evening, with the date set for a catch up as soon as the women returned from their weaving course in Scotland.

~

Early the next morning there was a loud thud which sent Darren racing to the bedroom window.

'Sounds like a car's been hit. Or my van.' Darren pulled back the curtains. 'Nope. It's a skip being dumped outside number 36.'

Throughout the day their neighbours, Luke and Alex, were carrying possessions out with the container rapidly filling.

The next morning, about to set off for a walk with Barnaby, Emma peered into the skip as Alex was leaving her house carrying a buckled lamp shade. 'I can't believe how much junk we've accumulated.'

'I can see why that's going.'

Alex dropped the hideous paisley shade onto the pile. 'It's been in the attic since Luke's grandmother died. I'm not sure why we kept it for so long, we were never going to use it. It's hardly a sentimental keepsake.'

Emma was eyeing the mound of goods. 'There must be quite a collection in that attic of yours.'

'Not everything is ours. There's been some sneaky fly tipping going on.'

'Emma had spotted a car exhaust, a pram with a missing wheel, plasterboard rubble and a roll of carpet. 'We had the same problem when we moved. In the end we had to get a second skip even though we were only offloading from a minuscule flat. When are you leaving?'

'Early next week. We'll let you know exactly when and give you our new address, of course.'

The Crabtrees and Robertsons never did get the date of the move or the new address.

Darren was the first to notice their departure on seeing the curtains missing and the car gone one afternoon when he was out with Tyson.

'They've left,' he told Kelly when he got home.

'Such a sweet couple.'

'Perhaps, though we hardly knew them.'

'I wonder what the new people will be like. The Halls, isn't it?'

'Yeah, I think that's what Luke said.'

'If I'm away when they arrive you'll be welcoming, won't you. Offer to help. Make them tea.'

'Of course I will.'

~

The weather turned dramatically for the better on the day Kelly and Emma were due to depart. There had been gales throughout March, but the wind dropped as if in recognition of the start of the new month. A warm sun burst through the dispersing clouds.

The men stood at the ends of their paths, dogs by their side, as their wives took off their coats and threw them onto the back seat of the taxi. Emma had won the battle to go by train rather than undertake a long, long drive, forcing Kelly to have a major rethink about what to take. Emma had reminded her that there was a washing machine on the premises which allowed a second suitcase of clothes to be culled.

'Aren't we lucky with the weather,' a beaming Emma called out, addressing both men who were now standing together outside the empty number 36.

'You look after yourself, Darren. And make sure you behave.' Kelly rushed back to Darren to give him another cuddle.

'Enjoy!' Andrew waved and Emma blew him a kiss.

'We'll call when we arrive. Bye, boys.'

And off they went, first stop Euston, leaving Darren and Andrew cursorily nodding before heading indoors.

Andrew was in high spirits. The draft of his new book had received a positive reception from the publishers with only minor edits needed and he was looking forward to the Manchester signing tour taking place after the Easter weekend.

Immediately Darren was feeling lost and lonely. He called the other Kelly, his accounts manager, and asked if she'd like to come over for a drink that evening. She couldn't – family stuff.

He knocked on Andrew's door. 'Maybe we can go to the pub tonight.'

'Not sure I can make this evening, Darren, but definitely before I head off on Tuesday.'

'Two weeks. I've never been apart from Kelly for that long.'

'Nor me from Emma.' But Andrew looked rather less perturbed than his near neighbour.

'OK. See you soon then,' Darren said with little enthusiasm to return to the silence of his house.

He didn't have time to close his front door. A sleek electric car, a VW, was pulling into a rare free space directly outside number 36.

A woman slid out and approached Andrew who had remained in his front garden pulling at weeds. 'Excuse me, do you by chance have a visitors parking permit that you could lend me? There's been so much to do, I haven't got round to applying for my residents permit yet.'

'I'm afraid not. We don't have a car and all our friends either walk, cycle or use public transport when they visit.'

It's like he's telling her off for owning a car Darren was thinking as he strode back up his garden path. He was remembering Kelly's request to be welcoming to his new neighbours as he pushed past Andrew to speak to this attractive woman. 'I've got one you can have,' he called out on reaching her.

'Thank you.'

'One sec, I'll dash home and get it.'

'No hurry,' the woman said as Darren turned away. 'I'm by the car so no one's going to fine me.'

Darren stopped in his tracks and swung round to face her. 'You don't know those bastard attendants. They're ruthless.' He started stepping backwards as he spoke. Tyson came bounding up behind him, sending his owner crashing down.

'Fuck. Sorry, I mean bother,' Darren said having judged that the woman might disapprove of an expletive.

Andrew had sped to his side and was attempting to pull him up. 'Are you OK?'

Darren didn't trust the man, the knight in shining armour was showing off. He sprang up with a rare demonstration of agility. 'Thanks. I'm as right as rain. I'll get the permit.'

His knee was hurting as he limped to his house. Keeping his distance Tyson followed him. He was glad to see the woman by the front door when he re-emerged with the permit. He handed it over.

'Thank you so much. I feel awful being responsible for your fall.'

'Not your fault, love. It was my stupidity.'

'Anyway, thank you for this. I'll replace it as soon as I get my act together.'

'No need. Accept it as a housewarming present.'

The woman examined the piece of paper as if she were assessing the value of a designer label gift. 'Well, obviously you've guessed who I am, the new owner of that lovely house. Mrs Hall. Cecelia.'

'Welcome to Brookland Gardens.' Andrew had appeared in Darren's garden and was shaking her hand. 'I'm Andrew Crabtree, your neighbour at number 38.'

'How do you do, I'm Darren Robertson from this house.' He extended his arm, reddening with embarrassment at having pretended to be posh with a false accent.

Mrs Hall took hold of his hand. 'I'm afraid there's blood seeping through your shirt.'

'Oh, it's nothing. I'll clean it up later.' Darren was not going to leave Andrew alone with the woman. He watched her lean into the car to place the permit on her dashboard. She had a top rate body, her legs snug in tight fitting calf-length jeans with turn ups. She was slim, much slimmer than Kelly, though not as thin as Emma who was all skin and bones. The loose fitting jacket she was wearing prevented further inspection.

Andrew had joined her by the car. 'I assume you'll be moving in soon then,' he was saying, his tone mellow and deep. This woman oozed class and Andrew was putting on a snobby air to impress. You could forget his la-di-da jolly hockey sticks pretence because Darren knew full well what Andrew was thinking. He was a bloke so the same as him, that Mrs Hall was a bit of alright.

'Correct,' Mrs Hall replied. 'I've popped in today to do some measuring. The removals are here on Monday.'

The attractive woman's alluring smile was directed at Andrew alone even though Darren had limped across to join them. He was not going to be excluded from this exchange; he would only be following Kelly's order to be welcoming. 'If you need any help on Monday, like mugs of tea for everyone …' he got in before Andrew could speak.

'How kind. I will ask if there's anything.'

'We should leave you to it,' Andrew said. 'I'm sure you have loads to do and I'd better take this thing for a walk.'

'What a lovely dog.' Mrs Hall crouched down to stroke him. 'What's his name?'

'Barnaby.'

'A great name. I love golden retrievers.'

'This is mine.' The dog had kept his distance from Darren but had come to his side on hearing a walk mentioned.

'What are these mixed breeds called? Labrapoodles?'

'Labradoodle.' Darren waited for Mrs Hall to pet his dog until it became apparent that wasn't going to happen. 'Alright Tyson, a walk for you too.'

Again Darren waited, this time for Mrs Hall to admire his dog's name. It became apparent that wasn't going to happen either.

'It's been lovely to meet you both, no doubt our paths will soon cross again.'

The men watched Mrs Hall go indoors before setting off side by side with their dogs.

'What do you reckon?' Darren asked.

'Reckon?'

'Our new neighbour.'

'She seems charming.'

'Charming! There's a word to put in your poems. Well I think Mrs Hall is a bit of alright.'

'I suppose she is quite attractive.'

'You really are a lost cause, aren't you?'

'Honestly Darren, I don't judge people by their looks.'

They stopped as Tyson peed against a hedge. Barnaby hung around sniffing.

'I bet you do. It's only normal.'

'It might be normal for you, but I'm more interested in a person's –'

'Sorry mate, I don't believe you.' They moved on in silence. 'I didn't catch her first name. See something our other, wasn't it?'

'Cecelia.'

'That's an odd name.'

'Not really.'

'I wonder whether there's a Mr Hall?'

Darren didn't get an answer. They'd reached a T-junction. 'I'm going this way for a change,' Andrew said.

'Fine. See you around.' Darren turned right.

24

When Mrs Hall's removal van pulled up early on the Monday morning both men were outside within minutes of the arrival.

Mrs Hall was already on the street, watching the driver reverse the van into a tight spot.

'This is it then,' Darren called out having won the race to get to her first. 'Can I get you a tea?'

'Or would you prefer a cup of coffee?' Andrew asked as he skipped along his path to reach them.

'I've made a thermos so I'm alright for now.'

'If you need help unpacking boxes or anything like that you only have to ask.'

'Thank you, Darren, that's very kind.'

'It's a pleasure. I've taken the day off in case I'm needed.'

Andrew edged closer to Mrs Hall, their shoulders close to touching. 'I'm a teacher so I'm on holiday. I'm around to help with whatever you need today or early tomorrow.'

'Again, very kind but I really do think –'

'But after that I'm off to Manchester for yet another book signing tour.'

'Book signing? Are you an author then?'

'Yes. Poetry.'

'How interesting. You'll have to show me what you've written when I've settled in.'

Darren stood there fuming. Couldn't she spot that Andrew getting in about being a poet was creepy boasting? "I'm off on a security alarms maintenance tour in north London next week" would hardly have the same pull.

A removal woman jumped out of the van and approached Mrs Hall, a youngster of slight build in dungarees and DMs and wearing a woollen hat.

'If you stand by the front door you can direct us where to put your stuff.'

'Will do, Sal.'

Sal called across to the two women standing by the rear of the removal van. 'OK girls – we're all set to roll.'

Their new neighbour went over to the van and chatted with the team. There was lots of laughter.

'Women doing removals? Now I've seen everything.'

'Don't be such a dinosaur, Darren. It's great that females do this type of work.'

'So you've seen hordes of women doing removals have you, Andrew?'

'I didn't say that.'

'Then what are you saying?'

'It's good that there are no gender barriers.'

'Gender barriers. Plastic carriers. I think I have my own poem in the making.'

'Very funny.'

Mrs Hall had returned. 'Time for my door duty.'

They watched her take up position to the side of her front door in time to instruct the two women carrying a sofa.

Darren was ready for an argument. 'She heard you call me a dinosaur. Don't you dare put me down in front of her again,' he began, jabbing his finger into Andrew's chest.

'I don't think she heard and I didn't say anything as a put down. If you thought that then apologies.'

'What about this, Cecelia?' one of the dungareed girls was asking. She was carrying a wooden cabinet, smallish but it looked heavy.

'Right, so she is called Cecelia. I thought that's what I heard her say yesterday but I wasn't sure.'

'Do you think they're lesbians? An all-girl team of removers, all of them in dungarees, including our new neighbour. You have to admit that's strange.'

'I've never heard such a ridiculous supposition!'

'I'll tell you what, Andrew, it's not nine o'clock yet and I've already had enough of you for today.'

'The feeling's mutual, Darren.'

'The feeling's mutual, Darren. Fucking posh woke.'

'You don't even know what the word means. Idiot.'

There was a reciprocal storming off, though Andrew was soon outside again in running gear, waving to Cecelia as he sped past with exaggerated acceleration.

'Enjoy!' she called out. 'I might be joining you one day.'

Andrew's only thought as he ran was that Darren was an obnoxious fool. His initial instinct when they first moved, to have nothing to do with him, had been correct. This was it now, no more doing Emma a favour for the sake of her friendship with Kelly.

He reached the park and slowed down; he wasn't quite as fit as he used to be. Would Emma now be faster than him? For some reason that thought was uncomfortable.

He switched to running across the grass to avoid the busy paths, this pleasant Easter day having brought out the crowds. Sometimes during the unyielding winter it had seemed like spring would never arrive, but here it was in all its pink and white magnificence – cherry blossom, magnolia, camellia, viburnum.

Andrew stopped for a rest on reaching Alexandra Palace and then walked home, his attention turning to the people rather than the scenery. Couples holding hands. Parents playing frisbee or football with their children. So much smiling and laughing. It struck him that everything he wrote was filled with doom and gloom, his poetry never portraying the joy that he was now witnessing around him. Perhaps he should capture the best of human nature, not the worst. He wouldn't know where to start though.

The van was still outside number 36 when Andrew got home, but Cecelia and the removal team were nowhere to be seen. He looked at his watch; it was around lunchtime. He imagined an enraged Darren spying on his fantasy group of lesbian, feminist, woke women feasting on hummus and pine nut sandwiches washed down with herbal tea. Andrew's smile was a malicious one.

He started packing for the Manchester trip. So strong was his dislike of Darren that not seeing his neighbour for a few days seemed more important than engaging on the book signing tour. He would have liked Emma with him though perhaps, as she'd suggested, it was no bad thing to have some time apart. 'I'll love you all the more when I come home,' she'd told him.

By coincidence she phoned as he was considering what she'd said. 'Sorry I didn't call yesterday; the journey was horrendous and we were exhausted.'

'No problem. Sending a text was fine.'

'This place is fabulous. You'd love it here; we must visit together.'

'I'm up for that.'

There was a ping and Andrew admired the lake, forests and mountains in the photo Emma had sent.

'That's sensational. I don't think any photo I send from Manchester is going to match that!'

'How are things there?'

'The new neighbour is moving in today. Cecelia Hall. She seems nice enough.'

'Only one person?'

'I haven't seen anyone else yet though there hasn't been an opportunity to find out.'

'Well, we'll soon know.'

'How's the weaving going?'

'It isn't yet; the course starts tomorrow. I'm looking forward to it but I'm terrified that I'll be useless.'

'You'll be fine, you're always quick to pick things up.'

'Not sure about that.'

'How's it going with Kelly? Is she being well behaved?'

'Well behaved? What do you mean?'

'It was a joke. Though Darren is not being well behaved. I'll fill you in when you're back.'

'OK. Have a good journey tomorrow and stay in touch. Love you.'

'Love you, too.'

~

While Andrew was out on his run Darren was sitting by his bedroom window spying. Watching the young women and his new neighbour manoeuvring heavy objects up the path had been a bit of a turn on –

the lifting, the carrying, the sweating, the sheer inappropriateness of it all. His fantasy was of taking a shower with the lot of them in his wet room. He'd thought he was well concealed by the net curtain until Cecelia waved.

Having been spotted he moved away from the window. To continue seeing what was going on he set about performing everyday tasks that took him outside. That morning there were two walks with Tyson, two trips to the local mini market, and front garden maintenance (which was anything but an everyday activity for him).

He timed it so that he would cross paths with the women.

'Are you OK with that, love?' he asked the youngster carrying a wide cardboard box. One of the straps on her dungarees had slipped down her arm.

'It's quite heavy so if you could step out the way it would help.'

With none of them prepared to engage he lost interest in seeing the women go back and forth from the van to the house. His attention switched to Andrew as he saw him turn into the street after his run. Not much of a run because the man was walking. Darren rushed indoors. He'd never known such a pompous, stuck up prick before. There would be no more dinner parties to keep Kelly happy, maybe not even a hello as they passed on the street. He switched on a sports channel and watched a discussion about the midweek fixtures. The panel expected United to win but he was less sure. A bet would have been sensible but he'd stick to the promise made to Kelly.

The next morning Darren rushed to his bedroom window when he heard a door slam; it was Andrew jumping into a taxi. He'd forgotten he was off to Manchester to sign books. Good riddance. A few days of having nothing to do with the man was more than welcome. It struck Darren that this left a golden opportunity to get to know Cecelia without having to worry about competition from Andrew.

He was unsure why getting to know Cecelia seemed so important. He was hardly going to have an affair simply because Kelly wasn't around. And anyway, the new neighbour wasn't his type. Judging by the way she'd connected with Andrew and excluded him, it was likely the feeling was mutual. But there remained some irresistible compulsion to flirt, whoever the woman might be. And if he could mess up any ambition that Andrew might have then that would be worth it.

That afternoon after work he put on a clean shirt, leaving the top two buttons undone, and rang her doorbell.

'Darren. What can I do for you?'

'It's more a case of what I can do for you. I was looking out at your back garden and wondered whether you'd like me to mow the lawn tomorrow after work. Grass is growing like mad now that the weather's improving. I'll be doing mine so it would hardly be any extra effort to cut yours too.'

'Well, if you're sure that would be most kind, particularly because I don't have a mower yet!' She giggled like a teenager. Darren refrained from admitting that he didn't have a mower either; he'd be using Andrew's.

'It would be best in the morning though,' Cecelia continued. 'I'm out after lunch and I'd rather keep the back gate locked when I'm away.'

This posed a problem, Wednesday being a regular work day for Darren and he'd been allocated a full schedule by his money grabbing new boss.

'No problem, I'll do yours first thing and mine later on. Is nine o'clock alright?'

'Perfect.'

'See you tomorrow then.' He winked. Cecelia looked puzzled.

At home he texted the boss he'd once trained. *Not going to be able to make it in tomorrow, I'm laid low with hay fever. I should be better once I get the medication. I'll do a double shift on Thursday.*

The reply was instant. *Pls make sure you're here by 7.30 on thurs.*

No "Hope you feel better" which annoyed Darren even though he wasn't actually ill.

It turned out to be a hectic three days getting to know Cecelia, or more to the point, getting to do jobs for her. In addition to the mowing, strimming included, Darren gave a helping hand weeding, repairing a fence panel and collapsing boxes for the removal company to collect. When they were together during short breaks for a coffee or tea, Cecelia questioned him while offering little information about herself.

'How long have you lived here?'

'Do you live all by yourself?'

'A weaving course – that sounds fun. For how long?'

'Do you have any children?'

'So is that *Stop Thief!* van yours then? What a clever name.'

Having moved on to a conversation about alarm systems, Darren explained the benefit of getting one installed.

'You've convinced me,' Cecelia said. 'Could you fit one for me when you have a slot?'

'If you're serious then you're in luck because I've had a last minute cancellation. I could do it tomorrow. I won't charge you.'

'Don't be silly, I insist on paying.'

'No really, there's no need.'

'I won't let you unless I can pay.'

'OK, but for the parts, not my labour.'

'You're so kind.'

'That's what neighbours are for.'

Darren had to lie to his boss about another hay fever attack but it was worth risking it to spend a whole day with Cecelia who was going to work from home during the installation.

The next morning she greeted him wearing a baggy shirt and an above knee-length skirt. Shapely legs he was thinking as she turned and made her way to the kitchen having offered to start the day with a coffee.

'I'll have to leave the front door open because I'll be in and out with stuff,' he informed her as they sat in the kitchen, two mugs resting on a glass-topped table.

'That's not a problem.'

'I'm just saying in case you need a jumper because of the draught.'

'That's thoughtful of you, but I'm sure I'll be fine. Tell me, what made you choose a career in burglar alarms?' She bent low to collect a crust of toast off the floor and Darren caught a glimpse of a white bra with lacy edging.

Cecelia fired questions at him as she had done previously and Darren decided to keep his answers brief.

'How's the business doing.'

'Pretty good.'

'Where did you live before moving to Muswell Hill?'

'A couple of miles down the road.'

'So what made you move?'

'Oh, it's a long story.'

'Tell me a bit about your wife.'

'She's called Kelly.'

'Have you been together long?'

'Yes, quite a few years.'

'You must be missing her.'

Darren thought enough was enough. 'I'd better make a start if we want to get it finished today.'

He was on the ladder connecting an alarm box when a taxi arrived and Andrew got out. If anything, the dislike of his near neighbour had intensified during Andrew's absence. He could hardly ignore him though, that would be infantile. 'Good afternoon, Andrew.'

'Afternoon, Darren. What are you doing up there?'

It was obvious; it didn't merit an answer. 'Good trip?'

At that moment Cecelia came out with a mug of tea, the fourth drink that day. 'I'll leave it at the bottom of the ladder,' she said before catching sight of Andrew. 'Hello. How did your book signing go?'

'Most successful. It's always such an eye opener to meet my fans, to discover what they love about my poetry.'

Darren squirmed. Here we go, la-di-da, aren't I wonderful.

'The tea's brewed. You're welcome to come in for a cuppa as long as you don't mind being surrounded by unsorted possessions.'

'I'd welcome that; the train buffet didn't arrive and I'm gasping.'

So in they went as friendly as could be, leaving Darren up the ladder. He the worker while the other two would be sipping tea while they discussed poetry. Probably in her bloody living room rather than in the kitchen.

He gave it five minutes then scampered down the ladder and entered the house. Confirmed – they were sitting in the living room. 'This'll be noisy,' he called out. 'I'm testing.' He set off the alarm needlessly.

'We'll close the door,' Cecelia said as she clicked it shut.

'And again,' he called out, drowning out their laughter with the shrill siren.

He opened the living room door holding a step stool. 'Sorry to disturb but I need to check the sensor.'

'I'd best get going.' Andrew stood up. 'Thanks for tea.'

'And thanks for telling me about that wonderful local café. Perhaps we could go there tomorrow morning.'

'Good idea.'

'Shall we say 10.30?'

'Perfect.'

Cecelia looked across to Darren. 'You too, of course.'

Darren nodded in agreement. 'I'm also leaving now. The alarm's done.'

'What about checking the sensor?'

'No need. I forgot I'd already adjusted it through the control panel.'

The two men had no option but to leave together, Darren having picked up his tool box and step stool. Andrew turned to the right and Darren to the left at the end of Cecelia Hall's path without a word spoken.

25

Saturday. 10.30 am.

Andrew and Darren left their houses in unplanned synchronicity, shoving each other as they made their way up Cecelia Hall's path towards her front door. There was a battle to press the bell. Darren won.

'Good morning, gents. What a lovely day, I'm not sure I'll need a jacket. What do you reckon?'

Darren was speechless. Kelly never asked him what she should wear.

'I'd take one just in case,' Andrew advised.

'So, tell me all about this wonderful café we're visiting,' Cecelia asked as they set off, sandwiched between the two men. 'Everyone on Facebook is raving about the place.'

All Darren could think of saying was that it was a posh café with a ridiculous name that he could never remember, that the drinks were too expensive, and that his wife liked it for some reason, maybe because she was a woman and it was a woman's kind of place. He decided it was best to let Andrew do the talking.

'It is perfect for the area, absolutely buzzing from early morning until late evening and the entertainment they provide is top notch. I think there's music on tonight but they also have art exhibitions, run a book club, host comedians – and poets of course. I was snapped up by my publisher at a café event. Or have I already told you that?'

'Several times,' Darren muttered.

'They show films too,' Andrew was rabbiting on. 'Not the blockbusters. Old black and white ones, even foreign.'

'Sounds wonderful,' Cecelia responded.

'Yes, David and Bridget have put together a brilliant package; they certainly know their clientele,' Andrew continued. 'Stunning décor, fabulous food, an impressive wine list, friendly staff – and as you're about to find out, the best coffee north of the Thames.' Imminently so because they had reached their destination.

Andrew drew to a halt with a look of horror on seeing David supervising two men up ladders attaching a Dream Café sign above the entrance. Broken bits of laminated lettering lay on the pavement. *A. eet. ame. Des.*

'What's going on?'

'Good morning, Andrew. It's our new name. The old one was confusing.'

'Not for me.'

'Then you're an exception. We asked customers and did a Facebook poll. The approval to change was near unanimous.'

'This is much better,' Darren said.

'That's exactly what your wife said.'

'Did she?' Darren had a rush of pride that his wife agreed with him.

'What about Emma? My wife?'

'Oh, she said you'd hate it, but you really are out on a limb. She thought it was a good idea to change.'

'I can see why you've renamed it. A Street Café Named Desire is clever but maybe too clever. Dream Café has a soft romantic feel to it. I'm Cecelia by the way, the in-between neighbour of these two gentlemen.'

'Welcome to our Dream Café!'

'I'm ready to try this world famous coffee of yours.'

Darren led the way with a light step and a broad smile, overjoyed to see the distraught Andrew sulking, head down, as he entered the café.

'They take orders at the counter,' Darren said cheerily. 'What can I get you, Cecelia?'

'I'll have a cappuccino please.'

'What about you, Andrew?'

'Double espresso.'

'Righty-ho, coming up!'

He skipped away from their table, returning with the coffees and a taster patisserie mix – small cubes of cheesecake, muffin, carrot cake and strudel.

'Mmmm, yummy,' Cecelia said as she bit into the strudel, Darren having offered her first choice.

Cecelia was facing the counter. 'Who's that serving, the one David's chatting to?'

'Bridget, David's business partner and they're married.'

'No they're not, they're just in a relationship.'

'Have a cake, Andrew.'

'I don't want one. Thank you,' the "thank you" a barked reprimand.

The tension between the two men was impossible to miss.

'Well, here we are and I'm impressed. I appreciate you two for bringing me.'

'A pleasure,' Darren said.

Andrew nodded.

'And of course I have more neighbours to meet – your wives. When are they back?'

'Still another week and then Emma will only have one day to get ready before returning to school. She'll be exhausted.'

'Perhaps not. Being away doing something different can be re-energising.'

'It's a massive journey from the uplands of Scotland back to London.'

'Are they driving?'

'No, trains.'

'Well that's fine then. They can relax, chat, read. How did that old advert go? "Let the train take the strain." So it's Emma, and I think you told me your wife is Kelly. Obviously they're good friends to go away together.'

'Like us,' Darren said with a pretence of delight, expecting a reaction from Andrew that would convey his true feelings.

'Yes, like us,' was all he got back.

'It's time I told you a little about me. You'll have seen that I'm in the house all by myself. I got divorced a few months ago. It was perfectly amiable and we're still friends. We'd simply had enough of living together and what with our youngest starting university, the time seemed right. So I bought my amazing house next door to you two while he's gone to live in the middle of nowhere in the Chilterns. God knows why. No shop, one pub – he'll hate it.'

She stood up. 'Let me get refills. Same again?'

Darren and Andrew watched as Cecelia made her way to the counter. The café was filling and Cecelia had to wait to be served.

'She is a stunner,' Darren said. 'And single, too. Some lucky bloke is going to be onto a winner.'

'Here you go again, everything coming down to sex. Why can't you simply see her as a charming lady. I can tell that her and Emma are going to get on well.'

Anger surged with Darren seeing this as an implication that Cecelia, not Kelly, was Emma's type of friend. 'You really are pathetic, Andrew. All I'm saying is that she's a stunner. There's nothing wrong with that and you'd be a liar to say you don't think the same. I can see the way you're looking at her. And it's not about sex – she's not my type and I've got Kelly.'

'Two Kellys from what I've seen.'

'You'd better button it.'

Returning with a tray, Cecelia saw the red-faced Darren pointing an index finger a short distance from Andrew's face.

'Everything alright, you two? Bridget told me you were a pair of rogues and seeing you now I think she might be right. Honestly, if looks could kill!'

'We're fine.' Darren's hand returned to its resting place on the table.

'Yes, we're fine.' Andrew handed out the coffees.

'Did you know that it's their music night tonight? I'm going. Do you fancy?'

~

Andrew had had more than enough of Darren for one day, (or one lifetime), but decided to go to the music night because he hadn't had enough of Cecelia. Describing his new neighbour as a "charming lady" when what he really thought was that she was gorgeous was deservedly mocked by Darren. Andrew fancied her. It was her eyes – dreamy, sultry, seductive – bedroom eyes was the expression he'd heard Emma use. Taking things further with Cecelia had entered his head, the thought in itself not a disloyalty to his wife, but what would he do if the opportunity arose?

He chuckled as the three of them were on their way to the music night at Dream Café.

The other two looked across at him. 'Want to share it?' Cecelia asked.

'It's nothing really.' It was something though, the term "taking things further". What he'd really been thinking of was plain and simple going to bed with her, though even that was inadequate. Going to bed could be due to tiredness and the need for a good night's sleep after a stressful day. Making love seemed old fashioned, something requiring toil and rationality. Sexual desire was not rational. Darren was right – sex was the word to use.

He let out a loud harrumph sound which got the other two looking at him in puzzlement again. The thing is, he was thinking, say Emma never came back (which was possible given the recent drift apart) and Cecelia was single (which she was) and liked him (which seemed to be the case). Then sex would be OK, wouldn't it? But was he wrong to get as far as that thought when Emma would be coming home after her short break in a week's time? But say Cecelia took the lead before then and suggested sex? Of course he'd say no.

The café was filling up fast, the audience predominantly young.

'Bridget told me that David's daughter's boyfriend is performing. I suppose a lot of the people here are his friends,' Cecelia said, articulating Andrew's observation of the average age of the audience.

'Quick, let's grab that table near the back,' Darren said pointing. 'I'll get the drinks.'

He returned with a bottle of red wine. As far as Andrew could remember, Darren rarely drank wine and never red.

'It's a Merlot. I hope that's acceptable. It's one of my favourites.'

Andrew fought off the temptation to inform him that the letter t was a silent t.

'Perfect,' Cecelia said as Darren filled to near the brim of her glass; Andrew hoping that the ignorance of the right quantity to pour would be noted by Cecelia. It had been the same faux pas at their dinner parties. When Andrew had remarked on it after their first social, Emma had told him not to be a snob.

There was applause as David emerged to introduce that night's band. *Up Above.*

Three youngsters came on stage carrying acoustic guitars. 'Well, we've finally made it to the best venue in Muswell Hill,' one of them said.

'The only venue,' another of them quipped.

'Seriously though. I'd like to thank Rachel's dad and Bridget for letting us play tonight. I promised we wouldn't drown out all conversation so this session is going to be acoustic.'

There was further applause as the first chords were struck. The music was good and for the first time that day Andrew felt relaxed. With the first bottle of wine empty he was up and at the bar to get a second. It was Cecelia's round next but Andrew insisted she was the guest of honour. Protesting, she pushed her chair back to stand, but Andrew rested his hand on her shoulder to make his point. That touch, on a woollen cardigan, not even skin, was sensual, shocking. When she looked at him with those bedroom eyes he had to flee to the bar for fear of stooping down to kiss her.

Standing there waiting to be served, his legs struggling to support him, he was unsure whether it was the alcohol or the woman that was the cause. The youngsters around him seemed to be buying the same concoction, a red liquid in a tall glass.

'What is that?' he asked Bridget.

'A lethal cocktail. I'd say it's not for you, Andrew. I've told the others to stop serving it before we have a serious crowd control incident!'

'Well, make the last three for us.'

'Really?'

'Yes, really.'

More cocktails followed and the trio were still drinking after the music had stopped and most of the audience had dispersed. David announced that they were about to close as he put on the main lights.

Andrew discovered that he couldn't stand up. Cecelia tottered. Darren seemed as right as rain and assisted the others.

They must have made it back to Brookland Gardens because Cecelia was inviting them in for a sobering up coffee as she put it. The men sat in the living room, Darren chatty, Andrew monosyllabic, while Cecelia was in the kitchen.

'What's got into you, mate? Never thought I'd see you downing so much booze.'

'Can.'

'I'd say can't. You're right out of it. Are you going to puke?'

'No.'

Cecelia came back with the coffees, unsteady as she handed them out, the tray angled precariously. Collapsing onto an armchair, she took off her shoes and stretched her legs.

Andrew was looking at her feet, her ankles, her calves, her show of thigh.

And that was it for him.

'He's passed out,' Darren stated, looking across at Andrew sprawled out on the couch with eyes shut, saliva speckled across his beard.

'Is he safe?'

'Well, he's still breathing.'

'I must say, my head is spinning.'

'Finish your coffee, that'll help, then I suggest you lie down.'

Cecelia gulped down the coffee. 'You're right, I do need to lie down. Now if you don't mind.'

'So you want me to leave?'

'Yes, I think so.'

'Do you need help getting upstairs?'

'No, I'm fine.'

'What about him though?'

'He's not going anywhere. He can stay the night.'

'Here? With you?'

'I really am shattered, Darren. I'm sure it'll be OK.' She smiled. 'He's hardly likely to attack me!'

That wasn't the issue as far as Darren was concerned. The two of them would be spending the night in the same house and Cecelia wouldn't be making it up to her bedroom. On the edge of consciousness she would be crashing out in the armchair next to Andrew on the couch. Everyone knew what drunkenness led to. And then in the morning they'd have breakfast together and she'd talk about her divorce and loneliness. Everyone knew where that conversation could lead to.

Now standing, he was assessing what to do. The only option was to leave them to it – and he wasn't happy.

26

Andrew stirred, hungover and disorientated. The curtains were open and light was streaming in. The magnolia outside was bursting with pink-tipped white bloom. Their fragility. Their beauty. He wanted to touch the delicate soft petals.

Beauty.

Touch.

Delicate.

Soft.

Cecelia!

He sprang up with the realisation that he wasn't at home. Sensing a stirring to his side he spun round to see Cecelia slumped in the armchair, one arm dangling over the side, the other stretched out above her head. Her tangled body, her tousled hair, her bare feet, her shapely legs – and he was alone in the room with her. What had happened? Had they …?

She opened her eyes, a look of shock followed by a smile. 'I was terrified for a sec.'

'And I was … well, I don't know what I was because my head is still foggy.'

'I'll make some coffee.'

Andrew was left to regain lucidity, his head still pounding. He scanned the room and noted the evidence of the recent move. Six columns of books were stacked against an empty bookcase. Two cardboard boxes were by the side of the fireplace, a red ceramic vase protruding from one of them. He would buy flowers to fill the vase to thank Cecelia for allowing him to stay the night. Surely they'd crashed out and nothing more.

Cecelia was back, following his gaze. 'It's still such a mess. I have made a start but there's loads more to do.' She set the tray with cafetière, two cups and saucers, milk jug and sugar bowl onto a low table with a grey smoked glass surface, either an original or 1960s retro. 'I'm starving. I'll put some toast on,' she said as casually as if a wife organising breakfast. 'You might want to freshen up before eating. The bathroom is the second door on the left upstairs.'

'I think I'm OK thanks. I'll have a shower as soon as I get home.'

'Why not splash some water over your face?'

This came out more as a command than a suggestion so Andrew did as requested. On looking in the mirror upstairs he could see why the order had been given; his beard was streaked with dried saliva. He cupped water into his hands and rubbed his face vigorously, the pressure easing his headache. He registered the rough feel of hands against beard and it crossed his mind that Emma's comment about discomfort when kissing had validity.

Emma! He was in another woman's house, in her bathroom, with no idea of what had happened the night before. And now he was regarding with interest the thin nightdress and skimpy pair of knickers on the hook behind the door.

He was close to certain that he – they – hadn't done anything, hadn't taken things further, that ridiculous phrase now seemingly embedded in his brain. He'd been drunk and crashed out in a neighbour's house. And it was hardly a crime to look at what was in a bathroom when you were there for the innocuous reason of needing to freshen up.

Then why was he opening the cabinet above the washbasin? Nothing exceptional there, the sort of stuff Emma used. It could almost be a man's cabinet – electric toothbrush, interdents, sun lotion, paracetamol. The razor was different to a man's one though. Small, dainty, pink. So she shaved. Under her arms? Legs? Private parts? Was it wrong to wonder about that, to visualise?

'I'm in the kitchen,' Cecelia called out.

Andrew closed the cabinet, pausing to check that all traces of dribble were off his face, before heading downstairs.

The table had been laid with napkins, pretty floral bowls for the butter and jam, and a plate of fruit and a pot of yoghurt to add to the toast and coffee on offer.

How come Cecelia was collected enough to put a breakfast together after an alcohol-fuelled evening and a night sleeping on an armchair, when he was so washed out?

'Thanks, this is lovely,' he said as he buttered a slice of toast. 'I'm sorry to have been such a nuisance.'

'You weren't, at least I don't think so because I was as comatose as you. I didn't even know you were still here until this morning.'

Although the coffee and food were restoring Andrew's clarity, he continued to feel guilty even though there was nothing to feel guilty about. He scanned the room, settling on the stack of books on the floor in the corner. 'More books. I noticed the pile of them in your living room. Is book sorting all that's left for you to do?'

'You must be joking, you should see the state of my bedroom.'

Andrew blushed on mention of her bedroom, the nightdress and knickers in his thoughts. He searched for something sensible to say. 'I suppose there's no rush to get everything done. After all, you have to do it all yourself.'

'I asked the children if they'd like to assist. Too busy of course. I was told they'd look at their schedules and fit me in as soon as possible. As usual I was too conciliatory; I should have insisted they come over to help.'

'Two boys, isn't it? I think that's what you said yesterday.'

'Yes, two boys, both now flown the nest. Do you have children?'

'No. We decided against what with the state of the world.'

'Meaning?'

'Overpopulation driving food shortages, squandering non-renewable resources – the imminent environmental catastrophe.'

'Help, that's a dramatic call. I'm glad we did have kids; they do add something important to one's life even if it's an uphill struggle from the day they pop out.'

As quickly as it emerged, Andrew expunged all thought of a baby popping out of Cecelia.

'Gosh, all these books. You must be an avid reader,' Andrew blurted out, wondering as he spoke whether this was the most banal line he'd ever uttered. He was a poet; he was supposed to be good with words. Did writing dystopian poetry prevent everyday chitchat? Thinking of the first lines of his latest poem he reckoned that could possibly be the case.

The great sickness has abated
Leaving those left huddled together
With vague memories of a happier past
Their future laced with fear

'Sorry, I missed that.'

'I was saying the books in here are for work. As soon as I can empty a room I'll have an office to put them in.'

'Mind if I take a look?'

'Sure, go ahead. More coffee?'

'Yes, please.'

Andrew knelt to read the spines.

Discovering Yourself or is it Yourselves?

The Road to Happiness.

The Psychology of Counselling: Attached or Detached.

'So you're a counsellor.'

'More psychology really.'

'A lecturer?'

'I dabble a bit.'

Replacing the books Andrew rejoined Cecelia at the table. The real Andrew was back, the serious and academic one, ousting the shallow and lecherous imposter. Cecelia was a clever woman who would understand the messages in his poetry. 'There's a fair bit of psychology in my writing. Philosophical thought too.' He had the urge to impress her, perhaps recite a line or two to illustrate his point?

They said they knew
They said they understood
But they knew they didn't know
And had no desire to learn

Or might reciting be presumptuous? Best not to; not now anyway.

'I look forward to reading your poems. I'll get the book.'

'I'm assuming you publish your research.'

'More dabbling. *Can men forgive easily?*'

'Pardon?'

'That's the title of what I'm working on. The first draft has a ridiculously long subtitle – *A comparative study of levels of antipathy, empathy and self-healing amongst men from different socio-economic backgrounds.*'

'Wow, sounds great.'

'It covers how men cope when their woman – wife or whatever – leaves them. How do you think you'd get on if Emma left you for good?'

Coming out of nowhere the question caught Andrew on the hop. He'd never been comfortable talking about personal concerns, even if theoretical. 'Fortunately I don't need to think about that because Emma is coming back.'

'But imagine it all the same. Could you cope?'

'I'm extremely practical so I'm sure I'd be fine. I'm not sure about Darren though.'

Why had he brought up Darren? His abrupt pause and Cecelia's frown suggested that she was also wondering why.

'So,' she said finally, elongating the word to two syllables. 'Is competition with other men an issue for you?'

'No, of course not. I don't know why I mentioned Darren.'

'But say his wife, Kelly isn't it, say Kelly also didn't come home. What would be more important to you? Showing that you were coping better than him or establishing a supportive network?'

'It goes without saying. The latter.'

'Interesting. My research indicates that the vast majority say what you have, but when it comes to the crunch men are fiercely competitive. Who will be the first to get a new woman? Who can get drunk the most often? Who'll buy the flashiest car?'

'Really? Well, I'm not your typical man then.'

Was he though? There was the man he liked to think he was, serious, intellectual, ethical, faithful to his wife. And there was the man now in this room who fancied Cecelia, who would like her naked by his side, who wanted to take things further. To have sex. A disgraceful man like Darren.

If this conversation was prolonged what would his psychologist neighbour be able to unearth? He had to end the discussion, but how?

Fortunately he was saved by the boom.

~

Darren had hardly slept, enraged as he was with Cecelia allowing – wanting – Andrew to stay the night. So much for innocent Andrew who in all probability had feigned unconsciousness.

Early morning he took a cup of tea up to his bedroom and sat by the window to spy on the comings and goings at number 36. When would Andrew be leaving?

One hour passed. Two hours passed. Two and a half. It was nine thirty.

Enough was enough. He crossed his garden towards the back alley and then on to Cecelia's gate. With a little lifting and shoving of the rotting wooden structure he managed to ease it open without causing much damage, nothing he couldn't repair later on. Returning home, he took his brand new mower out and pushed it into his neighbour's garden. With one pull of the cord the diesel engine kicked in with a roar and he moved up the lawn towards the house.

The kitchen door opened and Cecelia came running out. Andrew was behind her. Darren's immediate impulse was to punch the man but he managed to force a smile. 'All the rain and sunshine we're having. I thought it was time for another mow.'

'Don't you think the noise on a Sunday morning is a bit of an imposition on neighbours?'

With one of her neighbours doing the mowing and the other by her side this didn't seem a valid reason to stop, but since he was only in her garden to see if Andrew was still there he switched off.

'And haven't you already cut it once this week?'

The three of them examined the barely noticeable first strip of grass mowed. 'Fair dos. I'll leave you two in peace.'

'It's probably time I headed home,' Andrew said. 'Thanks Cecelia. For everything.'

Surely that was a deliberately inflammatory comment. Darren wanted to punch Andrew more than ever.

'I do appreciate you helping, Darren,' Cecelia said, 'and I can see that it could do with a trim. Perhaps tomorrow if you can fit it in.'

A trim like it was a haircut – Cecelia and Andrew had recognised why he'd shown up and he'd made a fool of himself.

'Thanks for showing me the books and telling me about your fascinating work,' Andrew was saying. A punch really was on the cards.

Darren walked off, dragging the mower behind him. Make sure you're nice to the new neighbour Kelly had told him, but now he was wondering whether to have anything further to do with Cecelia.

By the next day his competitive spirit had returned and there was no way he was going to let Andrew have a free ride.

After work he sped to Cecelia's garden, edging through the busted gate with his mower. Cecelia waved from the kitchen, using a hand movement to beckon him in for a drink. How posh is that he thought, her thumb and index finger holding an imaginary cup handle with her pinkie extended. Posh and sexy. He gave a thumbs up then extended his fingers to signal five minutes. That's all it took to mow a lawn that didn't need mowing.

'I went out earlier to open the gate for you but it was already open. It's damaged.'

'The wood's rotten. I'll see what I can do to patch it up.'

'It didn't seem that bad when I wheeled the bins out the other day.'

'It's kids. They're always out the back messing about. Good job you've got that alarm.'

Cecelia had lost interest in the subject. ''Help yourself to a biscuit.'

'Thanks.'

Darren felt a tension what with Cecelia observing him.

'Tell me, did it bother you Andrew staying here on Saturday?' she asked.

'Bother me? No, of course not.'

'Good. It's just that you weren't your usual jolly self yesterday morning.'

'I was a bit hungover; it was quite an evening!'

'You can say that again. Andrew and I were totally – what do they say these days? – Wasted.'

Me AND Andrew. She was implying that they were a couple. All Andrew's noble talk about loyalty and morality was a sham. Darren remembered that Andrew had thanked her for showing him her books and talking about her work when he'd overheard them the previous morning. Was this how to gain her admiration? Well. two can play at that game Darren decided having spotted a heap of books in the corner of the room.

'Books eh. You've got loads of them.'

'And they're only the ones for work.'

'What work is that then?'

'I'm at one of the London colleges.'

'That's nice.'

Cecelia seemed to be waiting for him to say something else. He wasn't sure what.

'I teach Psychology,' she continued.

'Seeing inside people's minds.'

'I guess that sums it up nicely. Actually, can I ask you the questions that I asked Andrew? Let's see if you have the same opinions.'

'Fire away.'

'I know this isn't the case, but how do you think you'd cope if Kelly left you for good?'

'She won't.'

'I know, I've said that. This is just to get you thinking what if. It's for research I'm doing.'

'But she isn't leaving me.'

'This is just pretend.'

'I'd hate it. I don't know what I'd do. I love her.'

'That's splendid to hear, good for you. But let's carry on pretending for a minute. Say Kelly did leave you and by coincidence, Emma left Andrew. What would be more important to you, making sure you were coping better than him or going flat out to help each other?'

'What's Andrew got to do with it? I wouldn't care what happened to him.'

'Interesting.'

'Not really.'

It was time to go; the woman was bonkers. When it came to women, he realised, looks weren't the only thing that mattered. He missed Kelly.

'I want to put everything away before it gets dark.'

'Sure. Thanks for helping,' he heard her call out as he went into the garden.

27

As they set off from Brookland Gardens Kelly had stretched across and given Emma a hug, slumping into her as they turned a sharp corner en route to Euston.

'Freedom! I'm so excited, I haven't been away without Darren for a big break since we met.'

'I've had a couple of trips with girlfriends but not to go on a course. Which I must say is scaring the living daylights out of me.'

'I know you'll be the star pupil. You even look arty.'

'What does that mean?' Emma was wearing warm layers to combat the predicted early April weather in the Scottish Highlands – black leggings under black waterproof trousers, beige Gortex ankle high trainers, a green fleece and a brown down jacket. That hardly constituted arty. Kelly had on a short sleeved dress, a cable knit cardigan, anything but sensible shoes, a light jacket, and enough jewellery to weigh her down and drown her were she to fall into a loch.

They had discussed what clothes to bring. Emma was wearing her thickest clothes to reduce the weight when lugging her suitcase on and off trains. Kelly claimed that all the sensible clothes were in her bulging suitcase.

The taxi pulled into Euston and they made their way through the crowded concourse to the platform.

'Well, here goes. I do hope Darren can survive without me.'

'Of course he can, it'll do him good. It's only for a couple of weeks.'

'I've left him ten meals in the freezer, not fourteen.'

'There are shops that sell food round the corner, rather a lot of them. And if he does need anything he's always got Andrew to help him out.'

They looked at each other and burst out laughing.

'You're confident about Andrew coping then?'

'Yes, he's totally self-sufficient. I'll come home and things will be more orderly than when I left. Anyway, he's away the first few days on his book signing tour.'

Kelly was restless on the long journey to Edinburgh and took to pulling out one of Emma's earbuds every so often to hear what she was listening to. 'More speaking. That's so boring.'

'It isn't. It's *From Our Own Correspondent*.'

'What's it about then?'

'Senegal. The government are thinking of clamping down on –'

'Here, take it back.' Kelly dropped the earbud into Emma's outstretched hand.

Minutes later, Kelly was shaking her head and swaying. Emma yanked off the headphones and put a side to her ear. 'Who's this then?'

'Harry Styles.'

'Isn't he for screaming pre-teen girls?'

'So what? I like it.'

'Actually, it's not bad.'

Because of a short delay on the four and a half hour journey to Edinburgh, the women had to leg it across platforms to catch the train to Inverness for their three and a half hour journey. The final stretch was from east to west, the views meriting their oohs and aahs as they sped through stunning scenery. It had taken eleven hours to reach Strathcarron; from there it was a short taxi ride to their final destination at Lochcarron.

The manager of the complex took them to their cabin, a simple single-storey wooden construction nestling by woodland. Emma stood by the huge picture window overlooking the loch, mesmerized by the sunset.

'Amazing,' Kelly declared having joined her to watch the sun sink behind a low hill, the sky an impossible mix of oranges and purples. 'You can't see anything like this in Muswell Hill.'

While Kelly was unpacking Emma stayed by the window as the sky darkened. Laden with stars, shimmering dots of light were reflected onto the water.

'Come back, Kelly, this is even more amazing. Switch the light off.'

Kelly returned. 'There are so many stars there's got to be life on one of them. Aliens with telescopic eyes are probably watching us this very minute. They probably know what we're thinking about.'

Emma couldn't decide if Kelly was being serious; she was so full of fun it was hard to tell. Andrew would have spoilt this moment by spouting some scientific evidence to prove the non-existence of outer beings. The difference between Kelly and Andrew wasn't about gender though because none of her other girlfriends had the same humorous take on things as Kelly.

'Let's get some food. I'm famished,' Kelly said. She'd had enough of the awesome view.

The communal building was a short walk from the cabin, another wooden structure with large picture windows and a slate roof. There were eight small round tables in the dining room; they had the pick because apart from them the place was deserted.

The man who came out the kitchen was the person who had shown them to their room. 'You'll be the vegetarians,' he said. 'It's macaroni cheese for you tonight.'

It wasn't gourmet food though they were impressed with the apple crumble and custard dessert.

'We should let the men know we've arrived,' Emma said when they got back to the cabin. 'I'm hoping Andrew won't mind if I just text to say we're here and that I'll call him tomorrow. I'm too shattered for a conversation now.'

'I'll do the same. The main thing is for them to know that we're here safe and sound.'

'What about this?' Emma read out her message. *'Arrived safely, shattered, going to bed, will call in the morning.'*

'A bit boring. Let's make them laugh.' Kelly read out her draft. *It's true, the Scots really don't wear anything under their kilts.*

'I'm not sure what Andrew would make of that.'

Emma began typing. *Ate haggis this evening – delicious. There goes being a vegetarian.*

'Darren wouldn't get that; he doesn't even acknowledge that I'm vegetarianish.'

They played the what-shall-we-text game for a little longer before settling on something similar to Emma's bland original message.

Emma got off the bed and returned to their large window. 'My God! Look!' It was a cloud-free night and a translucent sheet of mist was resting on the loch. 'I don't think I've ever seen anything so beautiful. It's like every bit of light possible has been squeezed from the darkness. I must try to capture it though it's a big ask for the phone.'

They crossed paths, the naked Kelly making her way to the window.

'Close the curtains! Someone might see you.'

'No one's out there.'

'What about your aliens?'

'Oh yes, I forgot about them. I wonder what their males are like.'

Emma was pulling the curtains shut ahead of stepping outside to take photographs. It gave her time to think. She had decided that what nearly happened last time wouldn't be an issue on this trip. Ahead of leaving, purely out of curiosity, she'd dipped into social media channels to discover that a hell of a lot of woman seemed to be experimenting in the LGBT+ world. It wasn't for her. Was it for Kelly though despite her saying how much she loved Darren.

'So tell me, are you bisexual?' she asked the naked Kelly as soon as she came indoors.

'Not really.'

'What does that mean?'

'It means I'm not but I have got this thing about you. When we're alone I just want to touch you. I think it's mutual but enough said. I won't hassle you.'

~

'Over the next two weeks you'll learn how to set up a small frame loom and to assess the variety of materials and warp settings required for designing. Once that's in hand you'll move on to control the weaving tension and to create shapes, angles, lines and texture in weave. The final step will be to learn how to mix and blend coloured yarns.'

'I'm already terrified,' Emma whispered.

'It might sound terrifying,' their tutor continued as if responding to Emma, 'but fear not. I'll be taking you through step by step with the help of Morag and Janet here. By the end of the two weeks you'll be competent weavers.'

There were five participants, four women and a man, not counting Fiona's two assistants who were of student age.

'We'll start by selecting the correct warp and weft thicknesses and I'll be showing you some basic tapestry techniques.'

'What's she on about? I don't think I can stay here; I really am terrified.'

It turned out to be a great morning, the pace unhurried, methodical and rhythmic. Kelly and Emma were instantly lost in the intensity of the activity, and at ease with the coaching team and fellow course members.

That first afternoon was free and the women went for a walk along the loch promenade. There was a bitter wind blowing so one of the fleeces, one of the hats and the down jacket that Kelly had squeezed into her suitcase were put to good use.

'How was your chat with Andrew this morning,' Kelly asked as they were walking along.

'To the point. He was glad I'd arrived safely. He told me he'd made linguine with roasted aubergine for dinner the previous evening. He was getting ready for his trip to Manchester. He's had a chat with the new neighbour who he was sure I'll like. He'd noticed slight damp under the bay window in the living room which he'll sort as soon as he's back from the book tour. He watched an Icelandic documentary about isolation and loneliness – it was brilliant and he's kept a note of the title in case I wanted to watch it. I half expected a report on his bowel movements over the past twenty-four hours. He was sure I'd do well on the course which was a nice thing to say.'

'You must have spoken for ages. Mind you, I did too. Poor Darren, he's so needy. I got asked how to change the temperature setting on the microwave – this from a security alarms engineer. Did I know whether there was a spare bottle of the shower gel he likes anywhere in the house? There are shops, I told him. I did have several I love yous and I miss yous which was nice. He's like a kid though; he asked when I was coming home. "I've only just left" I reminded him and we had a good laugh.'

Kelly had such a light way of describing everything and Emma could imagine her conversation with Darren, her friend rolling her eyes as they spoke, teasing her husband but with warmth.

'You've gone quiet,' Kelly said.

'Sorry, I was just thinking.'

'About?'

'Oh, nothing really.' But it was something. Emma was wondering why conversations with Andrew could be so sterile in comparison. When was the last time they stopped being serious? Talked rubbish. Messed around. Laughed aloud. Who's fault was that? As much mine as his she reckoned.

'Earth to Emma, did you hear what I said?'

'Sorry.'

'I was saying we should make this our last walk. From now on it's running.'

'Agreed.'

They settled into a comfortable routine, weaving in the mornings and then exercise in the afternoon. It wasn't always a run though, sometimes they went on a hike or cycled using bikes provided by the centre. Evenings were spent with the others in the group, tutors included, eating together then sitting in the bar where life journeys were revealed bit by bit.

'I don't think I've ever felt so relaxed,' Emma said when the two women were in their cabin one evening at the end of their first week.

'I know. We're doing loads and I should be exhausted but I've got masses of energy.'

'You've always got masses of energy.'

Sunday was a full day off and they decided on a cycle to an upland lake, taking a picnic with them. Part of the route was so steep they had to get off their bikes and walk, but when finally they reached the spot recommended by Ross, the centre manager, it was worth the effort.

'This could be paradise,' Emma said as they admired the stunning view, the placid lake turquoise, a waterfall cascading into it, the rock surfaces a rusty brown infused with lines of silver quartz. 'What are you doing?'

'Ross said if we reached this we had to skinny dip. It would be an experience of a lifetime.'

'The last experience of our lifetime because we'd die of hypothermia.'

Kelly was down to her underwear.

'You're mad. I'm not doing it.'

'Chicken.'

'You haven't even got a towel which ups the risk of death from probable to definite.'

'Yes I have,' Kelly said as she pulled two out of her rucksack. 'One for me – and one for you!'

Holding one of the towels, Kelly trod carefully over the uneven terrain to the shore, stepped into the lake and swam.

'OK, I'm coming in too.' Emma threw off her clothes and edged towards the water's edge, dipping her toes in. 'Done it. I'm coming out.'

'After three,' Kelly yelled. 'One. Two. Three … Four. Five. Just do it.'

It was mad. Wonderfully mad. Shocking. Mind-blowing.

They sat together on the hillock wrapped in towels and marginally warming up with the help of a flask of coffee with the added whisky recommended and provided by Ross.

'I could stay here forever. No, that's stupid, not forever, but definitely for longer than two weeks.'

'You've read my mind, Emma. You've read my mind.'

28

Cecelia Hall wasn't Mrs or Ms Cecelia Hall. She was Professor Hall, a distinguished lecturer who headed the Psychology department at a prestigious University of London college. She never introduced herself using Professor; it sounded too pompous.

Overwhelmed by deadlines, the last thing she had wanted was a move, but once the sale of the family home had gone through and assets divided, there was no choice. It had all been perfectly amicable; they'd gone as far as viewing each other's tentative choices of where to live and Charlie had even offered to help with her move. Yes, all perfectly amiable following twenty or so years of a pretty well strife-free partnership, but the spark had gone. Frank discussions about what to do resulted in the decision to go their own separate ways while remaining the best of friends.

Charlie had opted for a rural life, his new house tucked away in a sleepy village in the Chilterns encircled by sheep, cattle and horses. Cecelia could never give up the buzz of the city. Muswell Hill, with its village feel, was the perfect location. She could afford it, a considerably smaller property than the suburban mansion previously inhabited.

She recognised the irony in conducting research on the impact of marital separations given her own circumstances. Charlie was an exception because you couldn't ask for a more balanced and sensitive ex – male or female. But Charlie aside, there did seem to be substantial differences between men and women's responses to divorce, both emotional and practical.

The reaction from friends and family on finding out the topic for her research was either fear or boredom.

The fear came from those separated or divorced. 'If you're thinking of asking me to be one of the case studies in your research you can forget it. There's no way I'm going to hang out my dirty washing for all the world to see.'

'Everything is anonymised, Linda. The way you dealt with Ed's affair was amazing.'

'Forget it, Cecelia. I'll sue you if I'm in it.'

Boredom was the other response. Cecelia was over at Immy's a week or so after the conversation with Linda. They'd talked about loads of things before Cecelia mentioned her research.

Immy's eyes had glazed over. She sprang up and looked out the window.

'Sorry, Cecelia. It looks like rain and the washing's still out on the line. There's a dress I need for tonight's do so I'd better grab it. In fact, I need to start getting ready so shall we call it a day?'

Cecelia would have preferred honesty. "That is so boring. Can we please talk about something else?"

Her mother was the worst of the lot. She'd never quite forgiven Cecelia for her career choice. 'Art, music, design, any of those would have suited you, but no, you chose such a dreadfully dull subject.'

Since early childhood Cecelia had been fascinated by how the mind worked and the passion had stayed with her. It was anything but dull despite what her mother and some friends thought.

Given the sensitive nature of the subject Cecelia had instigated a hard and fast rule: she would keep her professional and social lives well apart. Until now that is because her new neighbours, with their backgrounds and personalities being poles apart, would make perfect case studies.

With the data analysis near complete based on a survey of four hundred carefully selected men, what was needed were in-depth interviews to illustrate the fascinating revelations exposed by the survey. It hadn't taken long for her to recognise that Andrew and Darren were prime candidates. While there was no reason to suppose that their wives wouldn't be returning, both men had relationship issues.

Can men forgive? A comparative study of levels of antipathy, empathy and self-healing amongst men from differing socio-economic backgrounds. Her research centred on those already separated or divorced, but with these two she would be able to add a fascinating new dimension – a consideration of how men think they might behave compared with how men have actually responded following separation.

But it would mean breaking Rule One, not to mix business with pleasure. Asking the men a few straightforward questions had already induced either suspicion (Andrew) or confusion (Darren). The fallout if they thought that her reason for socialising was devious would go far beyond Darren not cutting her lawn and Andrew not discussing poetry with her. These were her next door neighbours and the risk of antagonising them would be high. She wasn't stupid though; she'd noticed their glances. Lawn mowing and poetry chats were to impress her, the men possibly regarding her as an insurance should things not work out with their wives. They fancied her, she was pretty sure about that.

If they were using her it was reasonable for her to use them. Or was it? She needed to make the decision based on professional ethics rather than any notion about what was acceptable.

Surely including her neighbours was safe because case studies were anonymised. However, Andrew was showing interest and was likely to ask to see a copy of the published document. He would recognise his profile. And once Cecelia was aware of that risk she would be under pressure to tone down any revelations about his behaviour. That would make it pointless to include him as a case study.

What about Darren? It was unlikely that he would want to read the published work but what if Andrew told him about it. Then there'd be trouble.

God, how patronising she was in making that assumption – Andrew interested, Darren not – when she barely knew them. Was it based on their accents? Their vocabulary? Their jobs? So much for conducting unbiased studies, so much for the belief in a society without prejudices. She was as much a bigot as the worst of them.

So, do I include my neighbours in the study or not, this conundrum preventing sleep that Monday night? What an intriguing few days it had been, Saturday in the café with the boozy end; Andrew staying the night and their strained morning together until Darren had come barging in; she probing Darren the next day.

They were perfect candidates for the study.

A resolution to her conundrum came at the point when she had given up on sleep, grabbed her dressing gown and was heading downstairs to make a coffee. It was a sort of cop out – there was no need to decide yet. She could chat with the men informally, pick up information as a friend might do, record it as an academic must do, and make the decision down the line.

Eureka. Job done!

29

'Heard anything from the wife?' Darren asked Andrew as they crossed paths while walking the dogs late on the Tuesday afternoon.

'A bit. You?'

'A bit.'

'And?'

'She's having a good time.'

'Same with Emma.'

'I called Kelly this morning.'

'And?'

'Odd really. She said she'd like a bit of peace and quiet during the rest of the time away and I should only call in an emergency.'

'Really, she said that?'

'Yes.'

'Actually Emma said the same when we spoke last night. She's sending me postcards like it's the twentieth century.'

'I'm getting postcards too. Still, they'll soon be home. Got any plans to do anything with Cecelia?'

Andrew broke eye contact. 'No, nothing. You?'

'Also nothing.'

Barnaby tugged the lead as if picking up his master's wish to escape. 'Dogs, eh,' Andrew said as he pretended to be dragged along.

'Yeah, dogs.'

~

Nothing planned? The liar!

Darren had gone out to retrieve the thermos flask he'd left in the van. It was 7.23 pm. He looked up when he saw the security light that he'd fitted came on to illuminate Andrew at the door carrying a bunch of flowers, a bottle of wine and a book.

On red alert Darren sat by his open bedroom window with the lights off for much of the evening. He saw Andrew leave at 10.56 pm. At least he wasn't staying the night.

~

The following afternoon Andrew was returning home from a visit to the wine merchant. He stopped abruptly and ducked down behind a car on seeing Darren leave his house holding a bunch of flowers. Flowers and Darren? The two didn't go together. Spying through the car windows he saw Darren step over the low dividing wall and ring Cecelia's doorbell. His neighbour went inside and the door was shut.

Thankfully Darren hadn't spotted him.

~

Darren was struggling not to laugh as Cecelia opened the door. He'd seen Andrew diving down behind a car to snoop. What Andrew didn't know was that this visit was speculative; Cecelia might not be at home. It was worth a try though – Andrew wasn't going to win the race to befriend their new neighbour.

'A belated something to welcome you to your new home.'

The flowers he was handing over had cost a fortune at the exorbitant boutique florist on The Broadway. There was a touch of guilt that he'd never spent that much on flowers for Kelly.

'How kind.'

'Flowers are so lovely this time of the year. I thought these would brighten up your house.' He refrained from adding what the shop owner had mentioned when he'd complained about the price – ethically sourced, zero carbon footprint – even though he reckoned that Cecelia was interested in that sort of thing.

'Oh, do you think the house needs brightening up?'

'No, not at all. It's just that you must be so busy you haven't had time to think about flowers.'

'True enough. And they're gorgeous. Why not come in for a cup of tea?'

Cecelia had taken the bait and she led him to the living room. Andrew's poetry book was on her coffee table and presumably those were his flowers in the red vase.

'Have you read it?' she asked, noticing his glance and picking up the book.

'Not yet, but I intend to.'

'I suppose you have more free time with Kelly being away.'

Immediately Kelly was back as the topic of conversation.

How long had they been together?

How had they met?

What did they like doing together?

Darren was uncomfortable talking about Kelly without her being there to share the conversation.

At last there was the tiniest of lulls and he could switch topics to the reason for his visit. 'I would invite you over for a meal tonight but sadly my cooking skills aren't up to it.'

He waited in anticipation of the sought after response: "Why not come over to me."

'Never mind, we can arrange something when Kelly's back,' was what he got.

No further proof of favouritism was needed. Cooking a meal for Andrew was fine, cooking one for him wasn't.

'I'd better go, I've got loads to do.'

There would be no more cutting of her lawn.

~

During the period when Darren was at Cecelia's, Andrew was busy preparing dinner. He'd invited her to dine at his place towards the end of the evening at hers. 'Why not come over tomorrow,' he'd suggested.

'Perhaps we should wait until Emma's back,' she'd replied. 'I'm looking forward to meeting your wife; you've spoken so highly of her.'

'Of the two of us I'm the one who does most of the cooking so there's no need to wait.' Andrew paused, reflecting on whether his manipulative (and untruthful) boast would be recognised as wanting Cecelia over without Emma being around. A pity you couldn't rewind a conversation or delete it like in a text but now he had to think fast to make an offer that was hard to refuse. 'Of course Emma can cook too, she's very good, but as far as tonight goes, I've got a piece of halibut in the fridge that's far too big for one person. It would only go to waste …'

'… if you didn't have someone to share it with. That's an intriguing invite for a meal.'

'Gosh, that came across badly. You joining me would be a pleasure.'

'I'd hate to waste halibut so I'd better accept!'

Andrew liked her quick wit, it reminded him of Emma.

Early the next morning he had taken the halibut out the freezer and he was now garnishing it ahead of putting the fish in the oven.

~

When Darren heard Cecelia's door close he rushed to the open window. She had a bouquet of flowers – for an instant he thought they were the ones he'd given her. He continued watching as she entered Andrew's house.

His fury was so strong that his heart was racing, his hands squeezed into fists. He didn't know where to direct his anger, at Cecelia for rejecting him because she had another date that night or at Andrew for pretending that his thoughts about his neighbour were just that, neighbourly. Two dinners in two days, Andrew 2 versus Darren 0.

Would she be staying the night?

Loneliness overtook anger. He wanted to call Kelly but had been told not to. Turning on the television to take his mind off what was going on next door, *Love Island* didn't do the trick. Neither did the junk he continued watching on mute using subtitles so he could hear Cecelia leave, assuming she would be leaving. Finally he heard whispering and laughing, then light footsteps and his neighbour's door closing. It was 10.21 pm.

Even if Cecelia wasn't staying the night, a lot could have happened during their three hours together.

~

Andrew was being the perfect host. Charming, thoughtful and in the know about how to organise a dinner party. Seated in the living room he suggested an aperitif which Cecelia turned down. He proffered the bowls of cashew nuts and olives, cocktail sticks and a plate for stones on standby on the side table.

'Are you ready for a glass of wine?'

'Yes, that would be lovely.'

'It's a Pouilly-Fumé, a good fit with halibut.'

'Sounds fine.'

Andrew left to get the bottle and a couple of glasses. Having failed at two supermarkets he'd bought it at the ridiculously expensive wine merchant off The Broadway. 'It's a particularly dry Sauvignon Blanc,' he said on his return, showing Cecelia the label. She didn't seem attentive as he poured a drop, swilled and sniffed it, before filling Cecelia's glass.

'Dinner's ready so we can take our wine into the dining room.'

Andrew slid out a chair to help Cecelia sit at the table, something he realised he may never have done for Emma. Perhaps for the better though because the chivalrous act turned out to be a clumsy manoeuvre sending Cecelia plummeting down as he pushed her forwards.

The halibut he presented was substantially over-cooked, devoid of the soft flaky texture that the recipe called for. He watched as Cecelia attacked the solid lump.

'Do you take it in turns cooking with Emma?'

Suddenly, Emma had become the topic of conversation.

When and where did they meet?

Did she often go away by herself?

What were their shared interests?

He wasn't enjoying the conversation, talking about Emma when he was wanting to impress Cecelia. 'We used to do tai chi together until Emma took up running. I still go to classes though.' He didn't add, "but not for the last eighteen months".

'I've thought about giving tai chi a go but I've never got round to it.'

'Come along with me if you like.' Were classes still held at the same venue?

'Maybe down the line when I'm less busy.'

At last there was a pause and Andrew could turn the conversation to his own agenda – the new poetry publication; the praise received from fans during the book signing tour; his groundbreaking work with problem pupils at school; aspects of both the arts and the sciences to show that he was an all-rounder.

Somehow he lost control again and they were talking about Emma's teaching, her running, where she was staying during the course. 'And with Kelly. How lovely that they're friends. It seems more so than you with Darren.'

'We get on OK.' His tone suggested otherwise; he couldn't help it.

Cecelia thanked him for the lovely meal and left soon after ten o' clock, earlier than he would have liked. It had been a disappointing evening. In bed that night he fantasised about how it could have been a lot better.

~

Darren had two choices, give up and let Andrew monopolise Cecelia or battle it out until the bitter end. He was too competitive to select the first option.

He didn't write poetry, he couldn't cook (Andrew was probably of *Masterchef* quality), he didn't have the knowledge that Andrew was always showing off, so what could he offer Cecelia? It would need to be something way off Andrew's radar and different to anything Cecelia had ever done.

'QPR's a small club and they're playing a useless team so we'd definitely get in,' he explained while standing by Cecelia's door early on the Saturday morning.

'I don't get the Cupee-are. Aren't teams named after where they're located, like Manchester and Liverpool?'

'It's an abbreviation of Queen's Park.'

'Oh, I see. And the R?'

'Rangers.'

'It's a kind offer but I'm going to decline. Football isn't for me.'

Darren was searching for a more tempting offer when his phone rang.

'It's Kelly, I'd better take it,' he said as he backed away from the door. 'I'll catch you later.'

~

With a day to go before Emma's return, Andrew was clearing the fridge of food that Emma wouldn't approve of – smelly cheeses (stinking being her description), double cream, the original sugary Coca Cola – when his phone rang.

It was Emma.

30

On the Friday morning, a couple of days before their weaving course was due to end, a call came through from Kelly's boss.

'I'd better take it,' she told Emma. 'Back in a sec,' she called across to Fiona their tutor.

She was out of the room for ages; by the time she got back the coffee break was over.

Emma was sorting out yarns. 'Everything OK?'

'I'm not sure. Theoretically it's awful news but I don't mind.'

With the market rock bottom and the supply chain shredded, the global car sales company had instigated a rationalisation strategy at speed. The showroom where Kelly worked was to close, the business merging with a site ten miles away along the North Circular Road towards Essex.

'You're our star performer, Kelly,' her boss had told her, 'so I've made it clear that you have to be able to transfer, meaning it's good news for you if not for the others.'

'I need to think about this, Ron.'

'What's there to think about? I've had to fight to keep you employed, I would have thought you'd be delighted.'

'Thank you for your concern about me. Just give me a bit of time.'

'Three days. By Monday I need to know one way or the other.'

Kelly explained the situation to Emma.

'Is it the same type of work?'

'I suppose so.'

'Then what's the problem?'

'On a mundane level, the journey. Have you ever been on the North Circular during rush hour? It's a nightmare. And the showroom is near Romford, which I don't much fancy.'

Their tutor came out to check if they were returning soon. 'Another sec, Fiona. Kelly has a bit of sorting to do.'

Emma turned back to face her friend. 'Look, the solution seems easy to me. Say yes because at least it's a job, and you can start looking for something else straight away.'

'But do I want that? You know we joked about how nice it would be to stay here for a bit longer, how serious were you?'

'I love it here, not having a constant pressure to get through tasks. Being with you is loads of fun, I don't think I've laughed so much for years. And I'm enjoying the weaving, I'm finally improving. But –'

'That's a lot of plusses. Why the but?'

'Work for a start. And then there's Andrew, of course. Come on, let's go back in.'

It was impossible for Emma to concentrate on designing a new tartan because the thought of staying on was gathering momentum. Not forever obviously but why not for a little longer, maybe another month or so until summer? Then Andrew could join her during the half term holiday.

However, there was work, the inconvenience to the school if she took leave of absence. Not much though because the Italian A-level and French GCSE students would soon be on study leave. There was a young part-time foreign languages teacher who was always looking for more hours; she'd make a success of taking the final classes for the examination groups.

Without committing there was no harm sounding out the headteacher. She called.

'I'm confident Zara would be willing to cover for you,' Emma was told. 'We both know that she's an outstanding teacher, the pupils love her.'

This was moving too fast, beginning to look like a done deal. 'Nothing's definite yet.'

'No, of course not. But I was going to ask you to take on some sports teaching once your exam classes go. I believe you're a runner.' Yes, I do run, she wanted to tell him, but that doesn't mean I know how to teach athletics or tennis or hockey or whatever.

'To be truthful money is tight. If you want a term's sabbatical that would work well for us.'

'Fine, I'll see you in September then,' she blurted out, suffering from the weight of rejection. What had she done because staying on in Scotland was by no means certain?

Kelly was waiting for her outside the classroom. 'Well?'

'It's done. I'm staying.'

'Seriously?'

'Yes. You haven't changed your mind, have you?'

'Nope.' Kelly called work. 'Hi da-do-ra Ron, Ron. Oh, sorry, who is that? Could you put me through to Ron please? … Hi, Ron. I really appreciate you thinking of me but I've decided not to work at the other showroom. I'm going to take some time out ... Yes, a hundred and ten percent sure … No, it's not the money, a higher salary would have been nice, but it's still a no … I haven't left you in the lurch, it wasn't my decision to move to Romford … just get lost will you, Ron.'

Kelly cut the call. 'Tosser.'

'He won't want you back in a hurry.'

'Good riddance. He only wants me there to ogle at. But, and it's a big one, my salary was helping us financially. Darren won't be happy. And for that matter, he won't be happy about me not coming home on schedule.'

'I'm not sure what Andrew will think. Ahead of speaking to them we need to find out whether staying on is possible.'

At the end of that afternoon's session, Emma and Kelly discussed their plan with Fiona. Apparently they weren't the first to want to stay at the end of a course and the solution was easy. The next group weren't arriving until August so they could remain in their accommodation, attend the weekly classes for locals, and additionally use the workshop when convenient.

'And of course you'll be able to discover our beautiful countryside in better weather.'

'We're almost certainly staying, but if it's alright we'll let you know for sure tomorrow morning,' Emma said, hit by a wave of panic. What was she doing? Life in Muswell Hill was great, life with Andrew was great. Now she was abandoning him which risked ruining things for ever. But if life was so good why was she excited by the prospect of doing something different for a while?

'I'm going for a walk,' she informed Kelly.

'I'll come with.'

'I'd rather be alone for a bit.'

'Is everything alright?'

'Yes, I think so.'

Emma needed time to think. Would this be merely a few more weeks away or was it of life-changing significance? Assuming she was half way through her life this could be her very own midlife crisis. Did such a thing exist though because not a single friend reckoned they'd experienced one. But if she had another forty years left, wasn't it reasonable to take a break from her likely destiny for the rest of her time on this earth.

Wanting a breather wasn't wrong. She would tell Andrew that she was extending her holiday, that it was no big deal, and that she'd love him to join her as soon as school broke up.

Panic over.

31

'You what!' Darren screamed. 'I let you go for two weeks not for months.'

'You didn't let me go, I decided to go. And I've decided to stay on a bit longer. You're a, a … patriarch.'

'Party arse? What are you on about?'

'Maybe I mean misogynist.'

'What's that?'

'Look, a bully then. Stop bullying me.'

'Have I ever bullied you, Kelly?'

'No Darren, you haven't. But I do want a bit longer here. It's not forever, only a few more weeks. I don't want to argue, please just let me do this. Get your head round it and I'll call you tomorrow to go through the details. I've got something to tell you about work too. Tomorrow.'

That was it. Kelly had cut the call, leaving Darren staring at a blank screen.

His first thought was that Kelly was leaving him for good, that she'd met some kilt-wearing, ginger-bearded, haggis-eating, caber-tossing tosser. He was inclined to head straight up there to bring her home but it would end in failure, a wasted journey, because when Kelly decided to do something he'd never been able to get her to change her mind. So to all intents and purposes he was wifeless and that thought was alarming. Since living alone would be unbearable he'd have to find a new person and quick. Kelly from work? Cecelia? Hang on, those thoughts were ridiculous. He only wanted Kelly. He loved her.

~

'What about your job, Emma? Don't you think you have a duty to your pupils?' was the measured response when she told Andrew about her plan to stay on in Scotland. She wanted to scream down the phone, "Don't you mean what about us!"

Having spent the night fretting about her decision to stay there were no doubts now.

'I've sorted everything. School don't mind, in fact it sounded like they're glad to get rid of me.'

'I suppose your timetable will be on the lightish side once the exam kids have left.'

'That's exactly what the head said.'

Shouldn't Andrew be saying, "Don't be silly, you're a great teacher, you do fabulous work at the school" and "You're a wonderful wife and I'm struggling to cope without you."?

'Anyway, no need to worry about me. I've got plenty to get on with at school and writing.'

The conversation was infuriating though unsurprising. Andrew was simply being Andrew, emotionally deficient. Practical, caring, helpful, protective – there were positives too – but all the same.

'Do you miss me, Andrew?'

'Miss you? Of course I do.'

'Good, that's nice to know.'

'What an odd question. I love you.'

'I love you too. I'd best go, we're about to run up a rather steep hill.'

'Good luck with that.'

'Thanks. I'll call you tomorrow.'

When the profile picture of Emma disappeared from the screen Andrew went into the kitchen and switched on the kettle. The room was orderly – no magazines, letters and papers scattered across the table; no crockery stacked on the draining board; no packets, jars and tins of food left out on the worksurface. It hit him how much he missed Emma's untidiness. He hadn't handled the call particularly well; he should have urged her to change her mind. He was far more upset than he'd made out.

During a previous conversation she'd suggested that they could visit the place where she was staying together, but there had been no mention of that today. Maybe there was another man? Kelly was a bad influence so perhaps it was a case of two men.

Andrew took the cafetiere and mug to the kitchen table, sat down, and thought about what life would be like without Emma. He loved her, her sassy take on things, her good nature, the way she organised their social life, the sex. Yes that, he was missing that. Was this news some divine retribution for fantasising about Cecelia the night before? A daft thought.

He pressed the plunger and poured the coffee. There was no choice other than to accept Emma's decision. He'd immerse himself in school work and his writing. Or was it time to drop everything and relax a little? He'd worked hard over recent months – the writing, school, the move – he deserved a break. He could join colleagues for the social events they organised, something he'd turned down in the past. He could get in touch with old school and university friends who he hadn't seen for ages. There were locals to see though they were couples which would require awkward explaining about Emma's absence. Finally, his neighbours. Forget Darren, but what of Cecelia? They got on well. If he broke free from lustful drunken thoughts they could become close friends. Nothing underhand, just friends.

~

Darren and Andrew stepped out of their houses with their dogs at exactly the same time. Cecelia was in her front garden deadheading blooms on the camellia.

'Good Morning, gentlemen.' Neither spoke; they looked rather forlorn. 'Is everything OK?'

'I'm fairly certain I'm speaking for both of us,' Andrew began. 'Emma has decided to stay on in Scotland for another two or more months. I'm assuming that's the case for Kelly.'

'It is,' Darren confirmed.

'Isn't that a lovely idea?'

'I suppose so,' Andrew said. 'I've got loads to get on with so if that's what she wants to do then yes, fine.'

'Well, I'm not happy and if you were honest, Andrew, you'd admit you aren't either.'

'How do you know what I'm thinking?'

'I only have to look at you to see that. You're as fed up as I am.'

'The difference between you and me is that I welcome my wife's independence.'

'The difference between you and me is that I say things the way they are. Wives away for three months? That's not normal.'

'Maybe not in your social circle but in mine husbands and wives are off doing their own thing all the time.'

'If I was Emma I'd be desperate to do my own thing.'

'Stop bickering you two. All I can say is that I'm jealous. Having the opportunity to extend a holiday in a beautiful location with loads to do, weaving if I'm not mistaken, sounds brilliant. And it's only for a short while.'

Silence.

'If they're enjoying themselves why aren't you two doing the same? Go have some fun.'

More silence.

Cecelia returned to snipping faded flowers and dropping them into a bucket. The men stood watching for a while before moving on, Darren heading up the hill and Andrew downhill.

Cecelia considered the news from a work perspective. She sensed that the wives weren't leaving for good, but the men were reacting as if that was the case. Their predicament added a further layer to her study, starting with how men respond when they think their marriages are over and ending with how quickly they can adapt on discovering that isn't the case. Fascinating.

Putting work ahead of neighbourliness if not friendship was troubling though. The men were upset, indicated in their different ways, and she felt sorry for them. If only they could put aside the rivalry then when their wives returned they might form a pleasant group of acquaintances, the six of them, the two sets of neighbours, she and Julien.

She could sympathise with Darren and Andrew if their distress was anything like her own. Julien was in Mozambique doing research on post-colonial politics and after four months without him she was suffering.

Cecelia tipped the garden waste into the green bin and took the tools and bucket back to the shed. Thinking of work again (she never stopped) she reminded herself that she had yet to decide whether to include information about Darren and Andrew in her study – for now they were friends who needed support.

She was sure that it wouldn't be long before one or both of them made contact with her. She needed to make it clear that she wasn't available as a substitute for Emma or Kelly – it was time to tell them about Julien. That was a problem though because it might distort her findings. If she kept quiet about him and they chased after her, that would allow her to measure how long it took for them to seek a replacement sexual partner.

The fact that they hated each other was another problem.

Complicated.

Delicacy was needed.

~

It was Monday late afternoon and Dream Café was beginning to fill up with mothers (only women despite this being enlightened Muswell Hill) and their children gathered from local schools and nurseries.

David was in the back office wading through spreadsheets. *Message in a Bottle* played. He pressed the green icon to take the call.

'Hi, Bridget.'

'I'm running a bit late but I'll be with you in half an hour.'

'No problem, Mike's coping well. I've left him to it while I do the accounts.'

'Good figures?'

'More than good. Brilliant. I'll show you later.'

'OK. See you soon. Bye.'

'Bye, gorgeous.'

Bridget. His business partner and lover. Almost two years had passed since the school reunion when they'd met, technically re-met after twenty-five years, and he still sometimes reflected on his good fortune. He must once have loved Jane, his ex-wife, as much as he now loved Bridget, but he couldn't recollect having ever had such intense passion.

There was a knock on the door.

'Hi Mike. Everything alright out there?'

Mike was their trainee barista, a serious young man with a commendable sense of responsibility.

'I think so, but there are a couple of men arguing and it's getting a bit heated.'

'I'll come out and take a look.'

It was Andrew and Darren. It was unusual to see the men in without their wives and at this time of day, too.

David had followed Mike to the room in time to see spittle being showered over Andrew as Darren yelled at his companion.

'I've told you, mate, we've both got to forget the past. It's over. We have to bloody get out there and make something of our lives.'

David watched Andrew wipe his face dry with a handkerchief before rolling his eyes, shrugging his shoulders, yawning and turning away. If looks alone were anything to go by, Andrew was making a far better job of making something of his life than his friend. Darren's sallow, puckered face was showing the effects of long-term excessive alcohol intake. He was a squat, tubby man, his waistline expansive. Bridget had once remarked on how a man of his build could have such thin legs. His herbal tea drinking companion was slim and wiry, the epitome of good health, his racing bike secured against a lamppost outside. His beard was of the academic's rather than the hipster's style, his face narrow, his eyes intent, somewhat lacking in smilability.

'You're jumping to conclusions. There's nothing to suggest it's over. Be patient.'

David and Mike watched as Darren got up, walked round to the other side of the table and stooped down to within inches of Andrew's face.

'And I know bloody well what you're doing.' He was still shouting despite his close proximity. 'I've already told you, stop hogging her!' More spittle. It was disgusting. Andrew took out his handkerchief and wiped his face again.

David noted the four empty pint glasses on the table. Usually Darren was a tea drinker during early afternoons at the café; he'd gone straight for the beers that day.

Having returned his handkerchief to his pocket, Andrew paused, the epitome of calmness, before responding. 'Cecelia is a lovely woman but she's a friend. Nothing more.'

'Liar! I was the first to help her – mowing, the security alarm. I was the first to be friendly and you've been trying to steal her ever since with those cosy meals.'

'Dining together hardly constitutes stealing her.'

'And I was the first to take her somewhere when we went to see a film.'

'Film? Hardly. It was *Top Gun: Maverick*! I'm surprised she agreed to that.'

'If you must know she enjoyed it. And we had a meal out at that Waggi … Waggi …place.'

'Wagamama, that world renowned culinary experience! During our three delightful dinners together we've been able to discuss all sorts of things, we've been to an art exhibition together, and she's read my poetry – which she loves.'

'I've heard enough about your bloody poetry to last a lifetime. I gave her a housewarming present. Flowers.'

'So what? I brought flowers when I went over for dinner.'

'That wasn't a present though, was it? I was the first with a present.'

'Being the first is hardly significant. Trevithick was the first to invent a steam powered railway but it was Stephenson who everyone admires and remembers.'

'Railways? What are you on about?'

'I'm merely saying, Darren, that being the first doesn't necessarily mean being the successful one. Anyway, I'm not in this competition that you've created.'

'I've seen the way you look at her, you sly bastard.'

David had paused to reflect on the wisdom of Andrew's statement about the pioneers of railway development in nineteenth century Britain, but now he was moving towards the pair, keen to end the shouting. Darren had taken hold of Andrew by the collar of his tweed jacket and was pulling him out of his seat.

David noted other customers' looks of shock, the older children excited, the younger ones in tears.

He stepped forwards. Enough was enough. 'Darren, will you stop, please? For a start, let go of Andrew.'

Darren did let go with a shove and Andrew sank back onto his chair.

'Happy now?'

'Not really, no. This isn't the sort of behaviour I'm prepared to allow.'

'I'll behave however I want.'

'No. Any more and you'll have to leave.'

'And if I say fuck off I'm not leaving?'

'That's it, I want you out now. And I'm banning you from coming back in again.'

David wasn't expecting the punch. Had he been prepared he might have lifted an arm in self-defence, thereby protecting a jaw that received a blow so hard that it felled him.

He lay on the floor in a daze, half-aware of a scuffle, of Andrew and Mike grabbing hold of Darren to restrain him. He was dizzy, the room was spinning from the light grey and beige walls – Bridget's Nordic chic colour choices – to the scarlet alcoves which had been her concession for his preference.

Then, as if in a dream, he saw a vision of Bridget by the café entrance.

'What's going on?' the apparition asked.

'Oh, it really is you. Hello, Bridget.'

32

Darren stormed out of the café. Andrew remained, helping Bridget to lift David onto a chair while Mike rushed to the bar to get an ice pack.

'It's OK everyone, drama over,' Bridget announced to the audience of mums and kids. 'Leave me to it and get behind the counter, Mike,' she added in a whisper. 'Hopefully the customers will settle down and want serving.'

Bridget turned her attention to her partner who was clutching the ice pack against his chin. 'Can you speak?' she asked.

'Of corsh I can eak.'

'At least it's not as bad as the last time then,' Bridget joked, ruffling David's hair.

'Last time? Has Darren hit him before?' Andrew asked.

'No, it wasn't Darren. We got mugged in the West End soon after we'd started dating and this knight in shining armour overdid the bravery.'

'He fought them off.'

'No, nothing as noble as that. He started cracking jokes and the thief whacked him. We ended up in A&E.'

'Pleesh Idget, you don't have to tell everygoggy.'

'This is all my fault,' Andrew said. 'I was winding Darren up. I shouldn't have done that.'

'Whatever was said, that's no excuse for violence.'

'Perhaps not, but I do feel guilty. I'll go now if that's OK.'

'Of course. Today isn't going to stop you coming here I hope.'

'Nothing would ever stop me coming to this wonderful place.'

The script couldn't be better, Andrew having spoken loud enough for the surrounding audience to hear. Slowly the gathering was breaking up and people were returning to their seats rather than leaving.

'That was something,' Bridget heard a pregnant woman say to her companion. 'Fancy another macchiato?'

'Right David,' Bridget said. 'Let's get you into the office and check on the damage.'

~

Cecelia was on her way to the post office when she saw Darren approach from the other direction. Pausing in anticipation of conversation, all she got was a cursory nod as her neighbour strode past.

302

Her policy to be even-handed in terms of time spent with each of the men had led her to accept Darren's recent invitation to see a film together.

'What a lovely idea,' she'd said.

'You'll have seen the first *Top Gun* film, brilliant it was, but did you know there's a new one out? They're saying *Top Gun: Maverick*! is better, though I'm surprised he's still up to it given his age. I reckon they use extras for the action stuff.'

Cecelia warmed to Darren's boy-like enthusiasm. She had no idea which film he was talking about and she had no idea who the "he" could be. Robert de Niro?

'We could have a bite to eat out first,' Darren suggested.

Muswell Hill is crammed full of independently run restaurants but Darren opted for Wagamama. Cecelia had never been to one of the chain but had to concede that the food was reasonable even if loaded with God knows how many calories.

So the evening had gone well enough, they'd chatted, smiled and laughed. She could think of nothing that might have caused offence so why had Darren all but ignored her?

Stepping out of the post office she came face to face with Andrew.

'Hi there. How are you today?'

'I'm good thanks but I can't say the same about Darren. He's just punched David at the café.'

'Hit him? Why?'

'We were having a bit of an argument and Darren got angry. When David tried to calm things down Darren went for him.'

'That's awful. What were you two arguing about?'

'That's the thing. Nothing really.'

'I've just seen him; heading home. He didn't look happy.'

'Hardly surprising. I expect he'll be permanently banned from the café.'

Cecelia wondered whether she was detecting a smirk. Maybe not, Andrew's facial expressions were hard to interpret. 'That's where I'm on my way to. The café.'

There was an awkward silence as they faced each other, Andrew looking like he was about to say something. Finally he spoke. 'I enjoyed the exhibition at the Courtauld Institute the other day.'

'So did I.'

'It's always nice to have someone to discuss art with.'

'True enough.' Andrew hovered until Cecelia broke another silence. 'Take care then.'

'Yes, see you around.'

Inside the café, now filling with after work revellers, Cecelia headed for the office and tapped on the door. Bridget opened it.

'I heard what happened. Is David alright?'

Cecelia had become a regular customer over the short time she had been living in the area and she and Bridget got on well. They were kindred spirits, agreeing about everything, be it the arts, politics, music or favourite foods. Cecelia loved Bridget's paintings and had bought the one with blocks of colour depicting an autumn landscape that had been displayed in the café. Checking if David was alright was the natural thing for her to do.

He was sitting down, the ice pack now removed, a cut visible on his jaw. 'Poor you.'

'It's not the first time I've had to deal with him being punched in the face,' Bridget said.

'Oh. Surely not Darren.'

'No.'

'Who then?'

Bridget retold the story of the mugging in the London alleyway and the two women laughed.

'Shhop it, Idget.'

'Now we need to decide what to do about it.'

'I'm fine. It wash jush one of tho thingsh.'

'Hardly,' Bridget said. 'We can't have a customer hitting a member of staff and we can't have other customers witnessing that. I want Darren banned from entry, at least for a while.'

'I dishagee. As long ash he akologishes.'

'What would you do, Cecelia?'

'I don't think I'm in a position to suggest anything.'

'Except that it would help because we're divided at present.'

'What I would say is that Darren's going through a tough time what with Kelly being away and him fearing it's permanent – which incidentally I don't think is the case. I'm happy to chat with him, find out what was going on and see whether he's prepared to apologise. Then I'll get back to you.'

'Are you prepared to do all that?'

'Sure. He's a neighbour and we're friends of a sort. I'll see if I can discover exactly what went wrong today.'

'One free glass of wine coming up!' Bridget declared as she took hold of Cecelia's arm. She turned back to face David. 'And then I'm taking you home to rest.'

Cecelia stood by the counter nursing her glass of wine. The fracas was interesting in the context of her research. To what extent was the anger attributed to Kelly having left Darren alone? Or had he always had anger management issues? She was annoyed with herself. There was Darren needing support and she was considering the disturbance as ammunition for an academic paper.

'Let me get you another one, love.'

The man in a designer suit with tanned skin and a tidy salt and pepper hairstyle was standing too close for comfort.

'No thank you.'

'Come on. One for the road.'

'Go away.'

'Time to loosen up, darling.'

Cecelia saw red, briefly recognising the irony were she to slap him and be banned from the café.

'I think the lady would rather not speak to you, sir.'

She'd been saved by Mike, the trainee barista.

'Thanks,' Cecelia said after the man had tutted and moved away.

It was time to go home.

33

Cecelia had to wait three days before Darren came knocking at her door.

'Can I come in please? I need to tell you something.'

Darren was in his work clothes, a navy boiler suit, the front buttons undone to expose jeans and a crumpled shirt underneath. He was unshaven and looked tired, quite a change from their evening out when he'd dressed up in smart trousers, shirt and jacket.

'Sure. Come on in.' She led him to the living room.

'I ignored you the other day which was rude,' he began, still standing, shifting his weight from foot to foot.

'I know what happened at the cafe.'

'Andrew told you!'

'Calm down, it wasn't Andrew. I was in the café and Bridget said,' a lie but if she was going to reduce the antagonism between her neighbours it was best to keep Andrew out of it. 'Why not sit down and I'll get you something. Beer?'

Darren nodded and collapsed into an armchair. He'd rehearsed what to say based on Cecelia not knowing. He needed to rethink.

'OK, so what exactly did happen the other day?' Cecelia asked as she handed him his drink.

'I asked Andrew for a man-to-man chat to sort things out. I thought away from home, a neutral place, might be best and suggested Dream Café. It's not my favourite but I know he likes it there. So we did meet … and I lost my rag. He was taunting but I shouldn't have let it get to me.'

'What needed sorting out?'

'Oh, just things. Man things.'

That was as clear as mud. 'How was he taunting you?'

'By staying calm. Not saying anything.'

'Is that taunting or is it trying to reduce tension?'

'I might as well go. You're taking sides.'

'I'm not taking sides. Questioning is what I do whoever I'm talking to. If it was Andrew here I'd be asking exactly the same things. But if you feel I'm being unfair, I apologise.'

'The way he was looking at me, the smug things he was saying, that's what got me so angry. And then David, you know, the owner, he came up and immediately took sides, blaming me. So I hit him.'

'Probably not the most sensible thing to do. And then what?'

'I left.'

'Has anything happened since?'

'If you mean have I spoken to Andrew or David or been to the café, then the answer's no. I've been busy working. I suppose that's it as far as ever being allowed into the café again.'

'Maybe not. Have you thought about apologising?'

'It wasn't my fault.'

'You're the one who hit David.'

'There was a reason. Well, maybe not to hit him but Andrew deserved it.'

'So much anger, Darren, which surprises me because my first impression is that you're not like that. Do you think this has anything to do with Kelly being away?'

Darren's look was a suspicious one. 'What's Kelly got to do with it?'

'As I've said, I like to ask questions. I was wondering whether Kelly being away has affected you.'

'Maybe. How do I know?'

'Do you miss her?'

'That's a daft question. Of course. Loads.'

'Do you think she knows that?'

'She must do, though I don't think she misses me.'

'What makes you say that?'

'If she was she'd come home.'

'My boyfriend has been away for months but I know he misses me because he tells me whenever we speak or video call. It's lovely to hear.'

'Boyfriend? You never said you had a boyfriend.'

'Well I do. Julien.'

'You've not been honest then because I remember you telling us, Andrew included, that no one else caused your marriage breakup.'

'That's true, Julien wasn't the reason we decided to split. Can I ask you something?'

'Nothing's stopped you so far.'

'You're a great bloke –'

'That's not a question. I'm waiting for the "but".'

'There isn't one. I'm just interested in what makes you happy, what you enjoy doing.'

'Well, I can tell you what I don't like. Stroppy customers. Snobs who think they're better than me just because they …'

'Write poetry?'

'Yes, that.'

'La-di-da shops that sell rubbish that no one needs at ridiculously high prices. People who distrust anyone who hasn't got a white skin.'

'You're describing yourself in terms of what you don't like when I actually asked you what you do like. What's on your likes list?'

'Kelly is.'

'That's a nice thing to say.'

'I don't want to lose her.'

'Then you need to think about what would make her want to stay.'

'Such as?'

'I can't give you a list, it doesn't work like that. They have to be things you want to do, or things you know she likes to do that you might learn to enjoy.'

'Yeah, like shopping!'

'Even shopping. Let me tell you something about Julien and me. He's been bombarding me with calls and videos and at first it got on my nerves. I've got a hectic job and I just wanted to get on with it without wasting my time messaging. It took me a while to realise that that was what he needed and it took even longer to reciprocate. To start with I wasn't enjoying it, then I accepted it, and now I can't wait until the next time. I think what I'm trying to say is that once you do things that you know someone you love enjoys, you start enjoying it yourself.'

This was sounding like a sermon and Cecelia wasn't sure what Darren was making of it.

He drained his glass and stood up. 'Alright, I will apologise. To David and to Andrew. And I'll have more of a think about what Kelly likes.'

'That's a good idea.'

~

Cecelia expected Andrew to make contact after Darren had left but the speed took her by surprise. She was taking the glasses into the kitchen when her doorbell rang.

'Well, what did he say?' were Andrew's first words when still standing by the door.

'Good afternoon. And how are you today?'

Andrew looked puzzled as Cecelia stood fast, waiting for a response. Finally it clicked. 'Sorry, that was abrupt.'

'Just a bit.'

'May I come in though?'

'You can, but don't expect me to tell you about my conversation with Darren.'

'No. No, of course not.'

'Go into the living room and I'll get you something. Wine or beer?'

'A beer would be welcome thanks.'

Cecelia could see the funny side of having the two men using her as an agony aunt, one straight after the other, but by the time she had got the beer out the fridge she was questioning her glibness and the potential danger of delving into the emotions of men she barely knew.

'I will say one thing about Darren,' she said as she handed Andrew his beer. 'He's extremely upset about what happened.'

'And so am I.'

'He's missing Kelly desperately which might well explain his behaviour.' That was two revelations about her conversation with Darren. She would stop there.

'My God, I miss Emma so much and I don't think she realises.'

'What makes you say that?'

'Maybe because I haven't told her. I never tell her how much I love her, not anymore.'

'The anymore is interesting. Why not?'

'Familiarity I suppose. I think I've become over critical, too. The things a person once loved about someone can become irritating, can't they?'

'Perhaps. Like what?'

'Mundane ones like leaving clothes lying around on the bedroom floor for days. Keeping stacks of papers and letters on the table in the kitchen. Over-filling the washing machine.'

'Rather trivial compared to what really matters in a relationship.'

'Exactly. I've come to that conclusion. Now that Emma's left me I realise that I do still love the things that I thought were annoying. I even miss her untidiness.' There was a pause. 'I've been taking everything about her for granted.'

Andrew's face crumpled and tears welled up; instantly brushed aside with the back of his hand. He took a swig of beer.

Cecelia had been waiting for an opportunity to mention her boyfriend; both neighbours needed to know about him. 'That's the mistake I made with my ex. I'm determined not to do the same with Julien.'

'Julien?'

'He's my partner. You haven't met him because he's been away doing research since I moved in. He's back in a few weeks' time.'

'Oh, I see.'

As quickly as a glimpse of openness had come it was now gone. Andrew didn't want to hear about Julien and the conversation was clipped.

'I'd better go, loads to do,' he announced and was up and making his way to the front door before Cecelia had time to stand up.

She was on her laptop taking notes as soon as Andrew had left. There were two conversations to record and she found herself able to write down some points more or less verbatim. The men were displaying such a jumble of emotions – sadness, confusion, anger, weakness, resilience, remorse – and it would be fascinating to observe and record what emerged over the forthcoming weeks if and when their wives returned.

Her typing couldn't keep up with her racing thoughts as she logged their comments and added her perception of the hidden meanings of these complex men.

Abruptly she abandoned the keyboard, her hands dropping onto her thighs. Setting up Andrew and Darren as case studies felt underhand. Worse than that, despicable. Within a split second her mind was made up: her neighbours would not form part of her study. She closed her laptop without even saving the document just in case she considered changing her mind.

34

Andrew was distressed following the conversation with Cecelia. The severe self-critical reflections that had surfaced were draining. He was failing Emma. He was failing to offer her the fun she craved and deserved. He was failing to put her progress and interests ahead of his own. A selfish bastard, that's what he was, going on about *his* teaching triumphs while taking no interest in hers, bragging about his publishing successes and expecting her to tag along to poetry events.

Mr I-can-do-it, I'm-a-feminist Crabtree was a fraud. Would Emma give him the chance to put things right? And if he were given that chance, would he be able to change or was he too set in his ways?

A sleepless night was one thing, but he couldn't put his worries to the side at school the next day. His usual enthusiasm, sense of humour and banter were absent.

'Finished. What do I do now?' a cocky, inattentive boy called out.

'Read on, Drew,' Andrew said while wondering what Emma was doing up in Scotland that very minute.

'I'm already at the end.'

'Isn't there any homework you can do for the last few minutes?'

'That's not fair. If he can, why can't I?' Millie asked.

'Because you haven't finished.' It must be beautiful up there in spring.

'Actually I have. Just 'cos I haven't called out like big mouth over there, just 'cos I got … decorum.'

Her comment momentarily brought Andrew back from his daydreaming. Impressive memory from Millie; they'd read *Dulce et decorum est* during a First World War poetry session a couple of weeks ago.

'Not decorum. Big bum,' Noah quipped.

'Piss off, midget.'

The lesson was threatening to get out of hand, Andrew needed to sort this out. 'Enough thank you, Millie Glover,' he said using his fake stern teacher's voice.

'Willie-lover more like it.'

'And enough from you, Drew. Right, listen everybody. When you've finished reading the chapter I want you to write a synopsis.'

There were grumbles, kids always recognised pointless time-filling tasks.

'And if you get that done there'll be no other homework.'

All grumbling abruptly ceased. The subsequent tranquillity allowed Andrew to return to the core topic – himself.

Was there a parallel between his attitude towards Emma and these pupils – a pretence of caring when actually it was all about him? Cecelia had seen right through him, recognising an emotionally detached, conceited man. And if that's what she thought of him then God knows what she made of Darren. Why did he think about Darren so often?

'Can we go, Sir?'

'Maybe he's dead.'

'No, I saw him blink.'

'I think dead people can carry on blinking. They can definitely have their eyes open.'

'I saw a dead person's eyes move on TikTok. It was creepy.'

'Sir, the bell's gone. Can we go?'

Andrew snapped out of his reverie. 'Yes. Remember the homework you've got.'

'Done it.'

'Done it.'

There were several more "Done it".

'All of you?'

'You've been in some sort of weird trance for ten minutes.'

'Yeah. Troy and Shaz have been snogging at the back and you haven't even stopped them.'

'Sod off, midget.'

'Ok, that's enough. If you have finished I'll take your homework in now.'

Returning home from school with an unwanted pile of synopses to mark, he texted Cecelia with a request.

Her reply was instant. *We're friends and anyway I'm not a therapist!*

I know, but you're a great listener.

Sorry, still no way.

The request had been for a session to discuss his character flaws and to provide ideas for improvement. He'd wavered before sending the text and ended up relieved with her reply. It would take more than one conversation with a neighbour to put things right; this was something he would need to sort by himself.

Cecelia's reference to therapy got him thinking about how a therapist might explore his childhood. OK, here goes. I'm egotistical because I was indulged like a prince by my mother, telling me I was the best, the cleverest, the handsomest boy in the whole wide world. And I'm emotionally dead because when I was sent to boarding school I learnt to conceal all emotion, be it joy or sorrow, because bullying boys made me believe that I was the worst, the stupidest, the ugliest of them all. Maybe writing dystopian poetry was the inevitable aftermath. Or maybe digging up childhood stuff from over twenty-five years ago to explain his current state was bollocks.

Resigned to a quiet evening marking homework there was a knock on the door. It was Cecelia.

'Can I have a quick word? My texts were a bit abrupt.' They remained in the hallway. 'Perhaps stop being so hard on yourself,' Cecelia began. 'I think you're a good man and Emma's lucky to have you.'

'Thank you for saying that, but then why has she left me?'

'Well, she hasn't, has she? She'll be back after the short break.'

'But will she though? I'm not even allowed to speak to her.'

'If that's what she prefers for a while then respect her wishes. Don't see it as a slight on you, think of it as what Emma feels she needs.'

'I suppose so.'

'Anyway, what I came to remind you about is what I suggested a while back. Don't sit around moping until Emma's back. If you get out and enjoy yourself you'll feel all the better for her return.'

Cecelia lunged forwards and hugged him. Andrew wanted to kiss her. No he didn't. Anyway, she'd already pulled away.

'I don't want you thinking badly about yourself because of anything I've said. I'm a friend, not an analyst.'

~

Enjoy yourself Cecelia had advised. He wasn't sure that was possible but facing thirty synopses to mark he had to get out of the house.

There was a favourite pub, the Famous Royal Oak, a rare traditional one in an area monopolised by gastropubs and wine bars. He and Emma had spent many happy evenings there together, now he'd be going alone for one quick tipple.

He loaded his backpack with wallet, phone, keys and a just-in-case light fleece, clipped on his helmet, and cycled towards The Broadway on this pleasantly mild evening.

They'd always steered clear of the Famous Royal Oak on the events nights (or "Nites" as the staff liked to write) but now he was entering just as a quiz was about to start. The team at the table nearest to the door cheered when they saw him, urging him to join them. Apparently a friend had failed to turn up.

Why not, he thought, as an empty chair appeared. He found himself sitting with three men and two women. He didn't recognise anyone in the group and would have to say based on first impressions that they didn't seem his type. Introductions were made – they all used nicknames.

What Andrew didn't know at the onset but would soon be discovering was that it was a marathon quiz stretching over two hours, and his team would be consuming an astonishing quantity of alcohol while somehow staying focused on the task at hand. What his team members didn't know but were soon to find out was that Andrew was an encyclopaedia of knowledge.

The women on each side of him moved closer and closer. The more Belly Button edged towards him the more his shift away pressed him against Fifi. He was trapped.

'It's my turn,' Fifi announced. 'What you havin' mate?'

'Maybe a half of bitter, please,' Andrew requested. He'd only come in for one drink; there was school in the morning.

'Nah. Start with a G&T. It'll get your brain cells goin'.'

Fifi returned with a tray of G&Ts in large glasses, pink cocktails with wedges of orange and cucumber on the rims.

'Doubles,' she called out as she handed them over.

The quiz started: 'Name any ex-Soviet Union states beginning with the letters A, K or T.'

'Fuck knows. Is Transylvania one of them?' Bonzo asked.

'Yeah, could be,' Clipper declared.

'I don't think so,' Andrew said. 'That's a region in Romania. I do know a few though. Turkmenistan …'

'You what!' Belly Button called out. 'Here, take the paper, you write them down.'

She pushed the sheet along the table and handed him the pencil.

'Thanks. Tajikistan. Azerbaijan. Kazakhstan. Kyrgyzstan. I think that's it. Hang on though, wasn't Armenia part of the Soviet Union?'

'If you say so, mate.'

'Time for more booze,' Salted Peanuts said. He didn't ask what people wanted but returned with pint glasses.

The challenge, in addition to the quiz, seemed to be for each team member to order a different drink and in quick succession. Andrew opted for red wine when it was his turn. By then, Belly Button was kissing him every time he provided an answer and that was a lot of kisses. The first had been a peck on the cheek but by the time cider arrived she was attempting to go tongue to tongue with he determined to keep his own mouth shut. Initially that is because Andrew didn't want to offend and anyway, the alcohol was weakening his resistance.

The quizmaster spoke: 'Name any chemical element with a symbol beginning with an I.'

'Iron,' Clipper called out, his one attempted contribution that evening.

'I'm afraid not,' Andrew informed him. 'Iron is Fe.'

'That's ridiculous. It begins with I.'

'It's the Latin. You see –'

'Iodine,' Fifi butted in, gaining a round of applause from her teammates after Andrew had nodded and jotted it down.

'What next, genius?' Belly Button asked, lining herself up for a kiss. Her skirt had ridden up her podgy thighs.

'There's Iridium. And I think an Indium, too. You've got nice legs.'

Did he say that? Jesus, he was drunk.

'Irriderium.' Kiss.

'Indianium.' Kiss.

'Why are you called Belly Button?' he asked.

She lifted her blouse to expose a diamante stud on her belly button.

'Rhinestone,' she declared. 'Like it?'

'Interesting. Isn't it uncomfortable?'

'Nah.'

'My round again.' Fifi jumped up and was off to the bar. At first Andrew had been declining the offers of further alcohol but they'd ignored him and piled them up. The more he drank the less the inclination to turn the next one down. He liked being with these people, a bit fuzzy headed but feeling good about himself.

Fifi returned with a tray of tumblers of whisky which apparently had to be downed in one go.

Andrew couldn't quite remember the specifics but the quiz must have come to an end. There was a loud cheer, handshaking and a kiss from Belly Button. His team had won by a mile which meant that all their drinks were funded by the prize money. He attempted to stand up, helped by Belly Button and a couple of the others who seemed far less affected by the alcohol than him.

'You've got your helmet on back to front,' Belly Button said when they were outside. She helped him do it properly and as far as he could remember, he kissed her in gratitude. 'So, are you coming back to my place?' she asked.

Andrew shot back to sobriety. He had a wife – at least probably. 'No, I have to get home.'

'Up to you.' She didn't seem that bothered which disappointed him. 'Hey, you lot, wait for me.'

He watched as she trotted off with the others, leaving him to reflect on his new friends. Fun-loving, accepting, generous, humorous – all the things he would like to be.

Despite telling Belly Button that he had to get home, he couldn't face returning to that lonely place. What could he do though now that his new friends were out of sight.

Unsteadily he mounted his bike and set off towards Alexandra Park. It was time to escape humanity and reach nature. The bike swayed from side to side, his vision blurred, his balance wrecked. There was a left turn then a right. He was in a street he didn't recognise so he doubled back and took a right then a left. Racing round the corner he hurtled into a lamppost, flying off his bike and landing with a thud in the road.

An elderly man walking a dog was peering down at him.

'Are you alright? Should I call an ambulance?'

It was so bloody obvious Andrew didn't bother to reply.

35

Darren had been doing a lot of thinking since that chat with Cecelia. She was a clever one alright, understanding more about what made him tick than anyone else, Kelly included, possibly even himself. What an idiot he'd been to get involved in the ridiculous scrap at Dream Café. For three days he'd fretted about what to do until finally he'd built up the courage to see Cecelia to apologise for his rudeness. He'd half expected her to tell him to get lost, but instead she listened to his explanation and tried to understand his take on it.

That had been the easy part of the conversation because she already knew about the punch. Then came her flood of questions and his immediate reaction was annoyance that she was being so nosey. I'll apologise to Andrew, I'll apologise to David, I'll think more about Kelly, he'd told her, anything to get away from the uncomfortable interrogation.

Back home was when the thinking started and it hadn't stopped since. What Cecelia had said was making him view things from a different angle. He'd never thought much of himself so Cecelia telling him what she liked – his kindness, his willingness to help people – made him feel good even if he was unsure whether it was true. Making changes was up to him though, Cecelia clear that it wasn't for her to suggest what he should do.

Improving the relationship with Kelly was essential. He needed to pay more attention to the things she liked if he was to have any hope of winning her back.

Darren took encouragement from what she wrote on the postcards she'd been sending, the most recent, a cartoon image of a smiling Loch Ness Monster, was particularly reassuring. *I thought you'd like this. Things going well but looking forward to getting back to London – and you. Kelly xxx*. She would not be happy if she returned to Muswell Hill to discover that he'd had an argument with Andrew, punched David, and been banned from the café. Action was needed – he couldn't keep putting it off.

It took Darren a further week to pluck up the courage to return to the café. By chance David was on duty and he risked walking straight up to the counter, defying the ban.

'I'm here to say I'm sorry and embarrassed for what I did.'

'Apology accepted.'

'Really? Just like that?'

'Yes. There's nothing more to say about it. Except not again, Darren.'

'Of course not. It was totally out of character.'

'Good. Then welcome back and let me get you a tea.'

'Thank you for forgiving me, I feel terrible about it all. I can see there's a cut on your chin.'

'It's nothing.'

Darren spent longer than necessary at the café, sipping the one tea then ordering another. A further apology was needed, one he wasn't looking forward to making. What would he say to Andrew? Would "Sorry about the other day, mate" be good enough?

He would have liked a beer or two to give him courage but decided that ordering alcohol at the café wouldn't be a great idea for the time being.

When Andrew opened his door Darren blurted out, 'I want to apologise for my behaviour the other day. I was totally out of order.'

'David is the one who needs the apology, not me.'

'I've said sorry to David.'

'Good.'

'Fine.'

'Well, thank you for saying sorry.'

'That's OK. I'll be off then.'

What is wrong with my neighbour, Darren was thinking when he got home? Try as he might, he couldn't get on with him. Was there anything positive to say about a man who had a superiority complex, was a snob, sneaky and as boring as hell. It was a problem what with the two wives being such close friends. If he wanted to win Kelly back he needed to conceal his dislike of Andrew. How was that going to be possible?

He took a beer out the fridge, then another, another and another.

Dressed in a flowing white robe, he was sitting cross-legged on the floor opposite a guru with an abundant white beard. The man may have been spouting wisdom but since it wasn't in English Darren had no idea what he was going on about. He smiled and nodded in appreciation despite the lack of understanding. Cecelia joined them, her robe orange and see-through. She was carrying a tray of tea things which she set down onto a low table by their side. With her back towards him and bending low, it left nothing to the imagination. She poured the liquid into tiny brass tumblers but Darren wasn't given any time to drink. Cecelia took hold of his hand, yanked him up, and led him to a room with the floor covered in brightly coloured cushions. She unrobed. Darren couldn't wait to get his hands on her as he pulled off his own robe.

There was a ringing. Darren had an erection and was perturbed that he was at least in theory two-timing Kelly. The ringing continued.

He'd crashed out downstairs and was sprawled out across the couch. He reached across to grab the landline, a phone rarely used in the age of mobiles. 'I'm sorry Kelly. I wasn't going to do anything.'

'It isn't Kelly, it's me. Andrew.'

Darren remained silent, in the process of sorting out dream from reality.

'Are you still there?' Andrew continued. 'I've got a bit of a problem and Emma isn't here to help.'

Of course Emma wasn't there to help, she was away with Kelly. 'What's the problem, mate?'

He could hear beeping and shouting. Where was Andrew so early in the morning? At a railway station?

'I've had a bike accident and I'm in A&E. I've possibly broken my wrist.'

'What happened?'

'Could we leave the details for later, I've only got use of this phone for a couple of minutes? If you don't mind there are some things I'd like you to do.'

'Fire away, mate.'

'Well, top of the list is to pick up my bike and bag from Springfield Avenue, the end near the Alexandra Park entrance. That's where I crashed it. The thing is, I left my backpack there when the ambulance came and it's got my phone in it. I can't call Emma because I have no idea what her number is; on the mobile all I do is press her name. Luckily I remembered your home number because it's only one digit different to ours.'

'OK mate, I'll take the van to get your bike and bag and then I'll come over and you can contact Emma. Is that it?'

'There's stuff to collect from home if you don't mind. Pyjamas, dressing gown, slippers, toiletries, those sort of things.'

'You're staying in then?'

'They think for a night if I need surgery, though nothing's definite yet.'

Andrew was rabbiting on about other things he might need but Darren interrupted him. 'I'll need a key though, to get into your house.'

'My keys are also in the backpack; I drop everything in it when I'm cycling. You'll find my wallet too. Actually, while you're at the house maybe collecting my laptop would be useful.'

'Yeah, while you're hanging around in hospital you can write a distrop … disstop …'

'Dystopian.'

'That's the one. A dystopian poem about a bike accident.'

There was no laughter from the other end of the line. Didn't Andrew realise he was joking? Fair dos though, he'd had an accident so probably wasn't in the best of spirits.

'Let me get going, I won't be long. I'll come to A&E before the house so you can have the phone. Are you at the Whittington?'

'Yes. I might not be in A&E though, they're moving me to a ward if a bed becomes available.'

'No worries, I'll find you.'

'Err, Darren …'

'Yeah?'

'Thank you.'

'My pleasure, mate.'

Darren got dressed, skipped breakfast, not even a mug of tea, jumped into the *Stop Thief!* van and headed off. He felt good about doing a good deed even though it was for Andrew.

It was only a few minutes' drive to Springfield Avenue and he could see the bike as soon as he turned into the street. Resting against a lamppost, the front wheel was completely buckled and the bike was now U-shaped. It was a write off. He carried it into his van. There was no bag visible. He extended the search to behind low walls and bushes in nearby front gardens in case someone had hidden it for safety, but there was nothing. He feared the worst – with a phone and wallet in the bag it was a tempting picking.

There seemed little point driving to the hospital without the bag's two essential contents – phone and keys – until he was certain the bag was gone for good. Might someone have handed it in? Unlikely though that was, he walked round the corner to the small red-brick building that served as the police station.

Mentioning an accident was a mistake. The over-zealous policeman at reception wouldn't answer his straightforward question – has anyone handed in a backpack? – without filling out a form.

'Were you involved in this accident?'

'No.'

'Were you a witness then?'

'No.'

'So how do you know about it?'

Darren was wasting time having promised Andrew that he'd get to the hospital as soon as possible. He couldn't explain to the policeman what had happened because he didn't know. 'I've already said, I wasn't there. As far as I could see when I took the bike no one else was involved. He'd smashed it into a lamppost.'

'You took the bike?'

That led to wasted minutes of explanation to alleviate suspicion of theft. Finally, Darren was informed that nothing had been handed in and he could leave.

He drove to the hospital aware that without mobile, wallet or keys it was a pointless trip, but he could think of no other option. He'd see Andrew and they could plan what to do next.

Andrew was still in A&E, sitting in a crowded corridor.

'Hello, mate. How are you doing?'

'Not great. I do need a minor op. I'm waiting for them to find me a bed.'

'There was no backpack there and it hasn't been handed in, I asked the police. Someone must have nicked it.'

'That's a disaster.'

Darren had been considering solutions on the drive. 'I wanted to check this with you but I think there's one thing we can sort easily. If I call Kelly she can pass her phone over to Emma then the two of you can speak.'

'That's brilliant.'

Hardly. Darren dialled and shook his head.

'Hi Kelly. When you hear this please call straight back. There's a bit of a problem …' Darren looked across at Andrew who picked up the unspoken question and nodded. 'Andrew's had a bike accident, nothing serious, but he needs to speak to Emma. He's lost his phone so I'll leave this one with him. I hope you're having a good time. Miss you. Bye, love.'

'Are you sure about the phone?'

'No problem, I can collect it when I deliver stuff from the house. I'm sure Kelly will call back soon.'

'I'm so grateful.'

Darren smiled. He was enjoying being nice. 'But we need to work out how I can get into your house. I don't suppose you leave a key under a flowerpot or something?'

'No, but Cecelia has a spare.'

'Cecelia?'

'For emergencies. Don't look alarmed, she's never used it. And I'm fairly sure Emma gave Kelly a key too. Any idea where that might be?'

'I'll look when I get home.'

'Or simply get the key from Cecelia.'

'I'll try home first.'

Andrew handed over a list of what he needed, each item with a comment in brackets about location.

'Right, I'll get going. What's your passcode?'

'Passcode?'

'For the alarm.'

'Don't worry, it won't be on. I rarely use it.'

'Then what's the point … oh, never mind.'

36

Darren was not happy as he drove off from the hospital. It shouldn't matter that Cecelia had a key to Andrew's house but it did. Had there been an exchange of keys? Was their friendship more than platonic? You had to be suspicious of Andrew what with Emma being away.

He searched for the key at home. If Kelly had been given one she hadn't left it in the usual place. Would she have hidden it? All this key swapping was doing his head in. There was no choice but to get one from Cecelia but Andrew could wait a while; he'd grab some breakfast. No time to freshen up with a shower though so he slapped on some aftershave ahead of seeing his neighbour. Why did it matter that he smelled good? Why was he jealous that she had Andrew's key? Why had he had an erotic dream about the woman who had encouraged him to focus on his wife's needs? A funny thing, the mind.

Cecelia's welcoming smile was chased by a sneeze. And another.

'Sorry.' Her voice had taken on a croaky, squeaky pitch. 'I'm allergic to perfume.'

'It's aftershave,' Darren reassured her.

'Anything in particular?'

'Hugo Boss.'

'No, I mean the reason for you visiting me. Is there something you want because I'm not sure I can bear being close to you for long?' She sneezed.

'I need Andrew's key.'

'Why?' She sneezed.

'He's lost his. Well, it's probably stolen.'

Cecelia took a step outside, looked across to number 38, scanned up and down the street, and restored a distance between them. 'Where is he?'

'In hospital. He fell off his bike and broke his wrist.'

Darren provided an outline of what had happened, briefly since he was still unaware of the details.

'Poor thing, let me come with you to see him.'

'Best not. He's exhausted, he looks a right mess.'

'Isn't that when friends are most needed?'

'I'm only repeating his request that he'd rather not see anyone – except me. Not ahead of the operation.'

'Operation?'

'Look, for now let me have the key so I can get what he needs.'

He did not want Cecelia to see Andrew. Yes, a very funny thing, the mind.

Cecelia lifted a key from the hook by the side of the door and handed it to him.

'Thanks,' he mumbled.

'Send him my love.'

'Of course I will.'

Entering number 38, Darren picked up the postcard laying on the hall floor.

It's so peaceful here, I love it. Maybe we should move. Miss you. Emma xxx.

He turned the card. Stunning scenery on the Isle of Skye. No Loch Ness monster from Emma.

In the end he was grateful that Andrew had indicated where to find the items on his list, it sped things up. The pyjamas, dressing gown and slippers were designer label rather than the fuddy-duddy ones he'd expected. Returning home he picked up a charger, his old phone with a spare SIM card, a couple of ten pound notes and a bar of chocolate before returning to the hospital.

Andrew was in a ward by the time Darren arrived.

'Hello, mate,' Darren said, dropping the plastic bag onto the bed. 'I couldn't find a key at our place so I picked up Cecelia's. She sends her …' He paused, unwilling to say "love". 'Her best wishes.'

'This is great,' Andrew said as he was emptying the bag, as excited as a child opening birthday presents. 'Chocolate! A charger, clever you to think of that. And can I borrow this phone?'

'Yeah, it's a spare.'

'Here's yours. I tried to call Kelly again but she's still not answering.'

'That's odd.'

Darren dialled and shook his head after a few rings.

'Hi Kelly, me again. We're waiting for you to get in touch. Andrew's having an operation and wants to speak to Emma. I'll have my phone back so you can call me, but I've left my old one with Andrew. The number is …'

He looked across at Andrew. 'What's got into them?'

'I really don't know.' He was fingering the ten pound notes. 'No use, I'm afraid. They only use contactless.'

Darren slipped the notes into his wallet and handed Andrew a credit card.

'No, I can't have that.'

'No worries, it's not my only one and you can pay me back when you're out. I don't think you're the sort of bloke who does a runner.'

'Darren, I can't tell you how grateful I am for everything.'

'That's what friends are for.' Had he really called him a friend? 'And don't worry about Barnaby, he can stay at mine.'

A nurse was approaching them. 'All set, Mr Crabtree?'

'I'll be off then,' Darren said. 'Good luck with the op, mate.'

~

The operation was a minor one and Andrew was out of hospital the following day wearing a blue protective cast.

'Luckily it's my left arm so I should be able to do most things.' They were driving home in the battered Ford Fiesta. 'I'll need to do some food shopping as soon as I'm back.'

'We can stop off at a supermarket if you like, the one by the next roundabout.'

'Would you? Thank you so much,' this thank you adding to the ones for taking care of Barnaby, lending him a credit card, collecting everything for the hospital stay, and trying to contact Kelly. 'Her phone must be out of action. As soon as I'm home I'll call Emma and she can get Kelly to call you.'

Darren was pushing Andrew's trolley up and down aisles with unfamiliar stops to collect red wine instead of beer; rosemary and sage bites instead of crisps; muesli instead of cereal; and foreign cheeses from the deli counter.

'Remember you joking about me writing a poem about the bike accident?' Andrew said as they were waiting in the queue to pay. 'Well, I took you up on that this morning. There's no doom or gloom in it, just humour. And I'll tell you what, I don't think I've ever enjoyed writing so much. I was laughing out loud as I penned it.'

'Does that mean I'm in it – again?'

'You'll have to wait and see.'

When the Ford Fiesta drew up Cecelia rushed out with the two dogs by her side. 'Good to see you safe and sound; you must be glad to be home.'

'I am.'

She took hold of Darren's arm. 'And this man has been a star.'

'I know and I'm hugely grateful.'

'Now it's my turn to be of use. I'll be cooking this evening, for both of you.'

'No need, Cecelia, We bought food on the way back.'

'That's neither here nor there. I'm doing tonight and I won't take no for an answer.'

'I accept your invitation and you do too, don't you, Andrew?'

'Yes, of course.'

'Come on, let's get you inside and I'll bring in the shopping.'

'And I'll call Emma.'

When Darren came into the kitchen carrying the four bags, Andrew was finishing a voicemail. 'There's no answer from Emma either. Should we be worried? Perhaps we should be reporting them as missing persons.'

'It's only been a day. The police won't be interested for at least forty-eight hours.'

'How do you know that?'

'I've seen it on TV murders.'

'Exactly – murders!'

'Let's wait until we're at Cecelia's. She's full of good ideas.'

Cecelia wasn't concerned. 'They've either switched off their phones for some peace and quiet or their batteries are flat or they've gone somewhere with no reception. But if you are worried call where they're staying.'

'Do you know where that is, Darren?'

'No. Don't you?'

'No.'

'Honestly you two, didn't you even … oh, never mind. There can't be many locations offering weaving courses. Google and then phone round to find them.'

'That's a great idea. If you don't mind I'm going to head on home and get started,' Darren said.

'We might as well do it together. Shall I come over to yours?'

'Sure.'

Darren's phone rang. 'It's Kelly.'

Darren's spare phone rang. 'It's Emma.'

37

Four and a half weeks into their extended stay in Scotland and Kelly was laying the garment she had made across the bed. 'I'm rather proud of this,' she said, lifting up a corner of the turquoise and bottle green shawl.

'So you should be, it's beautiful,' Emma said. 'You are so talented.'

'Hardly. It's taken one full on two-week course and twenty afternoon sessions to get to this.'

Emma's first completed garment was tucked away in a drawer, a scarf with a subdued blue and fuchsia design. Rather than using wool she'd gone for Lyocell yarn made from wood pulp, this ticking her environmental concern box. Andrew would be pleased.

'So shall we go home now?' Kelly asked.

'Home?'

'Yes. I feel that we've done it, made something nice, so there's no reason to stay on.'

'But we're not even half way through our time here.'

'So what, we're allowed to change our minds. I'm missing Darren.'

This was a cue for Emma to state that she was missing Andrew; she sensed that Kelly was waiting for it. Was she though?

'Here's an idea,' Kelly continued. 'Let's hire a car, head north for a few days, and then go home after our road trip.'

She hadn't mentioned it to Kelly but going back had been on Emma's mind, too. She feared that the longer she left it the harder it would be to return to normal – what had been normal. A trip possibly was a good idea – what the hell, go for it. 'Agreed. A bumper end to our holiday and then back to Brookland Gardens.'

They decided to go ahead with that day's planned cycle ride, their favourite route along the bank of Loch Carron to Strome Castle, ahead of investigating road trip options.

Sitting by the side at the lake, it was such a still day that the water was reflecting the jagged hills on the other bank like a mirror. It's as if we're the only people in the world, Emma was thinking. Or maybe we really are. The women had decided to cut themselves off from the outside world – no newscasts, no TV, no social media, not even mobiles other than for photos. So God knows what was going on out there.

'Are we definite about leaving?' Emma asked.

'It's magnificent here and being with you is great, but I'm ready to go back to London, back to Darren.'

Emma was weighing up whether it was "Absence makes the heart grow fonder" or "Out of sight, out of mind" when it came to her thoughts about Andrew. Kelly was right though, it was time to move on, or move back to be precise.

'My Darren would hate it here but Andrew would love it, so you two should come back for a holiday together.'

'Maybe.' Emma stood up. 'Come on. Let's go.'

They cycled at speed; the women super fit after their afternoons and weekends of hiking, running and cycling.

Ross, the Centre Manager, joined them for dinner. After they'd finished he spread out a large map of the region on the table. There was so much to see, so much to do.

'How long are yers thinking of being away?'

'We haven't thought about that yet. What do you reckon, Kelly?'

'Maybe four nights.'

'That's fine by me.'

'Then this is what yers do, or what yers shouldn't do. The roads are slow and the ferries are slower so yers didnae have time to enjoy anything by travelling right up north and catching ferries to the islands up there. My advice is –'

'The Isle of Skye,' Emma pointed onto the map.

'That's what I was going tae say.'

'Then the Isle of Skye it is,' Kelly agreed.

'Great because I've been wanting to go over that bridge. It looks like something out of a Nordic Noir.'

'Wasn't there a programme when a part of a body was found on one end of a bridge and the other bit on the other side?'

'That was *The Bridge*.'

'Disgusting. Well, we won't come across that in peaceful, law abiding Scotland.'

'Our end could be more like in *Thelma and Louise*. It's the final day before returning to our husbands, we're on the cliff edge, we look to each other, think what the hell, nod and accelerate!'

'It's not that bad, is it?'

'No, it's not. I'm looking forward to getting home.' Emma realised she meant it.

'OK. Now we know where we're going I can hire a car. A four wheel drive in case we're off road at all. Thank you, Ross.'

'Yers kin take the map.'

By mid-morning the next day they were crossing Skye Bridge, Kelly letting out a piercing scream when they were about halfway along. 'A body! There!'

'Not funny, you scared the living daylights out of me.' But it *was* funny, Kelly was always funny, always making Emma laugh, feel good about herself. Didn't Andrew used to be the same?

She looked across at Kelly, down to her tanned slim legs. She was thinking about the legs, the lizard too, as she turned to peer out the window.

'Wake up, Emma.'

'I'm not asleep.'

'You sort of are with that word you use. Metaph something or other.'

'Metaphorically.'

'Yeah, that's the one.'

'Anyway, we're here.'

They had reached Uig, a tiny village on the far west of the island. Whitewashed buildings with slate roofs were dotted around the gentle hillside. Their hotel, the only one in the area, was the dominant building. Having booked in they wandered down to the harbour to admire the grandeur of the chain of islands further west.

Emma purchased what would be her final postcard to Andrew, a photo of the bridge they had crossed. *Remind you of anything? Our last few days away, we're coming back early. See you soon. Love, E xxx*

Kelly switched on her phone. 'I know I've already got a zillion photos but I want one of this.'

Before she could take a picture her phone was beeping like mad. 'What's going on?'

Emma lifted her own phone out of her backpack. She'd switched it off a couple of days before travelling to Skye having photographed to death the scenery around Lochcarron.

'Mine too. Voicemails and texts.'

'I've already heard my first one; you're not going to like this.'

There was no need to listen to more than the first message, the news had been given loud and clear.

Emma called, all set to apologise for being offline since the accident, but Andrew was remarkably light about the whole thing. It was a silly accident but everything was fine. When he told her that no one else was involved, Emma had further questions but decided against. 'I'll be home as quickly as I can.'

She heard Kelly say the same to Darren, adding that meant two days, one to return to their base at Lochcarron and the next to travel from Scotland to England.

Emma repeated the schedule for Andrew. 'Is that Darren I can hear?'

'Yes, we're together. Cecelia's cooking for us tonight.'

'Cecelia?'

'Our new neighbour. Mrs Hall. Well, Professor Hall actually.'

'Oh, I see. It should be me there helping. I feel awful being away with you injured.'

'Darren and Cecelia have made everything easy.'

Emma paused to take in Andrew's positive comment about Darren and his reference to the neighbour she had yet to meet. Being surplus to requirements came to mind but she dismissed the thought as paranoid. 'As soon as I'm back you'll be getting full on love and care. I'd best sign off now though, there's lots of sorting out to do. Bye love.'

'I can't wait to see you. I've missed you.'

'I've missed you, too.'

38

'I told you everything would be fine,' Cecelia said when Darren and Andrew returned to the living room, having taken their calls in private in the hall and kitchen respectively. 'They're safe and sound and soon they'll be home. Now you can relax and enjoy my mediocre cooking, it's never been my strong point.'

A meal consisting of charred spring onions with romesco, followed by a spiced root vegetable and lentil casserole and ending with a caramel and apple loaf cake suggested otherwise. Cecelia's diplomatic skill was in full force to ensure that the subjects covered as they ate were common ground. The likelihood of a rapid switch to electric cars. The attraction or otherwise of *I'm a Celebrity*. The current fad to grow beards and whether women liked or loathed them.

'I'm suddenly exhausted. If you don't mind I'm going to call it a day.'

'Not surprising you're tired, you have had an operation.' Cecelia began stacking the dessert plates.

'I'll go too. Or would you like help with the clearing up?'

'Thanks for the offer, Darren, but no. It won't take me long.'

The men left together and Andrew paused at the top of Cecelia's path. 'Hold on, Darren. In a couple of days I'll have Emma to look after me but I want to thank you for everything you've done up 'til now.'

'No problem, mate. I can't wait to see Kelly but I've been thinking. Let's surprise them.'

'Surprise them? How?'

'Tomorrow they'll be heading back to … wherever they were staying.'

'Lochcarron.'

'Then they're there overnight before travelling here the next day. We could drive up to meet them tomorrow to give them a surprise. Maybe we could even stay for a bit before coming home together? You told me it's your half term so it works perfectly.'

'It's a hell of a long way.'

'Agreed, but just think how shocked they'd be to see us. I'll book a car online, something posh so we can treat them like royalty.'

'Can I have time to think about it?'

'Not really, we need to set off bright and early tomorrow.'

'Yes, but what about –'

'I've decided, I'm going. It's up to you whether you want to join me.'

Spontaneity was not one of Andrew's strong points but Darren's suggestion had brought a rush of excitement. 'OK, let's do it.'

Darren booked the car as soon as he got home and then researched the journey. It was longer than he had thought, an estimated ten hours not counting stops. He went round to Andrew as soon as he'd logged off; there was something to check.

Andrew opened the door in his pyjamas and dressing gown. 'Is there a problem? I was upstairs packing.'

'No, all's good. The car's booked and I added you as a named driver, but then it struck me that you might not have a licence.'

'I do, but there is this.' He held up his injured arm.

'I know. It would only be in an emergency and I got an automatic so no gears to change. Fear not if it's only me driving. We can make lots of stops.'

Andrew had a restless night worrying about undertaking the long journey with a single driver because he didn't think he would be safe sharing the load. However, the next morning Darren seemed full of enthusiasm and energy as he stood by a black SUV with a shiny front grill and tinted windows. Inside, the seats were cream coloured leather. 'Pricey, but the girls are worth it. And we'll be needing a big boot for all Kelly's stuff.'

'Should we let them know we're coming?' Andrew asked.

'I'd rather it was a surprise. Kelly loves surprises.'

'OK, it's your call.'

Relaxed in each other's company but with little to say that could occupy even a fraction of the ten hours in the car, they listened to music on the eight-speaker audio system. Darren had mirrored his phone onto the dashboard screen and from there they took it in turns to choose albums from the Deezer menu. "That's not bad" and "I quite like that" were said, the tastes of the two men surprisingly close as they marched back in time to access music from their teenage years.

During a stop at a service station near Liverpool, Darren suggested switching to Talk Radio for a change, thereby subjecting Andrew to a new experience of listening to ordinary people expressing extraordinary opinions. Every so often Darren muttered, "Absolute idiot" or "They're talking a lot of sense" with Andrew frequently considering the so-called idiots to be spot on and those allegedly talking sense to be far removed from reality. The rhythm of the chat was soporific and he nodded off near the Scottish border.

Darren looked across at his sleeping neighbour and smiled at the lightweight. He was getting tired himself and wasn't looking forward to the return journey the following day. Then he remembered that Kelly would be with them and could share the driving, her imminent presence fuelling a surge of euphoria and renewed energy.

Having escaped the satellite towns north of Glasgow they reached spectacular countryside. 'The more I think about it the happier I'd be to stay up here for a few days,' he told the rejuvenated Andrew who was peering out of the window.

'Me too.'

'We can tell the girls as soon as we see them. They'll love to show us some of the places they've discovered.'

The last part of a long journey always seems to take the longest and that was definitely what it felt like for both of them despite passing through breathtaking pine tree woodlands and gorse lowlands against a backdrop of conical hills. Enough was enough; Andrew was sighing and Darren was puffing and blowing.

'Well done, Darren,' Andrew said as the satnav announced that their destination was three hundred yards away on the right hand side. It was a little after ten o'clock, the twilight hour, and they could admire the magnificent Lochcarron lakeside, the sun sinking below the distant hilltop.

'This is truly beautiful,' Andrew remarked but Darren was already out the car and racing to the reception to discover where Kelly was. There was no one at the desk. He was calling the out of hours number shown on a piece of card when Andrew joined him.

'No-one's picking up.'

'Then let's call Emma and Kelly to tell them we're here.'

'I'd rather not, I want to see their faces light up when we burst into their room.' They'd bought bouquets of flowers to present to their wives, the most expensive a service stop could provide. 'This note says to use the number in an emergency so someone's got to answer soon.'

Fifteen minutes and seven attempts later, a man took the call.

'We're here to see Kelly Robertson and Emma Crabtree. Which cabin is that please?'

~

'What are you looking up?' Kelly asked, glancing across to Emma tapping her phone keypad as they were driving back to Lochcarron.

'Travel options. It's a bit of a minefield but if the journey from here to Edinburgh is hassle free, we might be able to catch the night train and get to London early tomorrow morning.'

'I'd love to do that; the sooner we're home the better. Now that it's about to happen it's hit me how desperate I am to reach Darren. You must feel the same.'

'Yes.' Emma realised she meant it; she couldn't wait to see her husband. The train timetable investigation was over. 'Sorry, it won't work. There's a minimum of six hours of train journeys to get to

Edinburgh and that's if we're lucky and the connections work out.'

'Fuck. I so much wanted … I've had an idea. The car hire company is bound to have a branch in Edinburgh. We can drive and leave the car there then surely we'd be in time for that night train.'

Emma did more googling. 'It's four hours by car,' she announced. 'Cross country though. Are you up for it? You've already driven quite a bit today.'

'Absolutely up for it. We're almost at Lochcarron so a lightning pack then off we go. Call the car hire place and let them know our change of plans.'

The usually meticulous Kelly chucked all her possessions into cases and bags, Rapid though fond farewells followed and they were on their way to Edinburgh. The journey was traffic free, returning the car was easy, and the taxi ride from the car hire company to the station was short. They were all set to depart.

It was a little gone eleven o'clock.

~

'They've gone,' the person who'd finally answered the phone was telling Darren.

'What do you mean gone?'

'Gie's five minutes, I'll come over to the office.'

'He's coming over,' Darren told Andrew. 'I can hardly understand what he's saying.'

A tall muscular man joined them. 'Hello, I'm Ross, the Centre Manager.' He extended his arm for handshakes.

Darren took hold reluctantly. He wanted to sort out what was going on rather than waste his time with pleasantries.

Andrew was somewhat more conciliatory. 'Pleased to meet you, Ross. I'm Andrew, Emma Crabtree's husband. Now, could you explain exactly what has happened? They were due to have a final night here.'

'It's simple enough. They're aff to Edinburgh to catch the night train to London. Emma mentioned your injury,' he added looking at Andrew's arm. 'She wanted to get back to yer as quick as possible. An early morning surprise: they seemed quite excited about that.'

Andrew sensed he was being examined by this man with penetrating blue eyes. He wondered whether he should be jealous of his wife being in close proximity to Ross for several weeks.

'You didnae tell them you were coming here then?' Ross asked.

'No. it was a surprise.'

'Well' you're all getting a surprise nou.'

They turned their attention to Darren who was speaking to Kelly. 'Yes, I do mean we're here in Scotland … We didn't tell you because we wanted it to be a surprise … Agreed, there's nothing we can do tonight … I suppose it is funny … I love you too.'

'Too late then?' Andrew was asking the obvious.

'Too late by only a few minutes.' Darren turned to face Ross. 'If you'd picked up the phone the first time I called we would have been able to stop them before their train set off.'

Andrew was thinking that if Darren had taken his advice and spoken to Emma and Kelly on arrival there would also have been time to intercept. He didn't say.

Meanwhile, the calm Ross wasn't accepting the accusation. 'Number one, nae one was expected to arrive today and I was off duty except for emergencies. Number two, I was taking a shower, which I can do after working in the grounds all day. So let's move on, shall we? Yae won't be driving straight back tonight; in which case you're welcome to stay in Emma and Kelly's cabin. I won't charge yae because they've paid for this evening and the room hasn't been cleared up yet.'

'Thank you, we'd appreciate that,' Andrew got in ahead of any further complaint from Darren.

'Take a key and follow me. I'll show yae where it is.'

~

'Why didn't they say they were coming up to Scotland?' Emma asked.

'He wanted to surprise me. That's so lovely.'

'Lovely but silly.'

'You're forgetting something, we didn't tell them we were returning early. We also wanted it to be a surprise.'

'I suppose so.' Emma was back on the trainline app. 'There are three stops before London, Carstairs, Carlisle and Watford. Carstairs we just passed, getting off at Carlisle makes no sense, and Watford's so close to home it would be pointless. All we can do is head to London and home and then wait for them to get back.'

'Poor things, coming all that way. Darren's such a star.'

A rather rash one Emma was thinking but didn't say. 'Let's try and get some sleep.'

39

The taxi rolled up at Brookland Gardens and Emma and Kelly stepped out, Emma helping her friend unload and stack luggage onto the pavement.

'I'll text the boys to let them know we've arrived.'

Calls and texts had gone back and forth until the early hours of the morning, the four of them shifting from frustration to amusement about the men being in Scotland while the women were on their way to London – surely a story to tell for years.

They hesitated on the pavement as if unsure what to do next before Emma spoke. 'I guess it's a case of unpacking, putting a wash on and getting in some food.'

'And then waiting for ages because they won't be back until really late.'

Emma looked across to the neat gardens, the proud houses and the swish vehicles parked along the street. John Gilbert, the neighbour opposite, was washing his car on the forecourt that had proved so useful on the day of their moves. Emma waved and he waved back. He was probably unaware that she'd been away;

they'd rarely spoken beyond a "What a lovely day" or "What an awful day".

'This feels so strange. No more weaving in the wilds of Scotland.'

'Yeah, a bit different. It's going to take some getting used to.' Kelly added her own wave towards Mr Gilbert. 'It was great what we did though, I loved it all.'

'Me too.'

Suddenly they were hugging, clinging together.

'Good morning, ladies. Welcome home.'

They pulled apart.

The woman had appeared from the in-between house, restraining Barnaby and Tyson who were dragging her towards their owners. 'Andrew said you'd be back about now.'

Emma took hold of Barnaby who already seemed to have forgiven her for being away for so long. The ancient dog was leaping up and down like a puppy. However, her focus was on this attractive woman, not the dog.

'I'm your neighbour, Cecelia Hall. I was put in charge of the dogs when the men set off this morning. I'm not really a dog lover so it's a relief to hand them over.' Emma was questioning why Andrew had told this neighbour her arrival time; the dog explained it.

'And I believe you've been taking care of Andrew as well as our dog,' Emma said, her smile fake as she watched for a sign of culpability. There was none. 'Thank you for that.'

'Hardly me, it's your Darren who's been doing all the hard work,' she said, turning to face Kelly. Emma wondered how Cecelia could immediately pair the couples. Had she been in their house and seen a photo? There was one of her and Andrew together in the living room and one in the bedroom. The bedroom? No, surely not.

'I moved in a couple of days after you left.'

Ran away? Deserted Andrew? Is that what she was implying? 'Well, I'm back for good now.'

'I'm pleased. Andrew has missed you so much.' How much talking had been going on?

'It's been lovely meeting you but if you don't mind I'm desperate to get home.'

'Of course. But do come over for tea this afternoon once you've settled in.'

Kelly was saying they'd love to before Emma could get in that she had too much to do.

~

Having dropped her suitcase onto the hall floor at number 38, Emma went from room to room to check that everything was as she'd left it.

She made a mental note of the differences – two vases of flowers in the living room (unusual); beer as well as wine in the fridge (unusual); the double bed unmade (exceptionally unusual). Andrew had a thing about making the bed properly each morning which admittedly only meant straightening the duvet, but even then. His pyjamas were scrunched up on the floor rather than hanging on the hook behind the door. She inspected the bedlinen, smelled it too, for evidence of sex. She checked the bathroom bin for condoms. Nothing. He would have been in a hurry to leave which might explain the bed and pyjamas.

Once suspicion sets in it lingers. She entered Andrew's shrine, his office, in search of … of what? There was a stack of handwritten notes, his lettering looping and exaggerated. She flicked through the jottings, out of character humorous poems about a child misunderstanding parental instructions; a house party going wrong when the parents were on holiday (easy to see where that came from); a woman guiding two hopeless men in their quest to treat their wives with more consideration.

She'd find out more about her husband's writing soon enough. For now it was time to do food shopping.

~

Kelly was hit by a rich fragrance as she entered number 34. There was a massive bouquet in a huge smoked glass vase that she'd never seen before on the table by the entrance. There were more flowers on the coffee table, the dining table, the breakfast bar and a kitchen counter.

It was like a florist's, six vases of flowers, each with a carefully arranged, colour-coordinated bouquet.

Darren never did flowers. He must be setting her up for some terrible news.

Option One: they couldn't afford to live there anymore because his company had collapsed and his ex-trainee had no work for him.

Option Two: Tyson was at death's door, a vet having diagnosed a life threatening illness. He didn't look ill there by her side, his tail wagging madly. Kelly provided a perfunctory pat – she was too busy thinking to offer more.

Option Three: Andrew's accident was all Darren's fault, perhaps a deliberate act of violence and he was about to be prosecuted for the crime. Then why would they travel to Scotland together and what about Cecelia saying that Darren had been helping Andrew?

Option Four: Darren had found a new woman. He was in love and was leaving Kelly. Her husband had always had a roving eye but she was sure he'd stayed loyal in the past. Was it the accounts woman? She would be devastated if Darren left her.

She sent a text. *Love you. Love you. Love you. Miss you. Miss you. Miss you. xxxxx*

Ahead of popping out to get food for lunch and dinner she checked what was in the fridge. That could never be a Darren-filled fridge. It had to be Option 4, a new woman, one who didn't tolerate Darren's poor diet.

~

Cecelia was anticipating a fascinating first proper meeting with Kelly and Emma having developed a perception of them based on what their husbands had spoken about. She expected independent, outgoing women, comfortable with who they were, in contrast to their rather awkward husbands. Andrew and Darren were so different from each other. Would that be the case with their wives, and if yes, how come they'd gone away together and extended their stay for so long?

Kelly was the first to arrive, in an expensive looking dress with lots of make-up on, as if out for a special event rather than a pop next door for a cup of tea. Good for her though having just got back after what must have been a gruelling journey.

'Sorry, I should have brought something.'

'Don't be silly. Come on in. What an astonishing end to your trip.'

'Yes, it is.'

'Still, they're on their way back. I bet you can't wait to see Darren.'

'Can I ask you something?'

'Sure.'

'You might not want to answer which is OK. I can understand it if you'd rather not betray a person when you've been told something in confidence. Or found out about it.'

'Well, why don't you ask me the question.'

'Fine.'

There was silence.

'And the question is?'

'Has Darren been with another woman while I've been away?'

'Apart from seeing me, and not in that way I can assure you, as far as I can tell he hasn't.'

'Good because I love him.'

'And he's told me that he loves you – so there's a lot to look forward to.'

'How come he's told you that though? It's a pretty private thing to talk about with someone he's only recently met. And Darren is hardly brilliant at sharing emotions, even with me.'

'He mentioned it during a chat.'

'Yes, but how come –'

Saved by the bell really did apply, Cecelia's doorbell was ringing. She leapt up out of the armchair.

'That'll be Emma I expect. I'll get her.'

Kelly isn't quite as happy-go-lucky as I imagined Cecelia was thinking as she opened the front door. What would this one be like?

'Hello, Emma.' She took hold of the bunch of flowers. 'Thank you, they're lovely, though there was no need.'

'To be truthful I picked these up from the house; we have so many. You hadn't given Andrew these, had you?'

'Me? No. Come into the living room, Kelly's already there and I'll make the tea.'

Cecelia was bemused by the uneasy atmosphere, not what she expected from the two women. As soon as she left the room she heard whispering.

'Here we go,' she said cheerily on her return.

Emma's questioning began before she'd finished pouring the tea. 'How often have you seen Andrew?'

'A few times planned and then when we bump into each other on our way in and out.'

'What sorts of things have you done together?'

'The first thing, with Darren too, was a couple of visits to that lovely café.'

'Has he invited you into our house?'

'Well yes, once for a meal.'

'I hope he showed you the whole house, upstairs included.'

'No. I don't think a tour was needed. Do you?'

It was clear what all this was about; Emma was suspicious that she was having a fling with her husband. The notion needed to be quashed immediately. 'I've valued both Andrew and Darren's friendship. It's been a hard few months for me because my partner has been away working. He's finally back next week and I can't wait.'

The subsequent conversation about Julien brought to an end the interrogation that had verged towards an accusation. When the topic shifted to the women's trip away Cecelia sensed an intimacy that possibly extended beyond friendship, but that was probably all in the mind.

'It sounds brilliant. If you do anything like that again count me in.'

The stay extended to a glass of wine together, Kelly's toast being 'To our missing men.'

We can be friends, the six of us, Cecelia was thinking as the women were leaving.

'What did you make of her?' Kelly asked as they stood at the end of Cecelia's path.

'She's alright. I like her.'

'I thought that, too. And now we have to wait for the boys.'

40

'You. Are. Mad,' Andrew told Darren. 'Absolutely mad. But yes, let's do it.'

There weren't many shops in Lochcarron but one of them sold kilts and Darren had insisted on visiting it when it opened on the dot of nine before setting off back to London. He intended to greet his wife wearing one and thought it would be twice as amusing if Andrew did likewise.

'And as the myth or truth goes, we'll be wearing nothing underneath.'

'The fabric's so itchy, I don't think I can,' Andrew said as he came out the changing room in a green tartan number.

'Och, aye, then you'll be waiting until we're nearly home before slipping yer boxers off, ma auld chiel.'

'That is the worst attempt at a Scottish accent I've ever heard. And stop posing.' Darren was swirling in his red tartan model.

'They cost a fortune – and I'll never wear this again,' Andrew whispered as they approached the till.

'If it brings a single smile from Kelly I'll be satisfied.'

Andrew wanted to see Emma's smile again, her smile was a kind one, affectionate, teasing.

They texted their wives that they were leaving. It was already ten o'clock and Kelly texted back to ask Darren why they hadn't left yet.

Shopping

You shopping? Ha-ha.

On their way to the car Andrew offered to do some of the driving. He still had the cast on but there was no pain; he was sure it would be alright.

'A bit would be useful, but don't overdo it,' the considerate Darren said.

'Let me start and I'll stop as soon as anything aches,' the helpful Andrew said.

Considerate. Helpful. Polite too. Darren and Andrew?

The journey was long, arduous and boring even though they agreed that going the other way was bringing completely different and equally scenic views. This was true enough for the first three hours but was no longer the case when they hit the dual carriageways as they approached the suburbs of Glasgow. From then on it was monotonous motorways skirting urban settlements all the way to London. When at last they reached Junction 1 of the M1, this only minutes away from Muswell Hill, it was eleven o'clock and the summer sun had finally set.

'There's no point going in with a kilt on now.'

'I'm going to. Kelly's up, the lights are on, so she'll still be good for a laugh. Anyway, we can hardly take them off in the street.'

'I suppose you're right but I feel like an idiot going home wearing this.'

'I bet Emma will love it. Oh, have you taken off your –'

'No I haven't and I won't.'

'Coward.'

'Itchy. Well, I'll say goodnight now. Even though it didn't work out, travelling to Scotland to meet them was a good idea.'

'It was that. Goodnight, Andrew.'

~

Turning the key in the lock at number 38, Andrew was greeted by silence. He ran upstairs to reach Emma but she wasn't in the bedroom. Back downstairs he tried the living room first and there she was, asleep on the couch, the TV on mute. When he switched it off she stirred.

'You're back! I must have dozed.'

Emma leapt out of the sofa and flung her arms around her husband. Their kisses progressed from a salvo of pecks on cheeks to full on snogging.

'It's wonderful to be held tight again,' Andrew said as he pulled away. He lifted up his right arm. 'I'm afraid I can't hug you properly though.'

'Oh! Poor you, I forgot all about that.'

'It's on the mend. I even managed to drive a bit today.'

'Your whirlwind trip to Scotland!'

'In theory it made sense.'

'It was a lovely idea.'

Andrew was smiling, those twinkling eyes making him look mischievous, playful, attractive. Weeks earlier Emma had left a rather morose man but his demeanour now was bringing memories of his sense of fun during their early years together. She had been madly in love with him. Perhaps she still was.

'I'm sorry my accident ruined your … your time away.'

'It didn't, we were about to come home. Let me get us a drink, then we can chat. What would you like, tea or coffee?' Emma anticipated a reply that he needed to unpack first or maybe that it was a bit late for a drink.

'Sure. What about wine instead? There's a Prosecco in the fridge.'

'Coming up.'

Andrew seems different, he even looks different, Emma was thinking as she went to the kitchen to fetch the wine and glasses. Or am I imagining it. No, because he was smiling broadly as she returned and there definitely was a change, something apart from him smiling. It came to her.

'Your beard's gone.'

'Yes, I decided I'd had enough of it. I know you weren't keen, particularly when we, when we ...'

'Kissed?'

'Yes, that.'

She dropped down next to him. 'And I didn't even notice with our last kiss. Let's test it again.'

'God, I've missed you so much,' Andrew said during a pause to catch his breath.

'And a kilt – you're wearing a kilt!'

'You've only just noticed?'

''I suppose I wasn't looking at your legs but it is bonkers that I missed it.'

'It's Darren's idea of a joke, but somehow at around midnight it doesn't seem that funny.'

'I think it is. Stand up, let's see it properly.'

Andrew stood and pirouetted, his arms outstretched.

'Interesting though perhaps not to be worn in public unless it's fancy dress. Let me check on something.' Emma ran her hand up Andrew's thigh. 'Oh, that's a disappointment.'

'It's made of wool, itchy wool, so I kept them on.'

'Well here's an idea, I'm going to take them off for you, pick up the wine and lead you upstairs.'

~

All the lights were on in the open plan downstairs space at number 34 but there was no sign of Kelly when Darren stepped inside.

'Kelly,' he called out.

'I'm up here.' The voice was faint and tremulous, not at all like her.

'Is everything alright?' he called up.

'Not really, there's a problem.'

'I'm on my way.' He raced upstairs.

Kelly was in bed. When she saw him she burst out laughing. 'Trust you to get a kilt.'

'It was Andrew's idea.'

'Liar. You didn't get him to wear one, did you?'

'I did.'

'I wonder what Emma will make of it. Anyway, here's my problem.' Kelly pulled back the covers – she was naked. 'I was thinking you might be able to help.'

Darren laughed and began to unbuckle his kilt.

'Wait! I want to check something. Come here.'

She ran her hand up his thigh, took hold of him and began to stroke.

They had always made sex fun and that night was no different. Actually it was different Kelly realised as she lay next to her husband. It was more passionate than ever.

I love this man she was thinking as sleep overtook her.

41

'I'm so happy to be back,' Kelly said as they were coming downstairs for a late breakfast.

Darren took hold of her hand as they walked to the kitchen space. Kelly couldn't remember when they had last held hands. She studied the man who didn't look quite like the husband she had left behind a matter of weeks earlier. He'd left his hair to grow – it suited him. He was wearing a pristine olive green linen shirt – surely he hadn't done any ironing. His jeans were a slim fit and tapered at the ankles. Slim fitting! But yes, he'd definitely shed some weight around his midriff in that short period.

'All these flowers, they're gorgeous.'

'I thought it would be a nice welcome home.'

'It's certainly that.'

'You relax, I'll get everything ready,' Darren said as he began to lay the table.

'No, please let me help.' Kelly was by the fridge. She'd noted the contents with incredulity the day before.

Darren must have second guessed her thoughts. 'Not the usual food, is it? For a start I've cut down on meat.'

'But where did you buy all this?' she asked having seen artichokes, roasted peppers, gnocchi, couscous and feta. 'Not only where, but how did you know what to buy?'

'Most is from that deli on The Broadway. I volunteered to shop for Andrew after the accident and doubled up on the list he gave me.'

Kelly had opened the cupboard in search of jam.

'Not that one, we might as well chuck it. There's a sugar-free jam somewhere.'

Surely all this had to be leading up to the bad news. Kelly revisited her options. No work. No company. No house. A court appearance. Falling in love with another woman.

'Is there something you need to tell me?' she asked.

'Yes, I need to tell you to sit down because I'm the one making the breakfast.'

Kelly weighed up the possibility of Darren having an until now unknown identical twin who had descended on the household to replace him.

'Darren?'

'Yes?'

'Just checking.'

'Checking what?'

'Your name.'

'What are you on about? Here we are, one coffee coming up.'

Over breakfast Kelly found out more about Andrew's accident. She was told how Darren had collected his neighbour's wrecked bike before sorting out what was needed in hospital. He'd loaned him a credit card and a phone, done his shopping and some cooking, and even tidied the house.

'We are talking about doing that for Andrew?' Kelly asked.

'Of course. That's what friends are for. Well, neighbours.'

'So you're mates?'

'There were some difficulties while you were away but we're OK now.'

'What difficulties?'

'A bit of a bargy.'

'Come on, tell me.'

Kelly had to bite her tongue when Darren recounted the incident in the café and the threat of the ban.

'It's all sorted, I promise. Actually Cecelia was a big help.'

'I met her yesterday.'

'She's nice, isn't she? Me and her have been chatting quite a bit.'

If there was another woman could it be Cecelia? Kelly decided no way but remained curious. 'Chatting about what?'

'She got me thinking about how I connect with people. Hopelessly is what I reckon, especially with Andrew, but even with you. And I'm trying to change.'

'Well don't change too much because I love you just the way you are.'

'There is one thing you need to know …'

This was it, the devastating news. Kelly's stomach churned, her heart thumped.

'All that thinking is helping at work. I'm back to having a good laugh with customers like in the old days. It's earning me positive reviews, I'm up to an average of 3.6.'

Kelly was seeing all the wonderful things that had made her fall for Darren. The enthusiasm, the humour. Helpful, too – he was clearing the table and loading the dishwasher as he spoke.

Here was the man she loved. A lot.

~

'What happened exactly?'

It was mid-morning and they were still in bed, Emma having brought coffees upstairs.

Andrew kept his account of the accident and its aftermath brief – a cycle ride, an accident, an ambulance, A&E. The quiz night at the Famous Royal Oak and meeting Belly Button and the others was omitted.

'I don't understand. What made you decide to go for a bike ride in the middle of the night?'

'I couldn't sleep. Alone in bed, it's been difficult.'

Emma couldn't remember Andrew ever having had trouble getting to sleep, he was usually dead to the world as soon as his head touched the pillow.

'Anyway, there was another problem because my house keys, phone and wallet were in the backpack. When Darren collected the bike the bag was gone.'

'Nice of him to get the bike for you.'

'He's been brilliant. He picked up everything I needed from here for the night in hospital and he lent me a credit card and a phone.'

'How did he get in if you'd lost the keys? Oh, I know, I'd given Kelly a key.'

'He couldn't find it so he used the one I'd left with Cecelia.'

'Cecelia has one?'

'Yes, I thought it might be useful – and it turned out it was.'

Had Cecelia set out to mislead her with all the talk about having a partner the previous day? Doubts about the nature of the relationship between Andrew and this new neighbour resurfaced. Cecelia was attractive and seemed intellectual, possibly an academic, which was right up Andrew's street. She'd find out soon enough, one way or the other.

'She won't need a key now that I'm back and Kelly has one. Will she?'

Andrew skipped the question. 'She's really nice. You'll like her.'

'I've already met her. Yesterday.'

'And?'

'And what?'

'Do you like her?'

'She seems OK.'

'Darren and I helped her to settle in. We've taken her to our favourite café. You'll never guess what though – they've changed its name.'

'I knew they were going to do that.'

'I wasn't happy. Anyway, Cecelia loved the place so much we went there twice on the same day, coffee in the morning then an evening music event.'

'Good.' Emma wanted no further conversation concerning Cecelia. 'Any other Brookland Gardens news? You and Darren getting on well is pretty big news for starters.'

'That took time. We nearly had a fight at the café and when David intervened Darren floored him.'

'What!'

Andrew seemed reluctant to dwell on the incident but Emma pressed him for details.

'That's the gist of it. It happened and it's over so it's best to drop it,' Andrew concluded.

'OK then.'

'I suppose another bit of news is my writing.'

'You've got a ready-made subject what with your bike accident. Infection, disease, death. What rhymes with gangrene?'

'Nope, no more disease and death. I've sent the second collection to the publisher and told them I'm done with dystopia. There's enough unpleasantness in the real world, I don't need to write about it. I'm experimenting with humorous stuff, a book for children included.'

Emma had seen some lines of poetry when in his office but nothing had seemed suitable for children.

'Stay there,' Andrew said, pulling back the duvet. He returned with a sketch book and handed it to Emma. Two adjacent A4 pages were crammed full of text and sketches.

The sheep are talking
The tractors are walking
At this magical farm.
The cows are dancing
The pigs are prancing
At this magical farm.

The drawings that filled the sides of each of the pages were both skilful and comical – a tractor with four stout legs set in wellington boots; two plump cows waltzing; a gathering of sheep chatting earnestly.

'What do you reckon?'

'Different. And really good. I didn't know you could draw so well.'

'They aren't the final versions. I was thinking, if it gets published I'd like to donate all the sales revenue to a charity supporting youngsters with special needs.'

'That's a wonderful idea.'

She loved this man.

42

Julien showed up three days after the women had returned. The Robertsons and Crabtrees discovered this when Cecelia sent the men texts inviting them, with their wives, over for coffee to meet her partner.

'Perhaps Cecelia should have my number,' Emma said when Andrew told her about the invitation. Despite no longer being suspicious, she would rather be the principle liaison between the neighbours.

She texted Kelly. *Are you two invited over to meet Cecelia's man?*

Yes.

You going?

Yes. Will be interesting to see what he's like.

~

'We're only going next door for coffee,' Andrew reminded Emma as she was pulling out clothes from the wardrobe, trying them on and dismissing them.

'I need some new stuff, nothing fits properly anymore. I'm too fat.'

Andrew admired his slim wife parading in her underwear. "Don't be daft, you've already got loads" was his first thought as he viewed the stash of clothes in the cupboard and the pile heaped onto the bed. He wouldn't tell her that, of course.

Emma was trying on a skirt and cardigan. She inspected the outfit in the full length mirror. 'This will have to do, I suppose.'

'You look lovely, but if you want to get some new things we can go shopping this afternoon.'

'Would you come with me?'

'Of course.'

~

'Is that what you're wearing to go out?' Darren asked Kelly.

'Obviously it is because it's what I've got on.'

'But jeans.'

'It's only for a morning coffee at our neighbour's. Alright then, if you're going smart – and I must say, you look fantastic – then I'm not going to be your scruffy wife.' Kelly had taken off her jeans and was squeezing her shapely body into a dress.

During Kelly's absence Darren had assessed his clothes and concluded that he was stuck in an earlier decade, possibly a previous century. It was time to buy some new ones. The old Darren, the one of a couple of months ago, might well have purchased inappropriate gear from the trendy boutiques on The Broadway. The new Darren had stepped inside one of them and rapidly exited having realised that he didn't want low rise trousers, garish shirts and logoed hoodies anymore – he wanted fashionable outfits suitable for a man of his age and shape. That took him to the department stores at Brent Cross where he decked himself out in plain linen shirts, chinos reassuringly a size down from past purchases, and at considerable expense, statement casual jackets.

~

The doors at numbers 34 and 38 clicked shut and together the two couples walked along their paths and then up Cecelia's path.

Darren rang the bell and Cecelia greeted them.

An earnest looking man of slight build was standing behind her. He had a narrow face, round-rimmed glasses and a goatee beard. His trousers were light-coloured and baggy, his navy shirt crumpled. He wore sandals, no socks.

'Meet Julien,' Cecelia announced.

'My pleasure,' Julien said, inviting handshakes. His serious expression persisted as Cecelia steered everyone into the living room, leaving them there to go and make coffee. By the time she returned the quietly spoken Julien had come to life, chatting away about his time in Mozambique in an easy-going manner with no accent detectable. As he described the country's scenic beauty and unique wildlife, Cecelia interrupted with highbrow stuff about the dangerous political situation.

'There is no danger away from the capital city,' Julien said, steering the conversation back to describing the extraordinary natural world and the generosity of the people.

'You're making it sound wonderful. I'd like to visit,' Kelly said.

'It really isn't a safe place,' Cecelia warned. 'I'm thankful I have Julien back in one piece.'

'No, it is not like that.'

Andrew said something in French. Emma told him to stop being pretentious ahead of Julien having the opportunity to reply.

The conversation moved on from Julien's account of the Mozambique trip.

Darren spoke with pride when asked about his line of work.

Cecelia praised him for the security alarm installation at number 36.

Emma explained why she was changing jobs. Come September she would be teaching in a less salubrious area to help tackle the challenges that the children there faced. 'I know it will be hard, but I want to do it.'

Andrew added that it was a brave decision and he was proud of his wife.

Kelly said she was thinking about what to do next because she didn't intend to work in a car showroom ever again.

Darren reassured her that she could take her time deciding on the next job.

Cecelia announced that her research on the impact of separation on men was complete and she had submitted the paper for peer review.

Andrew asked what conclusions Cecelia had reached.

Emma suggested he leave that discussion for another day.

Cecelia mentioned that she and Julien were going to the comedy night at Dream Café that evening and asked if the others would like to join them.

'English humour. If I can ever understand that I'll be a hundred percent fluent,' Julien joked.

~

They congregated at the end of the number 36 path at a little before eight o'clock. The summer sun was above the rooftops, casting long shadows across the street.

They walked in pairs, Andrew with Darren, Kelly with Emma, and Julien and Cecelia hand in hand at the front.

'We've hardly had time to speak since we got back, have we? How's it going?' Kelly asked Emma.

'Actually brilliant. You know how nervous I was, but that went as soon as I was with Andrew. He's being lovely; something's got into him.'

Kelly looked ahead at Cecelia. 'Or someone. Darren's changed too and I'm wondering whether Cecelia is at least part of the reason.'

'I don't see how. I thought she and Andrew might be having an affair, but I'm certain that's not the case.'

'You're right, she's well and truly attached to Julien. What do you make of him?'

'On first impressions, nice. He looks like a botanist in a TV documentary about the environment.'

Kelly laughed as she took hold of Emma's arm. 'We're still friends, aren't we?'

'Us? More than that, really good friends. I've learnt a lot from you,' Emma added.

'What? You mean how to …'

'Very funny – stop it!'

'What are you two chuckling about.' Darren had joined them with Andrew close behind.

The pairs rearranged to leave the three couples walking on towards the café holding hands.

They entered the packed venue in time to catch the first comedian's final lines, a tirade of expletives which appeared popular judging by the round of applause.

'Quick, let's get to the bar before everyone heads there,' Darren said. 'Come on, Kelly.'

Kelly saw Bridget at the far end of the counter and there were nods of acknowledgement. The café owner would be interested to find out about her and Emma's trip but no way that night because Bridget was working flat out. It looked quite fun though, pouring drinks, mixing cocktails, engaging with the customers.

Kelly had never seen the young man who was serving them. He was polite enough, definitely competent, though perhaps a little abrupt as he switched attention from customer to customer. Not like Bridget who always got it dead right.

'Who's that bloke behind the bar?' Kelly asked Emma as soon as she got back.

'Andy, Bridget's son. He helps out when he's back from university.'

There had been standing room only but Andrew spotted a rowdy group getting ready to leave. Chairs were being pushed back, jackets lifted off the backs of them, remains of drinks downed at speed.

'Look. There.' Andrew made a dash to grab their table. 'Excuse me, are you leaving …?'

Having followed Andrew, the others were witnessing a strange silent standoff, the members of the group eyeing Andrew as he stopped dead in his tracks.

'The quiz genius,' Clipper called out. Andrew was turning bright red.

A woman flung her arms round him and kissed him on the lips. When she pulled away Andrew was brighter than bright red.

'The booze is too pricey so we're off to get slaughtered somewhere else. Fancy coming with?' Belly Button asked.

'No, not tonight.'

'Well, make sure you join us for the next quiz night. We miss you.' That was Bonzo.

'Too right,' added Salted Peanut. 'We came bottom last time.'

All seemed amiable enough as the gang he'd met at the Famous Royal Oak departed, but unsurprisingly it left the other inhabitants of Brookland Gardens bemused by Andrew's secret friends.

'Who were they?' Darren asked.

'Who's that woman?' Emma added. 'The one you kissed.'

'She kissed me, I didn't kiss her.'

'They're around our age but they're dressed like teenagers,' Kelly stated.

David was on the stage, the PA system buzzing like an angry wasp.

'The next act must be about to start. Shall we sit down?' Andrew suggested as he sank into a chair.

'You are going to tell me what's going on,' Emma whispered.

'Yes, later though. It's nothing important.'

'Maybe I'll be the judge of that.'

There was a cheer as David left the stage and a further cheer as a man in a lime green suit with a wild shock of orange hair came into view. 'Hello, you fuckers!'

Another cheer.

'Are you fucking OK?'

'Do you know what? I don't think I can be bothered to listen to this,' Emma said. 'It's either back home alone for me or we all head off to a quieter place.'

'Agreed.'

'Agreed.'

'Agreed.'

'But what about your love of English humour?' Julien asked.

Andrew had kept quiet; he was too busy formulating his explanation.

43

The six of them were sat sipping wine in a tranquil pub frequented by the middle aged. Andrew was explaining how he'd got to know the group they'd seen at the café, having decided that there was nothing to hide except the kissing with Belly Button. He'd been desperate to escape the house. He'd been coerced into joining the quiz team as they were a player short. He'd quite enjoyed his star role in answering the questions. A high volume of alcohol had been consumed.

'And that woman? Was kissing you just now a follow up to kissing you on the quiz evening?'

'She was affectionate that night but I rejected her advances.'

It took a while for the laughter to die down.

Emma pressed on with her teasing. 'OK, so now I know why you ended up cycling in the middle of the night and how come the most careful cyclist in the United Kingdom managed to have a bike accident when no one else was involved.'

'And it explains why I never got an explanation about how your bike ended up wrapped round a lamppost,' Darren added.

Emma took hold of her husband's hand. 'In all seriousness, it's a good job you were sober enough to put on your helmet otherwise it could have been far more serious.'

'I wasn't sober. I think Belly Button put it on for me.'

'Belly Button! What on earth are you talking about?'

'They have nicknames. One of them is called Belly Button.'

'Why Belly Button?'

'She has this big stud on it.'

'Which you saw?'

'Briefly.'

Despite further laughter Emma wanted to dig deeper.

'And she was the one kissing you tonight? Remind me why.'

'I told you. She seems to like me.'

'But were you leading her on that night?'

'No. Well, only by getting so many questions right.'

'If I was in a quiz team with a man I didn't know, it wouldn't cross my mind to kiss him every time he answered correctly.'

'I can see what you're getting at. Like I said, I was doing exceptionally well but I agree that's beside the point. Could we talk about something else?'

~

'What interesting neighbours you have,' Julien reflected as he and Cecelia lay in bed late that evening, their love-making paused. There had been no reticence on his return, the intimacy and passion of their time together before his work trip was stronger than ever.

'Perhaps this is what real love is all about,' Cecelia quipped as they lay in each other's arms.

'Perhaps.'

Again they made love.

There was a decision to be made – where to live. Cecelia had a lovely home with an unlovely high mortgage. Julien rented a fabulous flat within walking distance of the university and he had a sizeable sum of money available for a deposit, though he could never afford to buy in his current location. This left an obvious resolution – to live together in Cecelia's home with Julien taking part ownership by using his savings to reduce her mortgage burden.

A consideration of this option stretched on until the early hours of the morning.

Finally, Julien raised his until then unspoken concern. 'The thought of us living together is wonderful and I think it will happen but giving up my flat is a big step. Maybe we should pause for a while.'

'I was thinking the same but didn't want to say in case you thought I was getting cold feet.'

'*Pieds froids*. What a lovely expression.'

'Don't you say the same in French?'

'*Avoir la frousse* is the closest.'

'Well, whatever. So this is what I think. Let's carry on living in our own places, but for a maximum of six months. If we still aren't sure by then it would mean we'll never be sure.'

'Agreed. I think we will decide to speed things up.'

'Me too. I hope so.'

~

Despite their plan there was hardly a night not spent together, usually at Julien's midweek and at Cecelia's over weekends. Midweek, immersed with work, their social life was confined to occasional meals with colleagues. While at Brookland Gardens they often arranged something with their four neighbours – a walk, the cinema, the café, a meal.

'They are so different those men,' Julien said to Cecelia following a group discussion about film choice for that evening. A fast moving Hollywood action blockbuster and an indie tale of family tragedy were put forward as options by their neighbours.

'Diversity, Julien, it's all part of the fun of friendships. I do agree that they're an odd pair though. Did I tell you I was thinking of including Darren and Andrew in my research after finding out that their wives were taking time out?'

'Yes, you did mention it. I think the decision to leave them out was the right one and I do see what you mean by diversity. Kelly and Emma are very different but they get on tremendously well.'

'Exactly.'

~

Emma had wondered whether the friendship with Kelly would be as strong on their return from Scotland. Any doubts turned out to be unwarranted. They were together more than ever with Emma still on her school holiday break and Kelly considering what to do next. Regular running was back on track with a 10k event scheduled for early autumn. They spent time shopping – Emma's preference, she was fascinated by Kelly's knowledge of the retail industry. They visited galleries and museums – Kelly's preference, there was such a lot of catching up to do.

They chatted about how Darren had turned his business around and was now able to work full time for himself. They covered how Andrew had been offered a deal to write his children's book. For a while they avoided talking about their marriages, the conversation finally held during one of their post-run sessions at Dream Café.

'Do you think having our break has helped your marriage?'

'I didn't go away with that in mind.'

'True enough but from what you're saying about Andrew, and the same goes for me with Darren, it does seem as if us being away has made things better.'

'Agreed. Nothing was bad but there was complacency, from me as well as him.'

'That's a good way of putting it. The same goes for Darren and me.'

The café was quiet that day, the affluent clientele possibly away on summer holidays in distant lands. They were sitting at their regular table by the door, the one where they could keep an eye on Barnaby and Tyson tethered outside.

Bridget slumped down next to them. 'At last, some peace and quiet.'

'You do look shattered if you don't mind me saying.'

'I am, Kelly. Our bloody deputy manager is walking out on us without giving proper notice.'

'Doug? He seemed happy enough working here.'

'He was until he was headhunted to manage somewhere on a ridiculous salary. I don't blame him going, it's leaving us in the lurch that's so annoying.'

'Surely it won't be difficult to get a new person in. This is such a great place in a great location.'

'Finding good staff in the hospitality sector is … a needle in a haystack comes to mind. Andy's offered to help out over the rest of the summer. He's prepared to cancel his travel plans, even do the barista training and whatever else is needed, but he's worked so hard at uni this year I think it's unfair to accept.'

'If he wants to …'

'And there's another thing if he did help out. You'll have seen Rachel here some weekends and evenings. Well, now David's promised her full time employment until she starts at uni. So my son would be line managing his daughter and they'll be at each other's throats. They've never hit it off.'

'When is Doug leaving?' Kelly asked.

'On Friday.'

'I could do it.'

'That's a kind offer but we want someone to take it on permanently.'

'I know and I'll do that. I'm looking for a job that's worthwhile and enjoyable. This fits.'

'I don't know about enjoyable. It's hard work.'

'I like hard work.'

'We're looking for someone with experience.'

'I have experience dealing with customers and that's the most important skill, isn't it? I've seen you and the others working and I don't think anything here is rocket science.'

'She'd be great,' Emma chipped in. 'The customers would love her and she's super organised. I know she's a star at mixing cocktails, too!'

'I'll tell you what, if you're serious I'd be happy for you to come in tomorrow morning for a chat with David and me.'

'You mean for an interview?'

'I suppose so. Is that OK?'

'Yes. I just needed to know what to wear.' Kelly raised the hood on her sweatshirt and produced one of those smiles that got those around her smiling too. 'I'd best be off to prepare then. What time do you want me in?'

—

'I've got the job,' Kelly announced on arriving home late the following morning. 'On probation for six months to start with.'

'That's brilliant, love.' Darren had taken the morning off work to be there for Kelly on her return from the interview.

'It wasn't a done deal, in fact I was nervous with the two of them sitting on the opposite side of the table and David starting with, "This is our livelihood, Kelly, so we have to be fully professional in our decision making". When I looked across at Bridget she was nodding as serious as could be. "Which is understandable and just how I would expect this meeting to be" I told them. They liked that; the atmosphere softened a bit though they kept firing questions at me.'

'I'm sure you were brilliant; you're always spot on giving the answers that people want to hear.'

'I don't know about that but my trial starts on Monday with David training me on the basics of the management side, and his daughter on making the drinks. I can't wait.'

Kelly texted Emma and Cecelia to let them know the good news.

Shortly afterwards Emma and Andrew were at the door to present Kelly with a bouquet of flowers.

'Thank you, but blimey, that was quick.'

'I haven't sprinted down to the shops. I got them in advance because I knew you'd be a winner.'

'And I've booked a table for the six of us this evening at Chez Claude,' Andrew added. 'We'll leave you to it for now and catch up with the details later.'

'Perhaps you can fill me in with those details now,' Darren asked as soon as they were alone.

'Actually I'd welcome that because even though I'm excited I do have some concerns.'

'Fire away.'

Darren had a positive spin on anything she saw as a potential problem.

On the pay being less than at the car company: 'My business is doing well so money isn't the most important thing.'

On the need to work irregular hours including some late nights: 'You always were a night owl.'

On her lack of experience and fear of failure: 'I've never known you to be anything but a star, Kelly.'

By the time Darren left for work Kelly was reassured and was able to spend a pleasant afternoon googling about what was needed to make a success of working in a café.

44

Six months had passed, Julien having tolerated a summer of irregular sunshine interspersed with downpours followed by an autumn with gale force winds wrenching leaves from trees and sending them swirling.

Now it was winter, severe and long drawn out with a layer of snow clinging obstinately to the pavements of Muswell Hill. Having been brought up in the south of France where the sky was always blue, the winds always mild and the winters always short, this was the time of the year when he had most questioned the sanity of moving to England with its gloomy skies and incessant damp. But that was in the past because meeting Cecelia had been life-changing.

The agreed six-month pause before moving in together had ended with Julien about to sublet his flat to another academic at the university until his rental contract expired. The final step, sorting out his contribution and part-ownership of the Brookland Gardens home, was underway.

Sometimes after work he and Cecelia would meet at Dream Café to have a light-hearted moan about their day – lazy students, pointless administration, the Vice Chancellor's antics. He stepped inside the café, more French than anything he'd known in France, as a wave of sleet slammed against the window. His phone pinged as he was standing by the door.

Can't make it, unscheduled tutorial with a masters student. Sorry xxx

Heading home was an option; staying inside the warm and dry café the better choice.

Kelly was behind the counter. 'Hi Julien, Is it a coffee day or a wine day?'

Whack thudded the sleet against the giant picture windows. Outside there was a warped fusion of white and red lights as rush hour cars, buses and bikes passed by.

'Definitely wine.'

'Mind if I join you, I'm about to go off duty?'

'Of course.'

Kelly didn't have to ask which wine to bring over from the café's extensive menu, it was always the Malbec for Julien. She poured a glass for herself and carried them to his table, his favourite by one of the scarlet-coloured alcoves.

'Cheers,' he said as he lifted his glass. 'To English weather.'

'Santé,' Kelly joked. 'It's a bit of a celebration day for me, I've completed my six months' probation. I'm officially Deputy Manager.'

'Congratulations. That's no surprise, you always seem like the perfect person for this place.'

'Thanks. I do love it, though managing Bridget and David's children is a bit of a challenge.'

'The wild looking girl and the rather serious young man?'

'That's them. Rachel is David's daughter and Andy is Bridget's son. Actually despite the image Rachel's great when she's not around Andy. He's OK but I get the feeling I'm being judged.'

They looked up as Cecelia stormed through the door of the unusually quiet café. She stamped her feet and ran a hand through her wet hair before joining them. 'Don't say anything; I know I look like a drowned rat. I hate sleet.'

'I thought you couldn't make it.'

'My student didn't turn up. And not for the first time.'

'What do you want to drink?'

'What you've got looks tempting.'

Kelly stood up. 'I'll bring the bottle over, it makes more sense than ordering by the glass. Though this is on me.'

'Don't be silly.'

'It's fine, Cecelia, I have something to celebrate. Julien will tell you what.'

'Here's an idea,' Cecelia said when Kelly was back with them. 'I can't be bothered to cook this evening, you shouldn't be cooking because you're celebrating, and I'm sure the others will be happy not to have to cook. Let's go to that new pizza place.'

Cecelia was already messaging. *We're having pizza out tonight. Come to DC for a drink and we'll set off from here.*

There were three rapid replies.

From Darren: *Couldn't carry on working outside in this weather so already home. See you in a sec.*

From Emma: *On the bus approaching The Broadway now. See you soon.*

From Andrew: *Got drenched cycling. Quick clothes change then I'll be there.*

Darren was the first to arrive.

'Do you know what we're celebrating?' Julien asked him.

'Of course I do.' He looked across to Kelly. 'And it calls for champagne.'

Darren returned with a bottle and six flutes. 'It's on the house. Bridget said it's a celebration for them too, having such a star deputy manager.'

The fourth glass was being filled as Emma came in. She took off her coat and shook it by the door. 'Hi everyone,' she said as she sat down. 'They said it would stay dry today.'

'Have one of these to warm you up, or maybe both,' Julien said, holding up the bottle of wine in one hand and the champagne in the other.

'No, I don't think I fancy alcohol, thanks.'

'What instead?'

'Maybe a mint tea?'

Julien left them to place the order.

'Not like you to say no to wine, especially when it's a celebration day.' Darren missed the glance that passed between Emma and Kelly. 'You do know what we're celebrating, don't you? About Kelly?'

'Yes, I do. Her big promotion day.'

Julien was back. 'One tea on its way. Bridget's bringing it over.'

'Thanks, Julien.'

Darren was on his feet holding up his glass. 'I'd like to propose a toast to my lovely wife.' He paused. 'Or should we wait for Andrew?'

'No need, he could be ages. Here's my tea so I can represent the Crabtree family. Thanks, Bridget.'

They were clinking glasses and a teacup together as Andrew arrived, frowning as he joined them.

'Champagne, Andrew? We're celebrating.'

The frown lingered. 'It's OK,' Emma told him. 'This is for Kelly officially becoming deputy manager.'

'We have an announcement too,' Julien said, putting an arm round Cecelia's shoulders. 'I am now a permanent resident in Brookland Gardens. You have a new neighbour.'

'That's hardly news. You've been a neighbour for months,' Darren said.

'But now there's no turning back, he's given up possession of his flat. Which definitely merits another toast.' Cecelia refilled the flutes. 'Emma, ready for some alcohol now?'

'Not really. I'll stick with the tea, thanks.'

Emma looked across at Kelly. Apart from Andrew she was the only one who knew.

'Andrew and I also have something to announce.'

'What a day. Come on, out with it,' Darren urged.

'We're going to have a baby.'

'Wonderful,' from Cecelia.

'Merveilleux,' from Julien.

'I sort of knew,' from Kelly.

'Brilliant,' from Darren. 'Though it's a bit of a surprise.'

'I know I've been going on about overpopulation and the state of the world …' Andrew began but came to a halt. 'It was a big decision. I'm – we're over the moon.'

'You don't need to apologise,' Cecelia said.

'Exactly. As Andrew's said, we're over the moon despite being nervous. I'll probably be the oldest new mum in Muswell Hill.'

'Age doesn't matter. You can outrun the twenty year olds,' Kelly said.

'But not outpregnancy them.'

'I don't think that's a word,' Andrew said.

'Isn't it? Anyway, you can all have your alcohol and I'll finish my tea.'

'You'll be a great mum – and you'll be a great dad, Andrew.'

'Thanks, Darren, that's a lovely thing to say.'

Kelly stood up. 'Back in a minute, I'd better get my stuff from the office before I forget.'

'I'll help you.' Darren leapt up and the others watched them leave the celebratory group arm in arm.

'Nice for Emma and Andrew, isn't it?' Kelly said as she was gathering her bag and jacket from the office, but there was a sadness as she spoke.

'It's time we looked into options for being parents.'

'You serious?'

'Yes, I am. Whatever it takes – IVF, even adoption, because I think you'd be a wonderful mum. And I'd be an OK dad. And there's no way I'm going to let Andrew win by having a child, am I?'

They were still laughing as they joined the others.

Ingram Content Group UK Ltd.
Milton Keynes UK
UKHW040931240523
422269UK00001B/8